MARGARET ATWOOD

Margaret Atwood is the author of more than forty books of fiction, poetry and critical essays, including *The Handmaid's Tale*, the Booker-winning *The Blind Assassin*, the MaddAddam trilogy and *The Heart Goes Last*. Her work has received many awards around the world. She has also worked as a cartoonist, illustrator, librettist, playwright and puppeteer.

Her first encounters with Shakespeare took place in the 1950s at her Toronto high school, and she has consistently named him as one of the most important influences on her own work. 'The Tempest is, in some ways, an early multi-media musical. If Shakespeare were working today he'd be using every special effect technology now makes available. But *The Tempest* is especially intriguing because of the many questions it leaves unanswered. What a strenuous pleasure it has been to wrestle with it!'

ALSO BY MARGARET ATWOOD

Novels

The Edible Woman
Surfacing
Lady Oracle
Life Before Man
Bodily Harm
The Handmaid's Tale
Cat's Eye
The Robber Bride
Alias Grace
The Blind Assassin
Oryx and Crake
The Penelopiad
The Year of the Flood
MaddAddam
The Heart Goes Last

Shorter Fiction

Dancing Girls
Murder in the Dark
Bluebeard's Egg
Wilderness Tips
Good Bones and Simple Murders
The Tent
Moral Disorder
Stone Mattress

Poetry

Double Persephone
The Circle Game
Speeches for Doctor Frankenstein
The Animals in That Country
The Journals of Susanna Moodie
Procedures for Underground
Power Politics
You Are Happy
Selected Poems: 1965–1975
Two-Headed Poems
True Stories

Interlunar
Selected Poems II: Poems Selected
and New, 1976–1986
Morning in the Burned House
Eating Fire: Selected Poetry,
1965–1995
The Door

Non-fiction

Survival: A Thematic Guide to
Canadian Literature
Days of the Rebels: 1815–1840
Second Words
Strange Things: The Malevolent
North in Canadian Literature
Negotiating with the Dead: A
Writer on Writing
Moving Targets: Writing with
Intent, 1982–2004
Curious Pursuits: Occasional
Writing
Writing with Intent: Essays,
Reviews, Personal Prose, 1983–2005
Payback: Debt and the Shadow
Side of Wealth
In Other Worlds: SF and the
Human Imagination

For Children

Up in the Tree
Anna's Pet (with Joyce Barkhouse)
For the Birds
Princess Prunella and the Purple
Peanut
Rude Ramsay and the Roaring
Radishes
Bashful Bob and Doleful Dorinda
Wandering Wenda

MARGARET ATWOOD

Hag-Seed

The Tempest Retold

VINTAGE

7 9 10 8 6

Vintage
20 Vauxhall Bridge Road,
London SW1V 2SA

Vintage is part of the Penguin Random House
group of companies whose addresses can be found
at global.penguinrandomhouse.com

Penguin
Random House
UK

First published in Vintage in 2017
First published in hardback by Hogarth in 2016

penguin.co.uk/vintage

A CIP catalogue record for this book is
available from the British Library

ISBN 9780099594024

Printed and bound by Clays Ltd, St Ives Plc

Penguin Random House is committed to a sustainable future
for our business, our readers and our planet. This book is
made from Forest Stewardship Council® certified paper.

MIX
Paper from
responsible sources
FSC® C018179
FSC
www.fsc.org

Richard Bradshaw, 1944–2007
Gwendolyn MacEwen, 1941–1987

Enchanters

"This is certain, that a man that studieth revenge, keeps his own wounds green, which otherwise would heal, and do well."

– Sir Francis Bacon, "On Revenge."

". . . although there are nice people on the stage, there are some who would make your hair stand on end."

– Charles Dickens.

"Other flowering isles must be
In the sea of Life and Agony:
Other spirits float and flee
O'er that gulf . . ."

– Percy Bysshe Shelley, "Lines
Written Among the Euganean Hills."

Contents

III. These Our Actors

IV. Rough Magic

V. This Thing of Darkness

Epilogue: *Set Me Free*

Prologue:
Screening

Wednesday, March 13, 2013.

The house lights dim. The audience quiets.

ON THE BIG FLATSCREEN: *Jagged yellow lettering on black:*

THE TEMPEST
By William Shakespeare
With
The Fletcher Correctional Players

ONSCREEN: *A hand-printed sign, held up to the camera by Announcer, wearing a short purple velvet cloak. In his other hand, a quill.*

SIGN: A SUDDEN TEMPEST

ANNOUNCER: What you're gonna see, is a storm at sea:
Winds are howlin', sailors yowlin',
Passengers cursin' 'em, 'cause it gettin' worse:
Gonna hear screams, just like a ba-a-d dream,
But not all here is what it seem,
Just sayin'.
Grins.
Now we gonna start the playin'.

He gestures with the quill. Cut to: Thunder and lightning, in funnel cloud, screengrab from the Tornado Channel. Stock shot of ocean waves. Stock shot of rain. Sound of howling wind.

Camera zooms in on a bathtub-toy sailboat tossing up and down on a blue plastic shower curtain with fish on it, the waves made by hands underneath.

Closeup of Boatswain in a black knitted tuque. Water is thrown on him from offscreen. He is drenched.

BOATSWAIN: Fall to't yarely, or we run ourselves aground!
  Bestir, bestir!
  Yare! Yare! Beware! Beware!
  Let's just do it,
  Better get to it,
  Trim the sails,
  Fight the gales,
  Unless you wantin' to swim with the whales!
VOICES OFF: We're all gonna drown!
BOATSWAIN: Get outta tha' way! No time for play!
A bucketful of water hits him in the face.

VOICES OFF: Listen to me! Listen to me!
  Don't you know we're royalty?
BOATSWAIN: Yare! Yare! The waves don't care!
  The wind is roarin', the rain is pourin',
  All you do is stand and stare!
VOICES OFF: You're drunk!
BOATSWAIN: You're a idiot!
VOICES OFF: We're doomed!
VOICES OFF: We're sunk!

Closeup of Ariel in a blue bathing cap and iridescent ski goggles, blue makeup on the lower half of his face. He's wearing a translucent plastic raincoat with ladybugs, bees, and butterflies on it. Behind his left shoulder there's an odd shadow. He laughs soundlessly, points upward with his right hand, which is encased in a blue rubber glove. Lightning flash, thunderclap.

VOICES OFF: Let's pray!

BOATSWAIN: What's that you say?

VOICES OFF: We're goin' down! We're gonna drown!
   Ain't gonna see the King no more!
   Jump offa the ship, swim for the shore!

Ariel throws his head back and laughs with delight. In each of his blue rubber hands he's holding a high-powered flashlight, in flicker mode.
The screen goes black.

A VOICE FROM THE AUDIENCE: What?

ANOTHER VOICE: Power's off.

ANOTHER VOICE: Must be the blizzard. A line down somewhere.

Total darkness. Confused noise from outside the room. Yelling. Shots are fired.

A VOICE FROM THE AUDIENCE: What's going on?

VOICES, FROM OUTSIDE THE ROOM: Lockdown! Lockdown!

A VOICE FROM THE AUDIENCE: Who's in charge here?

Three more shots.

A VOICE, FROM INSIDE THE ROOM: Don't move! Quiet! Keep your heads down! Stay right where you are.

I. Dark Backward

1. *Seashore*

Monday, January 7, 2013.

Felix brushes his teeth. Then he brushes his other teeth, the false ones, and slides them into his mouth. Despite the layer of pink adhesive he's applied, they don't fit very well; perhaps his mouth is shrinking. He smiles: the illusion of a smile. Pretense, fakery, but who's to know?

Once he would have called his dentist and made an appointment, and the luxurious faux-leather chair would have been his, the concerned face smelling of mint mouth-wash, the skilled hands wielding gleaming instruments. *Ah yes, I see the problem. No worries, we'll get that fixed for you.* Like taking his car in for a tuneup. He might even have been graced with music on the earphones and a semi-knockout pill.

But he can't afford such professional adjustments now. His dental care is low-rent, so he's at the mercy of his unreliable teeth. Too bad, because that's all he needs for his upcoming finale: a denture meltdown. *Our revelth now have ended. Theeth our actorth . . .* Should that happen, his humiliation would be total; at the thought of it even his lungs blush. If the words are not perfect, the pitch exact, the modulation delicately adjusted, the spell fails. People start to shift in their seats, and cough, and go home at intermission. It's like death.

"Mi-my-mo-moo," he tells the toothpaste-speckled mirror over the kitchen sink. He lowers his eyebrows, juts out his chin. Then he grins: the grin of a cornered chimpanzee, part anger, part threat, part dejection.

How he has fallen. How deflated. How reduced. Cobbling together this bare existence, living in a hovel, ignored in a forgotten backwater; whereas Tony, that self-promoting, posturing little shit, gallivants about with the grandees, and swills champagne, and gobbles caviar and larks' tongues and suckling pigs, and attends galas, and basks in the adoration of his entourage, his flunkies, his toadies . . .

Once the toadies of Felix.

It rankles. It festers. It brews vengefulness. If only . . .

Enough. *Shoulders straight,* he orders his grey reflection. *Suck it up.* He knows without looking that he's developing a paunch. Maybe he should get a truss.

Never mind! Reef in the stomach! There's work to be done, there are plots to be plotted, there are scams to be scammed, there are villains to be misled! *Tip of the tongue, top of the teeth. Testing the tempestuous teapot. She sells seashells by the seashore.*

There. Not a syllable fluffed.

He can still do it. He'll pull it off, despite all obstacles. Charm the pants off them at first, not that he'd relish the resulting sight. Wow them with wonder, as he says to his actors. *Let's make magic!*

And let's shove it down the throat of that devious, twisted bastard, Tony.

2. *High charms*

That devious, twisted bastard, Tony, is Felix's own fault. Or mostly his fault. Over the past twelve years, he's often blamed himself. He gave Tony too much scope, he didn't supervise, he didn't look over Tony's nattily suited, padded, pinstriped shoulder. He didn't pick up on the clues, as anyone with half a brain and two ears might have done. Worse: he'd trusted the evil-hearted, social-clambering, Machiavellian foot-licker. He'd fallen for the act: *Let me do this chore for you, delegate that, send me instead.* What a fool he'd been.

His only excuse was that he'd been distracted by grief at that time. He'd recently lost his only child, and in such a terrible way. If only he had, if only he hadn't, if only he'd been aware . . .

No, too painful still. Don't think about it, he tells himself while doing up the buttons of his shirt. Hold it far back. Pretend it was only a movie.

Even if that not-to-be-thought-about event hadn't occurred, he'd most likely still have been ambushed. He'd fallen into the habit of letting Tony run the mundane end of the show, because, after all, Felix was the Artistic Director, as Tony kept reminding him, and he was at the height of his powers, or so they kept saying in the reviews; therefore he ought to concern himself with higher aims.

And he did concern himself with higher aims. To create the lushest, the most beautiful, the most awe-inspiring, the most inventive, the most numinous theatrical experiences ever. To raise the bar as high as the moon. To forge from every production an experience no one attending it would ever forget. To evoke the collective indrawn breath, the collective sigh; to have the audience leave, after the performance, staggering a little as if drunk. To make the Makeshiweg Festival the standard against which all lesser theatre festivals would be measured.

These were no mean goals.

To accomplish them, Felix had pulled together the ablest backup teams he could cajole. He'd hired the best, he'd inspired the best. Or the best he could afford. He'd hand-picked the technical gnomes and gremlins, the lighting designers, the sound technicians. He'd headhunted the most admired scenery and costume designers of his day, the ones he could persuade. All of them had to be top of the line, and beyond. If possible.

So he'd needed money.

Finding the money had been Tony's thing. A lesser thing: the money was only a means to an end, the end being transcendence: that had been understood by both of them. Felix the cloud-riding enchanter, Tony the earth-based factotum and gold-grubber. It had seemed an appropriate division of functions, considering their respective talents. As Tony himself had put it, each of them should do what he was good at.

Idiot, Felix berates himself. He'd understood nothing. As for the height of his powers, the height is always ominous. From the height, there's nowhere to go but down.

Tony had been all too eager to liberate Felix from the rituals Felix hated, such as the attending of cocktail functions and the buttering-up of sponsors and patrons, and the hobnobbing with the Board, and the facilitating of grants from the various levels of government, and the writing of effective reports. That way – said Tony – Felix could devote himself to the things that really mattered, such as his perceptive script notes and his cutting-edge lighting schemes and the exact timing of the showers of glitter confetti of which he had made such genius use.

And his directing, of course. Felix had always built in one or two plays a season for himself to direct. Once in a while he would even take the central part, if it was something he'd felt drawn to. Julius Caesar. The tartan king. Lear. Titus Andronicus. Triumphs for him, every one of those roles! And every one of his productions!

Or triumphs with the critics, though the playgoers and even the patrons had grumbled from time to time. The almost-naked, freely bleeding Lavinia in *Titus* was too upsettingly graphic, they'd whined; though, as Felix had pointed out, more than justified by the text. Why did *Pericles* have to be staged with spaceships and extraterrestrials instead of sailing ships and foreign countries, and why present the moon goddess Artemis with the head of a praying mantis? Even though – said Felix to the Board, in his own defence – it was totally fitting, if you thought deeply enough about it. And Hermione's return to life as a vampire in *The Winter's Tale*: that had actually been booed. Felix had been delighted: What an effect! Who else had ever done it? Where there are boos, there's life!

Those escapades, those flights of fancy, those triumphs had been the brainchildren of an earlier Felix. They'd been acts of jubilation, of a happy exuberance. In the time just before Tony's coup, things had changed. They had darkened, and darkened so suddenly. *Howl, howl, howl . . .*

But he could not howl.

His wife, Nadia, was the first to leave him, barely a year after their marriage. It was a late marriage for him, and an unexpected one: he hadn't known he was capable of that kind of love. He was just discovering her virtues, just getting to really know her, when she'd died of a galloping staph infection right after childbirth. Such things happened, despite modern medicine. He still tries to recall her image, make her vivid for himself once more, but over the years she's moved gently away from him, fading like an old Polaroid. Now she's little more than an outline; an outline he fills with sadness.

So he was on his own with his newborn daughter, Miranda. Miranda: what else would he have named a motherless baby girl with a middle-aged, doting father? She was what had kept him from sinking down into chaos. He'd held himself together the best way he could, which was not too well; but still, he'd managed. He'd hired help, of course – he'd needed some women, since he knew nothing about the practical side of baby care, and because of his work he couldn't be there with Miranda all the time. But he'd spent every free moment he could with her. Though there hadn't been many free moments.

He'd been entranced with her from the start. He'd hovered, he'd marvelled. So perfect, her fingers, her toes, her eyes! Such a delight! Once she could talk he'd even taken her to the theatre; so bright she'd been. She'd sit there, taking it all in, not wriggling or bored as a lesser two-year-old would have been. He'd had such plans: once she was bigger they would travel together, he could show her the world, he could teach her so many things. But then, at the age of three . . .

High fever. Meningitis. They'd tried to reach him, the women, but he'd been in rehearsal with strict orders not to be interrupted and they hadn't known what to do. When he finally got home there were frantic tears, and then the drive to the hospital, but it was too late, too late.

The doctors had done everything they could: every platitude had been applied, every excuse offered. But nothing worked, and then she was gone. Carried off, as they used to say. But carried off where? She couldn't have simply vanished from the universe. He'd refused to believe that.

Lavinia, Juliet, Cordelia, Perdita, Marina. All the lost daughters. But some of them had been found again. Why not his Miranda?

What to do with such a sorrow? It was like an enormous black cloud boiling up over the horizon. No: it was like a blizzard. No: it was like nothing he could put into language. He couldn't face it head-on. He had to transform it, or at the very least enclose it.

Right after the funeral with its pathetically small coffin he'd plunged himself into *The Tempest*. It was an evasion, he knew that much about himself even then, but it was also to be a kind of reincarnation.

Miranda would become the daughter who had not been lost; who'd been a protecting cherub, cheering her exiled father as they'd drifted in their leaking boat over the dark sea; who hadn't died, but had grown up into a lovely girl. What he couldn't have in life he might still catch sight of through his art: just a glimpse, from the corner of his eye.

He would create a fit setting for this reborn Miranda

he was willing into being. He would outdo himself as an actor-director. He would push every envelope, he would twist reality until it twangled. There was a feverish desperation in those long-ago efforts of his, but didn't the best art have desperation at its core? Wasn't it always a challenge to Death? A defiant middle finger on the edge of the abyss?

His Ariel, he'd decided, would be played by a transvestite on stilts who'd transform into a giant firefly at significant moments. His Caliban would be a scabby street person – black or maybe Native – and a paraplegic as well, pushing himself around the stage on an oversized skateboard. Stephano and Trinculo? He hadn't worked them out, but bowler hats and codpieces would be involved. And juggling: Trinculo could juggle some things he might pick up on the beach of the magic island, such as squids.

His Miranda would be superb. She would be a wild thing, as it stood to reason she must have been – shipwrecked, then running all over the island for twelve years, most likely barefoot, for where would she have come by shoes? She must've had feet with soles on them like boots.

After an exhausting search during which he'd rejected the merely young and the merely pretty, he'd cast a former child gymnast who'd gone all the way to Silver in the North American championships and had then been accepted at the National Theatre School: a strong, supple waif, just coming into bloom. Anne-Marie Greenland was her name. She was so eager, so energetic: barely over sixteen. She had little theatrical training, but he knew he could coax what he wanted out of her. A performance so fresh it wouldn't even be a performance. It would be reality. Through her, his Miranda would come back to life.

Felix himself would be Prospero, her loving father. Protective – perhaps too protective, but only because he was acting in his daughter's best interests. And wise; wiser than Felix. Though even wise Prospero was stupidly trusting of those close to him, and too interested in perfecting his wizardly skills.

Prospero's magic garment would be made of animals – not real animals or even realistic ones, but plush toys that had been unstuffed and then sewn together: squirrels, rabbits, lions, a tiger-like thing, and several bears. These animals would evoke the elemental nature of Prospero's supernatural yet natural powers. Felix had ordered some fake leaves and spray-painted gold flowers and gaudy dyed feathers that would be intertwined among the furry creatures to give his cape extra pizzazz and depth of meaning. He would wield a staff he'd found in an antique shop: an elegant Edwardian walking stick with a silver fox head on the top and eyes that were possibly jade. It was a modest length for a wizard's staff, but Felix liked to juxtapose extravagance with understatement. Such an octogenarian prop could play ironically at crucial moments. At the end of the play, during Prospero's Epilogue, he'd planned a sunset effect, with glitter confetti falling from above like snow.

This *Tempest* would be brilliant: the best thing he'd ever done. He had been – he realizes now – unhealthily obsessed with it. It was like the Taj Mahal, an ornate mausoleum raised in honour of a beloved shade, or a priceless jewelled casket containing ashes. But more than that, because inside the charmed bubble he was creating, his Miranda would live again.

All the more crushing for him when it had fallen apart.

3. *Usurper*

They'd been on the verge of rehearsals when Tony had shown his hand. Twelve years later Felix can still recall every syllable of that encounter.

The conversation had begun normally enough, at their regular Tuesday afternoon meeting. At these meetings Felix would present his list of errands for Tony to do, and Tony would update Felix on any items requiring his attention or signature. Usually there wouldn't be many of these because Tony was so efficient he'd already have taken care of the truly important matters.

"Let's make this short," Felix had opened, as was his habit. He'd noted with distaste the pattern of alternating hares and tortoises on Tony's red tie: an attempt at wittiness, no doubt. Tony had a taste – an increasingly foppish taste – for expensive bagatelles. "My list for today: number one, we need to replace the lighting guy, he's not giving me what I need. Also, about the magic garment, we have to find –"

"I'm afraid I've got some bad news for you, Felix," said Tony. He was wearing yet another dapper new suit; usually that meant a Board meeting. Felix had got into the habit of skipping these: the Chair, Lonnie Gordon, was a decent man but a paralyzing bore, and the rest of the Board was a bunch of rubber-stamping sock puppets. He didn't waste much thought on them, however, because Tony had them well in line.

"Oh? What's that?" Felix asked. Bad news usually meant a trivial letter of complaint from a disgruntled patron. Did Lear have to take off *all* his clothes? Or it might be a dry-cleaning bill from a front-row theatregoer's unwilling interactive participation in a splatter scene: Macbeth's gore-drenched head flung too vigorously onto the stage, Gloucester's gouged-out eyeball slipping from the grasp of its extractor, with vile jelly staining the floral silk print, so hard to get out.

Tony would handle such peevish plaints, and he'd handle them well – he'd apply the appropriate dollop of apology mixed with smarm – but he liked to keep Felix in the loop in case of a close encounter of the unpleasant kind at the stage door. If criticized, Felix might overreact with a surplus of ripe adjectives, said Tony. Felix said his language was always appropriate to the occasion, and Tony said of course, but that was never good from a patron perspective. Also it could get into the papers.

"Unfortunately," said Tony now. There was a pause. He had an odd expression on his face. It was not a smile: it was a downturned mouth with a smile underneath. Felix felt his neck hairs prickling. "Unfortunately," said Tony at last in his suavest voice, "the Board has voted to terminate your contract. As Artistic Director."

Now it was Felix's turn to pause. "What?" he said. "This is a joke, right?" They can't do that, he was thinking. Without me, the whole Festival would go up in flames! The donors would flee, the actors would quit, the upscale restaurants and the gift shops and the bed-and-breakfasts would fold, and the town of Makeshiweg would sink back into the obscurity from which he'd been so skilfully plucking it, summer after summer, because what else did it have going for it besides a train-switching yard? Train-switching was not a theme. You couldn't build a menu around train-switching.

"No," said Tony. "I'm afraid it's not a joke." Another pause. Felix was staring at Tony, as if seeing him for the first time. "They feel you're losing, you know, your edge." Yet another pause. "I explained to them that you've been in shock, ever since your daughter . . . ever since your recent tragic loss, but that I was sure you'd pull out of it." This was such a low blow that it left Felix breathless. How dare they use that as an excuse? "I tried everything I possibly could," Tony added.

This was a lie. They both knew it. Lonnie Gordon, the Chair, would never have dreamed up a putsch like this, and the rest of the Board members were ciphers. Picked men, picked by Tony. And picked women, there were two of those. Tony's recommendations, every single one.

"My edge?" Felix said. "My fucking *edge*?" Who had ever been edgier than him?

"Well, your contact with reality," said Tony. "They think you have mental health issues. It's understandable, I told them, in view of your . . . But they couldn't see it. The animal-skin cape was a bridge too far. They saw the sketches. They say you'd have the animal rights activists down on us like a swarm of hornets."

"That's ridiculous," said Felix. "Those aren't real animals, they're children's *toys*!"

"As you must realize," said Tony with condescending patience, "that isn't the point. They look like animals. And the cape isn't the only objection. They really draw the line at

Caliban as a paraplegic, they say it's way beyond bad taste. People would think you're making fun of disability. Some of them would walk out. Or get wheeled out: we do have a substantial number of . . . Our demographic is not the under-thirties."

"Oh for cripes' sake!" said Felix. "This is political correctness gone way out of control! It's in the text, he's misshapen! If anything, in this day and age Caliban is the favourite, everyone cheers for him, I'm just –"

"I understand, but the thing is," said Tony, "we need to fill enough seats to justify the grants. The reviews of late have been . . . mixed. Especially last season."

"Mixed?" said Felix. "The reviews last season were sensational!"

"I kept the bad ones away from you," said Tony. "They were numerous. I have them here in my briefcase, if you'd care to take a look."

"Why in hell did you do that?" said Felix. "Keep them away? I'm not an infant."

"Bad reviews make you irritable," said Tony. "Then you take it out on the staff. It's bad for morale."

"I am *never* irritable!" Felix shouted. Tony ignored this.

"Here's the termination letter," he said, drawing an envelope from his inside jacket pocket. "The Board has voted you a retirement package, with thanks for your many years of service. I tried to make it larger." There was a definite smirk.

Felix took the envelope. His first impulse was to rip it into shreds, but he was in some sense paralyzed. He'd had rows during his career, but he'd never been terminated before. Ejected! Tumbled out! Discarded! He felt numb all over. "But my *Tempest*," he said. "That goes forward?" Already he was begging. "At least?" His best creation, his wondrous treasure, crushed. Trampled on the floor. Erased.

"I'm afraid not," said Tony. "We – they felt a clean break would be best. The production will be cancelled. You'll find the personal effects from your office out by your car. I'll need your security pass, by the way. When you're ready."

"I'm taking this to the Heritage Minister," Felix said weakly. He knew this was a non-starter. He'd gone to school with Sal O'Nally, they'd been rivals at the time. There had been a clash over a pencil-stealing incident that Felix had won and Sal had evidently not forgotten. He'd given it as his opinion – in several TV interviews aimed straight at Felix's crotch – that the Makeshiweg Festival should be doing more Noël Coward comedies and Andrew Lloyd Webber, and other musicals. Not that Felix had anything against musicals, he'd started his theatrical career in a student production of *Guys and Dolls*, but a whole diet of musicals . . .

The Sound of Music, said Sal. *Cats. Crazy for You.* Tap dancing. Things the ordinary person could understand. But the ordinary person could understand Felix's approach perfectly well! What was so difficult about *Macbeth* done with chainsaws? Topical. Direct.

"In point of fact, the Heritage Minister is in full agreement," said Tony. "Naturally we ran our decision by Sal – by Minister O'Nally – before the final vote, to confirm that we were taking the right path. Sorry about this, Felix," he added insincerely. "I know it's a shock to you. And very difficult for all of us."

"You'll have a replacement in mind, I suppose," said Felix, forcing his voice down to a reasonable level. *Sal.* First-name basis, then. So that's how things stood. He would not lose his cool. He would salvage the rags of his dignity.

"Actually, yes," said Tony. "Sal . . . The Board has asked, ah, me to take over. In the interim, of course. Until a candidate of suitable calibre can be found."

Interim, my ass, Felix thought. It was clear to him now. The secrecy, the sabotage. The snake-like subterfuge. The stupendous betrayal. Tony had been the instigator, he'd been the implementer start to finish. He'd waited until Felix had been at his most vulnerable and then he'd struck.

"You devious, twisted bastard," he shouted, which was some satisfaction to him. Though a small one, considering everything.

4. Garment

Two men from Security came into the room then. They must have been waiting outside the door listening for their cue, which most likely was Felix shouting. He kicks himself now for having been so predictable.

Tony must've rehearsed the Security guys beforehand: he was nothing if not efficient. They stood to either side of Felix, one black, one brown, their muscled arms crossed, their expressions impenetrable. They were new hires: Felix didn't know them. More to the point, they didn't know Felix and would therefore have no loyalty. More of Tony's handiwork.

"This is unnecessary," Felix said, but by that time Tony was well beyond feeling the need to reply. He gave a small shrug, a nod – the shrug of power, the nod of power – and Felix was escorted, politely but firmly, out to the parking lot, a hand of iron hovering beside each of his elbows.

There was a stack of cardboard boxes beside his car. His red car, a Mustang convertible he'd bought second-hand in a fit of mid-life defiance, back when he'd still been feeling sporty. Back before Miranda and then no Miranda. It had been rusting even then, and had since rusted more. He'd been planning to trade it in, get another car, a more sombre car. So much for that plan: he hadn't opened the severance envelope, but he already knew it would contain the bare minimum. Not enough for splurges, such as semi-new cars.

It was drizzling. The Security men helped Felix load the cardboard boxes into his rusting Mustang. They didn't say anything and neither did Felix, because what was there to say?

The boxes were sodden. What was in them? Papers, memorabilia, who knew? At that moment Felix didn't give a rat's ass. He contemplated a grand gesture, such as dumping everything out onto the parking lot and setting fire to it, but with what? Gasoline would be needed, or some kind of explosive, neither of which he had, and anyway why give Tony any more ammunition? (Fire department called, police summoned, Felix hauled off in chains gibbering and screaming, then charged with arson and creating a disturbance. Psychiatric expert brought in, paid by Tony. Diagnosis given. *See?* Tony would say to the Board. *Paranoid. Psychotic. Thank heavens we were able to divest ourselves of him in time, before he went postal right at the theatre.*)

As the three of them were stuffing the last of the soggy boxes into Felix's car, a lone, plump figure came trundling across the parking lot. It was Lonnie Gordon, Chairman of the Festival Board, holding an umbrella over his sparsely tufted, wattled head and carrying a plastic bag, some kind of stick, and what looked like an armful of skunks topped by a dead white cat.

The treacherous old geezer. Felix did not deign to glance at him.

Shuffle shuffle, waddle waddle, splish splash through the puddles, up came fat Lonnie, wheezing like a walrus. "I'm really sorry, Felix," he said when he was level with the back of the car.

"In a pig's ear," said Felix.

"It wasn't me," Lonnie said dolefully. "I was outvoted."

"Horse pookey," said Felix. The stick was his fox-head cane; the dead cat was his false Prospero beard; the skunk item, he saw now, was his magic garment. What would have been his magic garment. It was damp, the fur bedraggled. Its many plastic animal eyes gazed beadily out at him through the fur, its many tails drooped. In the grey light of day it looked stupid. But onstage, finished, interwoven with foliage, spray-painted with gold accents, highlighted with sequins, it would have been splendid.

"I'm unhappy you feel like that," said Lonnie. "I thought you might want to have these." He thrust the cape, the beard, and the walking stick at Felix, who kept his hands by his sides and simply glared. There was an awkward moment. Lonnie was truly distressed: he was a sentimental old coot, he cried at the end of tragedies. "Please," he said. "As a memento. After all your work." He held out the items again. The black security guard took them from him and crammed them in on top of the boxes.

"You needn't have bothered," said Felix.

"And this," said Lonnie, holding out the plastic bag. "It's your script. For *The Tempest*. With your notes. I took the liberty of looking at . . . it would have been wonderful," he went on, his voice quavering. "Maybe this will come in handy sometime."

"You're hallucinating," said Felix. "You and that cesspool, Tony, have ruined my career, and you know it. You might as well have taken me out and shot me." This was an exaggeration, but it was also a relief for Felix to be able to rub someone else's nose in his own misery. Someone with a soft heart and a weak spine and therefore susceptible to nose-rubbing, unlike Tony.

"Oh, I'm sure everything will work out for you," said Lonnie. "After all, such creativity, such talent . . . There must be a lot of, well, other places . . . A new start . . ."

"Other places?" said Felix. "I'm fifty, for cripes' sake. Past the sell-by date for new starts, wouldn't you say?"

Lonnie gulped. "I do see what you . . . We'll be moving a vote of thanks to you at the next Board meeting, and there's a proposal for a statue, you know, like, a bust, or maybe a fountain, in your name . . ."

Creativity. Talent. The two most overused words in the business, Felix thought bitterly. And the three most useless things in the world: a priest's cock, a nun's tits, and a heartfelt vote of thanks. "Stuff your bust," he said. But then he relented. "Thanks, Lonnie," he said. "I realize you mean well." He stuck out his hand. Lonnie shook it.

Was that actually a tear, rolling down the too-red cheek? Was that a quiver of the jowl? Lonnie should watch his ass with Tony at the helm, thought Felix. Especially if he keeps displaying such blubbery compunction. Tony would have no qualms; he'd crush any opposition, punish any hesitation, surround himself with thugs, lop off the deadwood.

"Any time you need a recommendation," said Lonnie. "I'd be happy to . . . or . . . I understand there's a . . . maybe after a rest . . . You've been working too hard, ever since your, your terribly sad, I was so sorry, it's way been too much, no one should have to . . ."

Lonnie had been at the funeral; at both funerals, Nadia's first. He'd been very upset about Miranda. He'd thrown a little bouquet of pink tea roses into the tiny grave, rather theatrically Felix had thought at the time, though he'd appreciated the gesture. Then Lonnie had broken down entirely, hiccupping into a white handkerchief as big as a tablecloth.

Tony had been at the funeral too, the sneaky rat, in a dark tie and a mourning face, though he must have been perfecting his coup even then.

"Thanks," said Felix again, cutting Lonnie short. "I'll be fine. And thanks," he said to the two Security men. "You've been helpful. I appreciate it."

"Drive safe, Mr. Phillips," said one of them.

"Yeah," said the other. "We're just doin' our job." It was an apology of sorts. They probably knew what it was like to get fired.

Then Felix climbed into his unsatisfactory car and drove out of the parking lot, into the rest of his life.

5. *Poor full cell*

The rest of his life. How long that time had once felt to him. How quickly it has sped by. How much of it has been wasted. How soon it will be over.

Leaving the Festival parking lot, Felix didn't have the sensation of driving. Instead he felt he was being driven, as if blown by a high wind. He was cold, although by this time the drizzle had stopped and the sun was shining, and also he had the heat turned on. Was he in shock? No: he wasn't shivering. He was calm.

The theatre, with its fluttering pennants and water-spewing dolphin fountain and outdoor patio and landscaped floral surroundings and festive ice-cream-licking play-goers, soon vanished. The main street of Makeshiweg, with its priccy restaurants and its pubs ornamented with the heads of archaic poets and pigs and Renaissance queens and frogs and gnomes and roosters, and its Celtic woollen-goods outlets and Inuit carving shops and English china boutiques, and then its handsome Victorian yellow brick houses with their occasional bed-and-breakfast signs, petered out into a string of drugstores and shoe repairs and Thai nail bars. Then, after a few more traffic lights, the carpet outlet warehouses and the Mexican food joints and the hamburger heavens of the strip mall on the outskirts were also left behind, and Felix was adrift.

Where was he? He had no idea. All around him stretched rolling fields, the tender green of spring wheat, the darker green of soybeans. Islands of trees extruded their feathery or glistening leaves around the century-old farmhouses, their grey wooden barns still serviceable, their silos punctuating the horizontals. The road was gravel now, and not in good repair.

He slowed down, looked around him. He longed for a den, a hidey-hole, a place where he knew no one and no one knew him. A retreat where he could recuperate, for now he was beginning to acknowledge to himself how badly he was wounded.

In a day or two, three at the most, Tony would plant some lying story in the newspapers. It would say that Felix had resigned as Artistic Director to pursue other opportunities, but nobody would believe that version. If he stayed in Makeshiweg, ill-intentioned reporters would sniff him out, relishing the fall of the mighty one. They'd phone him, lurk in ambush, corner him in one of the town bars, supposing he was foolish enough to go into one. They'd ask him if he cared to comment, hoping to provoke some yelling from him, considering his irascible reputation. But yelling would be a waste of breath, for what would it accomplish?

The sun was declining; its light slanted, grew yellower. How long had he been out here? Wherever *here* was. He drove on.

At some distance from the road, at the end of a disused laneway, there was an odd structure. It looked as if it had been built into a low hillside, enclosed by the earth with only its front wall showing. It had one window, and a door standing agape. There was a metal chimney pipe protruding from the wall, then elbowing upward, with a tin cap on the top. There was a clothesline, with a single clothespin still gripping a scrap of dishcloth. It was the last place anyone would expect Felix to land.

No harm in looking. So Felix looked.

He parked his car on the roadside, then walked down the laneway, damp grass and weeds swishing at his pant legs. The door creaked when he opened it wider, but a drop of oil on the hinges would fix that. The ceiling was low, with beams made of poles, whitewashed at one time, now spiderwebbed. The interior smelled not too unpleasantly of earth and wood, with a hint of ash: that was from the iron stove, with two burners and a small oven, rusty but still intact. Two rooms, the main room and another room that must have been the bedroom. It had a skylight – the glass looked somewhat new – and a side door, hooked shut. Felix unhooked the door and opened it. There was an overgrown path, then an outhouse. Thankfully he would not be reduced to the digging of a latrine: others had done that for him.

There was no furniture apart from a heavy old wooden armoire in the bedroom and a Formica-topped kitchen table, red with silver swirls. No chairs. There was a wide-planked floor: at least it wasn't mud. There was even a sink, with a hand pump. There was an electric light, and, miraculously, it turned on. Someone must have lived here more recently than, say, 1830.

It held less than the bare essentials, but if he could locate the owner, strike a deal, fix the place up a bit, it would do.

By choosing this shack and the privations that would come with it, he would of course be sulking. He'd be hairshirting himself, playing the flagellant, the hermit. *Watch me suffer*. He recognized his own act, an act with no audience but himself. It was childish, this self-willed moping. He was not being grown-up.

But in reality what were his options? He was too notorious to be able to find another job; not one of equal stature, not one he'd want. And Sal O'Nally, with his hand on the treasure chest of grants, would subtly block any senior appointment: Tony wouldn't want a rival, with Felix outdoing the Makeshiweg Festival from some other vantage point. Tony and Sal, working together as they obviously had already, would make sure his head stayed underwater. So why give them the satisfaction of trying?

He drove back to Makeshiweg the way he'd come and parked in front of the small brick cottage that he'd sublet for the current season. Ever since that unthinkable stretch of time . . . ever since he'd no longer had a family, he'd chosen not to own a house. He'd rented the homes of others. He still had a few pieces of furniture: a bed, a desk, a lamp, two old wooden chairs that he and Nadia had picked up at a yard sale. Personal bric-à-brac. Things left over from what had once been a complete life.

And the photo of his Miranda, of course. He always kept it near him, where he could look at it if he felt himself starting to slip down into the dark. He'd taken that picture himself, when Miranda was almost three. It was her first time on a swing. Her head was tipped back; she was laughing with joy; she was flying through the air; her small fists gripped the ropes; the morning light aureoled her hair. The frame around her was painted silver, a silver window frame. On the other side of that magical window she was still alive.

And now she would have to stay locked behind the glass, because, with the destruction of his *Tempest*, the new

Miranda – the Miranda he'd been intending to create, or possibly to resurrect – was dead in the water.

Tony hadn't even had the decency to allow him to meet with the staff, the technical support, the actors. To say goodbye. To voice his regret that his *Tempest* would not happen. He'd been hustled off like a criminal. Were Tony and his minions afraid of him? Afraid of a general rebellion, a counter-coup? Did they seriously think Felix had that much power?

He called a moving company and asked how soon they could come. It was an emergency, he said; he needed everything packed up and stored as quickly as possible; he'd pay extra for the rush. He wrote a cheque to the owner of his sublet, covering the balance of the term. He went to the bank, deposited Tony's shitty kiss-off money, informed the manager that he would shortly have a different address and would notify them by letter.

Luckily he had some savings. He could remain invisible to the world at large, for now.

His next task was to locate the owner of the hillside dwelling. He drove back out to the gravel road, then tried the nearest farmhouse. A woman answered the door; middle-aged, middling looks, of middle height, with neutral hair scraped back into a ponytail. Jeans and a sweatshirt; behind her on the linoleum-tile floor, a child's plastic toy. Felix's heart gave a tiny lurch.

The woman crossed her arms and stood blocking the doorway. "I seen your car before," she said. "Up at the shanty there."

"Yes," said Felix with what he considered his most charming manner. "I was wondering. Do you know who owns it?"

"Why?" said the woman. "Not us. We're not paying no tax on it. That old thing, worth nothing. Left over from the pioneers or whatever, before they had any money. I told Bert it should've been burned down years ago."

Ah, thought Felix. A deal can be made. "I have been ill," he said, which wasn't entirely a lie. "I need a rest in the country. I think the air would do me good."

"Air," said the woman with a snort. "There's a lot of air around here, if that's what you want. It's free, last time I looked. Help yourself."

"I would like to live in the little cottage," Felix said, smiling in a harmless manner. He wished to give the impression that he was dotty, but not too dotty. A loony but not a maniac. "I would pay rent, of course. In cash," he added.

That changed everything, and Felix was asked to come in and sit at the kitchen table, and they got down to business. The woman wanted the money, she made no secret of it. Bert – the husband – couldn't make enough off the alfalfa and was driving the propane route to make ends meet, plus he cleared driveways in winter. He was away a lot, leaving her to cope with everything. Another snort, a toss of the head: "everything" included loonies like Felix.

She said that folks had lived in the shanty off and on, the latest being "two hippies, him a painter, her whatever you'd call what shacks up with painters" – that was a year ago. Before then, a poor uncle of hers; and before that, an aunt of Bert's who was a few bricks short of a load and had to be put away. Earlier than that she didn't know, because it was before her time. Some folks said the little house was haunted, but Felix should pay no attention to that rumour, she said derisively, because those people were ignorant and it wasn't true. (She clearly thought it was.)

It was agreed that Felix would have the use of the shanty,

and could make whatever improvements he wanted. Bert would plough the laneway in winter so Felix wouldn't have to walk through the snow all the way up. Maude – the wife – would handle the cash, in an envelope every first of the month, and if anyone asked it never happened, because Felix was her uncle and was living there for free. She and Bert would supply the wood for the stove: their teenage son could haul it over on the tractor. She'd already figured the cost of that into the price. If Felix liked, she could do his wash for him, extra.

Felix thanked her, and said they should wait and see. On his part, he stipulated that she not tell anyone about him. He was lying low, he said. He had his own reasons, but they were not criminal ones.

She looked sideways at him; she didn't believe him about the criminality, but she didn't care about it either. "Trust me on that," she said. Oddly, he did trust her.

They shook hands at the door. She had a tough grip, more like a man's. "What's your name?" she said. "I mean, what name should I say, in case?"

Felix hesitated. *None of your business* trembled on his lips. "Mr. Duke," he said.

6. Abysm of time

It didn't take Felix long to discover that it was easy to disappear, and that his disappearance was borne lightly by the world at large. The hole his sudden absence left in the fabric of the Makeshiweg Festival was filled soon enough – filled, indeed, by Tony. The show rolled on, as shows do.

Where had Felix gone? It was a mystery, but not one that anyone appeared dedicated to solving. He could imagine the chit-chat. Maybe he'd had a breakdown? Jumped off a bridge? The intensity of his sorrow when his little girl had died – so tragic – and then the way he'd immediately become obsessed over that frankly crack-brained *Tempest* of his, you had to wonder. But you didn't have to wonder very long, because for everyone doing the wondering, other, more pressing concerns would have flowed into the empty space left by Felix's departure, and the ripples of gossip must quickly have subsided. There were careers to be advanced, there were parts to be memorized, there were skills to be honed.

Here's to the mad old bugger, he could imagine them saying in the Toad and Whistle or the King's Head or the Imp and Pig-Nut, or wherever else the actors and factotums of the

Festival were in the habit of lifting a glass in their off-hours. *To the Maestro. To Felix Phillips, wherever he is.*

Felix moved his bank account to a branch in Wilmot, two towns away, where he also rented a post office box for himself. He was, after all, still alive; he would need, for instance, to file his tax return. Nothing would set the dogs on his trail so quickly as a failure to comply. Such was the minimum price to be paid for the privilege of walking around on the earth's crust and continuing to breathe, eat, and shit, he thought sourly.

He opened a second bank account in the name of F. Duke, claiming this was a nom de plume. He was, he explained to the bank, a writer. It pleased him to have an alter ego, one without his own melancholy history. Felix Phillips was washed up, but F. Duke might still have a chance; though at what he could not yet say.

For tax-paying purposes he kept his own name. Simpler that way. But he was "Mr. Duke" to Maude and Bert, and to their scowling little daughter, Crystal, who clearly thought Felix was a child-devourer, and to Walter, their surly teenage son, who, for the first few years – before he moved out west to work in Alberta – did indeed haul a few loads of firewood over to Felix's modest abode every fall.

For a time, Felix tried to amuse himself by casting Maude as the blue-eyed hag, Sycorax the witch, and Walter as Caliban the semi-human log-hauler and dishwasher, in his own personal *Tempest* – his *Tempest* of the headspace – but that didn't last long. None of it fitted: Bert the husband wasn't the devil, and young Crystal, a podgy, stubby child, could not be imagined as the sylph-like Miranda.

And there was no room for an Ariel in this ménage,

though Felix paid Bert – who was handy with tools – to add an extra electrical cable in from their farmhouse, alongside the surely illegal one that was already there. With that he could run a small heater on cold days, and also a bar fridge and a two-burner hotplate, though he could not have them all on at once without causing a blackout. He bought an electric kettle too. Maude estimated how much power he used and overcharged him accordingly. If the Maude family was anything in *The Tempest*, they were lesser elementals: a source of power, though not very much of it, he joked to himself.

Apart from the envelope of cash that Felix delivered into the roughened fist of Maude on the first of every month, he had little contact with his landlords, if that is what they were. The Maude family minded their own business. And Felix minded his.

But what was his business?

He made an attempt to avoid news of the theatre, and reading about the theatre, and thinking about the theatre. It was too hurtful. But his attempts were rarely successful. He found himself buying the local papers, and even the ones from nearby cities, scanning the reviews, then ripping them up for fire-starters.

During this early period of mourning and brooding he turned to the improvement of his rustic dwelling. The activity was therapeutic. He tidied up the inside space, swept away the cobwebs, got his few things out of storage and moved them in. With a little oiling and priming and a new rubber gasket, the hand pump worked. There was no mystery to the outhouse: it was functional, and so far not smelly. He bought a package of a brown granular substance advertised as being the right thing for outhouses and dumped some in periodically. He added a rug to the bedroom floor. He added a night table. The photo of Miranda perched brightly upon it, laughing with joy.

Despite his pathetic attempts at domesticity, he slept restlessly and woke often.

He bought a few implements at the hardware store in Wilmot: a hammer, a scythe. He cut the weeds in front of the shanty; he cleaned the window and, more precariously, the skylight. He thought of digging a garden, planting some tomatoes or other vegetables. But no: that would be going too far. Still, he kept himself busy. He worked at it, this busyness of his.

It wasn't enough.

He went to the library and took out books. Surely he should use this opportunity to read all those classics he'd never made it through in youth. *The Brothers Karamazov, Anna Karenina, Crime and Punishment* . . . But he couldn't do it: there was too much real life, there was too much tragedy. Instead he found himself gravitating to children's stories in which everything came out all right in the end. *Anne of Green Gables, Peter Pan.* Fairy tales: *Snow White, Sleeping Beauty.* Girls left for dead in glass coffins or four-poster beds, then brought miraculously back to life by the touch of love: that was what he longed for. A reversal of fate.

"You must have grandchildren," the nice librarian said to him. "Do you read to them?" Felix nodded and smiled. No sense in telling her the truth.

But even this resource was exhausted for him after a while. He began to spend a reprehensible amount of time sitting in the shade, in a striped deck chair he'd found at a garage sale, staring into space. When you did that long enough you began to see things that weren't there strictly speaking, but this didn't alarm him. Shapes in clouds, faces in the leaves. They made him feel less lonely.

The silence began to get to him. Not silence, exactly. The bird songs, the chirping of the crickets, the wind in the trees. The flies, buzzing so contrapuntally in his outhouse. Melodious. Soothing. Sometimes, to escape that ongoing semi-music, he'd climb into his increasingly unreliable car and drive into Wilmot and buy something at the hardware store, just to hear the sound of an ordinary human voice. After a few years, he had an accumulation of Krazy Glues and a small junk-pile of loose screws, hooks without eyes, and picture hangers. Had he begun to shamble? Was he regarded as a harmless local eccentric? Was he a subject of tittle-tattle, or did anyone notice him at all? Did he even care?

And if not, what did he care about? What did he want, in the way he had once wanted, so passionately, to be a mover and shaker in the world of the theatre? What was his purpose now? What did he have to live for? His occupation was gone, and the love of his life. Both of his loves. He was in danger of stagnating. Losing all energy. Succumbing to inertia. At least he kept out of the liquor store, and the bars.

He could become one of those aimless late-middle-aged men – past the snares of romanticism, past ambition – wandering here and there on the earth. He could take himself on trips: he could more or less afford it. But they would not be numerous, these trips, or interesting to him, because where did he want to go? He could hook up with some lonely woman and have a fling, and make both of them miserable. Starting a new family was out of the question, because no one could supply the place of the lost, the vanished one. He could join a bridge club, a camera club, a watercolour painting club. But he hated bridge, he no longer wanted to take photographs, and he couldn't paint to save his life.

But did he want to save his life? And if not, what then?

He could hang himself. He could blow his brains out. He could drown himself in Lake Huron, which was not that far away.

Idle speculation. He wasn't serious.

Therefore?

He required a focus, a purpose. He gave this much thought while sitting in his deck chair. Eventually he concluded that there were two things thing left for him – two projects that could still hold satisfaction. After a time he began to see more clearly what they were.

First, he needed to get his *Tempest* back. He had to stage it, somehow, somewhere. His reasons were beyond theatrical; they had nothing to do with his reputation, his career – none of that. Quite simply, his Miranda must be released from her glass coffin; she must be given a life. But how to do it, where to find the actors? Actors did not grow on trees, numerous though the trees were around his hovel.

Second, he wanted revenge. He longed for it. He daydreamed about it. Tony and Sal must suffer. His present woeful situation was their doing, or a lot of it was. They'd treated him shabbily. But what form could such revenge possibly take?

Those were the two things he wanted. He wanted them more each day. But he didn't know how to go about getting them.

7. Rapt in secret studies

His *Tempest* would be forced to wait, *faute de mieux*: he didn't have the wherewithal. So first he would concentrate on the revenge.

How would it work? Would he lure Tony down into a dank cellar with the promise of a cask of Amontillado, then brick him up in the wall? But Tony wasn't a foodie. He wasn't much interested in gourmet eats and drinks for their own sakes: they pleased him only as status markers. And he would never be so stupid as to go down into a dark place with Felix unsupported by a couple of armed guards, since he would be well aware of Felix's justified resentment.

Would Felix seduce Tony's wife or, better, hint that some young stud had seduced her? But Tony's wife was a showpiece made of frozen alabaster: she was most likely a robot, and unseducible. And, even suppose her invisible chastity belt could be safe-cracked, why be unfair to the innocent young stud, whoever he might be? Why bring down upon him the ire of Tony, now the wielder of considerable career-incinerating weaponry? Young studs had a half-life and should be allowed to enjoy their prime time in the swimming pools and scented sheets of the demi-matronly while that time was still theirs to enjoy. Before wilt set in, before drooping, and an inability to focus.

Would he sneak into Tony's house/office/favourite restaurant and spike Tony's lunch with a toxic agent that would give Tony an incurable illness or inflict upon him a lingering and painful death? Then Felix could disguise himself as a doctor and appear in Tony's hospital room and gloat. He'd read a murder mystery in which the victim had died from eating daffodil bulbs. They'd been disguised in an onion soup, as he recalled.

No, no. Mere fantasizing. Such revenges were far too melodramatic, and in any case well beyond his capabilities. He would have to be more subtle.

Know thine enemy, all the best authorities advised. He began to trace the movements of Tony: where he went, what he was doing, his pronouncements, his television appearances. His list of achievements; Tony liked accumulating achievements, and was careful to ensure that they were acknowledged.

At first this indirect stalking was easy: all Felix needed to do was get the Makeshiweg papers – of which, in those days, there were two – and look up the theatrical news and the social notes. Tony had been much in demand for soirées and fundraisers at that time, and was an affable granter of interviews. Felix ground his teeth over the Arts Entrepreneur of the Year Award, then over the Scholastic Outreach Award, given to Tony for the Festival program that bussed kids in from the surrounding area and made them sit through *Hamlet*, whispering and giggling, as the bodies piled up onstage. That program had been Felix's idea. In fact, most of the items Tony was getting awards for had originated in the brain of Felix.

In Year Five of Felix's exile, here was another award: the

Order of Ontario. La-de-da, Felix growled to himself. Another dingbat to wear on your lapel. Imposter!

In Year Six, Tony changed direction. He resigned from the Festival and ran for political office, right in the town of Makeshiweg, where he was a familiar face in public life, and he won a seat in the provincial legislature and became an Honourable. The Heritage Minister was still Sal O'Nally, so now they were both in the same nest, no doubt assiduously feathering it. How cozy for both of them.

It wouldn't be long before Tony would wiggle his way into Cabinet, thought Felix. Already he was being spoken of as up-and-coming. In his photographs, he had a ministerial air.

Then technology added a new telescope to Felix's meagre arsenal of spyware: the snoop gremlin, Google. Felix had once had a computer, but it had belonged to the Festival and had been impounded when Felix was deposed. For a while he'd lurked around in the Internet café in Wilmot, following Tony's activities as best he could. He'd closed his work email account when he'd left the Festival – how galling it would have been to receive all those hypocritical messages of commiseration on it – but now he opened two new accounts, one for himself and another one for Mr. Duke, who had acquired a couple of credit cards. He thought about getting Mr. Duke a driver's licence, but that would've been pushing it.

He felt he was becoming too visible in the Wilmot café – he might be suspected of watching porn – so he bought a cheap personal computer, second-hand. He had a telephone line run into his hovel from the Maude household and used dial-up. But after a while cable was installed along his back road, so he upgraded to an Ethernet connection and a router, which increased both the speed and the privacy of his Internet access.

It was amazing how much you could learn about a person over the Net. There was Felix, alone in his neglected corner reading the Google Alerts, and there were Tony and Sal, bustling about in the world, not suspecting that they had a shadower; a watcher, a waiter, an Internet stalker.

What was Felix waiting for? He hardly knew. A chance opening, a lucky break? A pathway toward a moment of confrontation? A moment when the balance of power would lie with him. It was an impossible thing to wish for, but suppressed rage sustained him. That, and his thirst for justice.

He realized that his spying was a little deranged, though only a little. But he'd gradually been opening another space in his life that verged on full-blown lunacy.

It began when he was counting time by how old Miranda would be, had she lived. She'd be five, then six; she'd be losing her baby teeth; she'd be learning to write. That sort of thing. Wistful daydreaming at first.

But it was only a short distance from wistful daydreaming to the half-belief that she was still there with him, only invisible. Call it a conceit, a whimsy, a piece of acting: he didn't really believe it, but he engaged in this non-reality as if it were real. He returned to his habit of checking out kids' books from the Wilmot library, only now he read them out loud in the evenings. Partly he enjoyed it – his voice was still as good as it had ever been, it kept him in practice – but partly he was indulging his self-created illusion. Was there a small girl listening to him? No, not really. But it was soothing to think that there was.

When Miranda was five, six, seven, he helped her with her schoolwork; she was home-schooled, naturally. They'd sit at the Formica table, he in one of his old wooden chairs, she in the other one. "Six times nine?" he'd quiz her. She was so sharp! She almost never made a mistake.

They began having their meals together, which was a good thing because otherwise he might sometimes have forgotten about meals. She scolded him gently when he didn't eat enough. Finish what's on your plate, she would say to him. Her own favourite was macaroni and cheese.

When she was eight, he taught her to play chess. She was a quick learner, and was soon beating him two times out of three. How seriously she would study the board, chewing on the end of the long braid she'd learned to make all by herself. How delighted he would be, secretly, when she won, although he'd pretend to be downhearted. Then she would laugh, because she knew he was only fooling. If he really had been downhearted, she would have been all sympathy. Such an empathetic girl. He tried never to show his anger to her, the anger he was hoarding up against Tony, against Sal: it would have confused her. When he was following their antics on the Internet, muttering out loud to himself, she was always out of the room.

During the day she was often outside, playing in the field beside the house or in the woodlot at the back. He would see a cloud of butterflies lift in the meadow: she must have startled them. When blue jays or crows would make a fuss in the woods, he'd conclude that Miranda had been walking there. Squirrels chattered at her, grouse whirred away at her approach. In the dusk, fireflies marked her path, and owls greeted her with muffled calls.

In the winters, when the snow drifted in the laneway and the wind howled, she'd slip outside without a second thought. She didn't dress as warmly as she ought to have done, despite his nagging about mittens, but nothing happened as a consequence: no colds, no flu. In fact, she was never ill, unlike himself. When he was sick she tiptoed around him, anxious; but he never had to worry about her, because what harm could possibly come to her? She was beyond harm.

She never asked him how they came to be there together, living in the shanty, apart from everyone else. He never told her. It would have been a shock to her, to learn that she did not exist. Or not in the usual way.

One day he heard her singing, right outside the window. He didn't daydream it, the way he'd been semi-daydreaming up to then. It wasn't one of his whimsical yet despairing fabrications. He actually heard a voice. It was not a consolation. Instead, it frightened him.

"This has gone way too far," he told himself sternly. "Snap out of it, Felix. Pull yourself together. Break out of your cell. You need a real-world connection."

8. *Bring the rabble*

Therefore, in Year Nine of his exile – when Miranda was twelve – Mr. Duke took a job. It wasn't a high-status job, but that suited Felix: he wanted to keep a low profile. Getting back into the world, re-engaging with people – he hoped it would ground him. He'd been going stir-crazy, he could see that now. Too much time alone with his grief eating away at him, too much time gnawing on his grievances. He felt as if he were waking up from a long and melancholy dream.

The job came his way via one of the local online papers. A teacher in the Literacy Through Literature high school level program at the nearby Fletcher County Correctional Institute had suffered a sudden illness – a fatal illness, as it turned out. A vacancy needed to be filled at short notice. It would be a temporary position. Some experience was required, although – Felix assumed – not much. Those interested . . .

Felix was interested. Using Mr. Duke's email account, he sent an initial note registering his willingness. Then he cobbled together a fraudulent resumé, forging decades-old letters of reference from several obscure schools in Saskatchewan, signed by principals who might be expected to have died or moved to Florida. He was ninety percent certain that these would never be checked: he'd be, after all, just a stopgap. In his covering letter he said he'd been retired for some years but felt the need to give back to the community, since he had been given so much in life himself.

He was summoned by email for an interview almost immediately, by which he divined that there weren't any other applicants. So much the better: they were probably desperate, and he'd get the job by default. By this time he really wanted it, he'd talked himself into it. It had, perhaps, some potential.

He cleaned himself up – he'd been letting himself get ratty – and bought a new dark-green plebian-looking shirt at the Mark's Work Wearhouse in Wilmot. He even trimmed his beard. He'd grown it over the years; it was grey now, almost white, and he had long white eyebrows to match. He hoped he looked sage.

The interview took place not at Fletcher Correctional itself but at a McDonald's nearby. The woman interviewing him was forty-odd and making efforts: the streak of pink in her grey-blond hair, the shining earrings; the careful nails, a fashionable silver. Her name was Estelle, she offered. The first name was a positive signal, she wanted them to be friends. She didn't work at Fletcher herself, she explained: she was a professor at Guelph University and supervised the Fletcher course from a distance. She also sat on various advisory committees, for the government. The Ministry of Justice. "My grandfather was a Senator," she said. "It's given me a certain access. I know the ropes, you could say, and I have to share with you that the Literacy Through Literature program has been more or less . . . well, my special baby. I've lobbied quite hard for it!"

Felix said that was admirable. Estelle said we all did what we could.

The teacher who'd died had been such a fine person, she said; he'd be missed by so many, it was so sudden, a shock. He'd really tried, up at Fletcher; he'd accomplished . . . well, he'd done his very best, under conditions that were . . . no one could go into it expecting too much.

Felix nodded and um-hummed at the right places, and looked sympathetic, and made eye contact. In return, Estelle's smiles multiplied. All was as going as it should.

The preliminaries over, Estelle launched into the interview proper. She took a breath. "I believe I recognize you, Mr. Duke," she said. "Despite the beard, which I must say looks very distinguished. You're Felix Phillips, yes? The famous director? I've been attending that Festival since I was a kid, my grandfather used to take us; I have a *big* collection of the programs!"

So much for alter egos. "Indeed," said Felix, "but I'm going under Mr. Duke for this job. I thought it would be less intimidating."

"I see." A smile, more tentative. A weaponless, elderly theatre director, intimidating? To the hardened Fletcher inmates? Really?

"If anyone on the hiring end knew who I was, they'd say I was way overqualified. Too professional for this position." A bigger smile: Estelle found this more convincing. "So it can be our secret," Felix said, lowering his voice, leaning across the table. "You can be my confidante."

"Oh, what fun!" She liked it. "A confidante! It's like a Restoration play! *The City Heiress*, or . . ."

"By Aphra Behn," said Felix. "Except the confidantes are burglars." He was impressed: it was an obscure play, not one he'd ever done.

"Maybe I've always longed to be a burglar," she laughed. "But seriously, this is quite an honour! I must have seen almost all of your plays, over at Makeshiweg, when you were there. I loved your *Lear*! It was so, it was so . . ."

"Visceral," said Felix, quoting one of the more enthusiastic reviews.

"Yes," said Estelle. "Visceral." She paused. "But this position . . . I mean, you are of course way overqualified. You realize it's only part-time – three months a year. You wouldn't expect a commensurate –"

"No, no," said Felix. "Standard pay. I've been retired for a while, I'm bound to be rusty."

"Retired? Oh, you're too young to retire," she said, a reflex compliment. "That would be a waste."

"Too kind," said Felix.

There was a pause. "You do understand that this is a prison," she said at length. "You'll be teaching, well, convicted criminals. The goal of the course is to improve their basic literacy skills so they can find a meaningful place in the community once they're back in the world. Wouldn't you be rather wasted on them?"

"It would be a challenge," said Felix. "I've always liked challenges."

"Let's be frank," said Estelle. "Some of these men have very short fuses. They act out. I wouldn't want you to . . ." She clearly had a vision of Felix lying on the floor with a homemade shiv sticking out of his neck and a puddle of blood spreading around him.

"Dear lady," said Felix, resorting to one of his posh-aristocrat stage accents, "in the early days of the theatre, actors were regarded as next door to criminals anyway. And I've known many actors – that's what they do, they act out! Stage rage. There are ways of handling that. And, studying with me, they'll be guaranteed to learn more self-control."

Estelle was still wavering, but she said, "Well, if you're willing to give it a try . . ."

"I'd need to do things in my own way," said Felix, pushing his luck. "I'd want considerable latitude." It was the beginning of the semester and the dead teacher had barely got started, so Felix himself would have room to create. "What do they usually read for this course?"

"Well, we've relied on *The Catcher in the Rye*," said Estelle. "Quite a lot. And some stories by Stephen King, they like those. *The Curious Incident of the Dog in the Night-Time*. Many of them identify with that, and it's simple to read. Short sentences."

"I see," said Felix. Catcher in the bloody Rye, he thought. Pablum for prep school juveniles. It was a medium- to maximum-security facility; these were grown men, they'd lived lives that had driven them far beyond those parameters. "I'll be taking a somewhat different tack."

"I hesitate to ask what tack," said Estelle, cocking her head archly. Now that she'd accepted him for the job, she was relaxed enough to flirt. Watch your trousers, Felix, he admonished himself. She doesn't have a wedding ring, so you're fair game. Don't start anything you can't finish.

"Shakespeare," said Felix. "That's the tack."

"Shakespeare?" Estelle, who'd been leaning forward, sat back in her chair. Was she reconsidering? "But surely that's far too . . . there are a lot of words . . . They'll get discouraged; maybe you should choose things more at the level of . . . To be frank, some of them can barely read."

"You think Shakespeare's actors did a lot of *reading*?" said Felix. "They were journeymen, like" – he snatched an example from the air, possibly a bad one –"like bricklayers! They never read the whole play themselves; they only memorized their own lines, and their cues. Also they improvised a lot. The text wasn't a sacred cow."

"Well, yes, I know, but . . ." said Estelle. "But Shakespeare is such a classic."

Too good for them, was what she meant. "He had no intention of being a classic!" Felix said, adding a tinge of indignation to his voice. "For him, the classics were, well, Virgil, and Herodotus, and . . . He was simply an actor-manager trying to keep afloat. It's only due to luck that we *have* Shakespeare at all! Nothing was even published till he was gone! His old friends stuck the plays together out of scraps – bunch of clapped-out actors trying to remember what they'd said, after the guy was dead!" When in doubt, he told himself, just keep talking. It was an old trick for when you froze onstage: throw out a line, anything that sounded good, to give the prompter time to toss you the real one.

Estelle looked puzzled. "Well, yes, but what does that have to do with . . ."

"I believe in hands-on," said Felix as authoritatively as he could.

"Hands on what?" said Estelle, truly alarmed now. "You have to respect their personal space, you're not allowed to . . ."

"We'll be performing," said Felix. "That's what I mean. We'll be enacting the plays. That's the only way you can really get inside the parts. Oh, don't worry, I'll fulfill the official criteria, whatever they are. They'll do assignments and write essays and all of that. I'll mark those. I suppose that's what's required."

Estelle smiled. "You're very idealistic," she said. "Essays? I really . . ."

"Pieces of prose," said Felix. "About whichever play we're doing."

"You really think so?" said Estelle. "You could get them to do that?"

"Give me three weeks," said Felix. "If it's not working out by then, I'll do *The Catcher in the Rye*. Promise."

"All right, agreed," said Estelle. "Good luck with it."

The first few weeks were a little rough, granted. Felix and Shakespeare had needed to work their way uphill over some fairly thorny ground, and Felix discovered that he was less prepared for the conditions inside than he'd thought he would be. He'd had to assert his authority, draw a few lines in the sand. At one point he'd threatened to walk out. There'd been some quitters, but those who'd stayed had been serious, and in the event the Fletcher Correctional Shakespeare class was a hit. In its own modest way, it was cutting edge; it was also, you could say – and Felix did say it to his students, explaining the term carefully – avant-garde. It was cool. After the first season, guys lined up for it. Astonishingly, their reading and writing scores went up, on average, by fifteen percent. How was the enigmatic Mr. Duke getting these results? Heads were shaken in wonder, fraud was suspected. But no, objective testing backed him up. The effect was real.

Estelle was given much credit, out in the wide world where academics gathered and conferences were held and theories were proposed and ministries approved budgets, but Felix didn't begrudge her that. He was too busy. He was back in the theatre, but in a new way, a way he'd never anticipated in his earlier life. If anyone had told him then that he'd be doing Shakespeare with a pack of cons inside the slammer he'd have said they were hallucinating.

*

He'd been at it now for three years. He'd chosen the plays carefully. He'd begun with *Julius Caesar*, continued with *Richard III*, and followed that with *Macbeth*. Power struggles, treacheries, crimes: these subjects were immediately grasped by his students, since in their own ways they were experts in them.

They had their informed opinions about how the characters could have conducted their affairs better. So dumb to let Mark Antony speak at Caesar's funeral, because it gave him an opening, and then look what! Richard went too far, he shouldn't have assassinated just about everyone, it meant nobody helped him out with his battle when the time came. You want to be the kingpin, you need allies: no-brainer! As for Macbeth, he shouldn't have trusted those witches because it made him overconfident and that was a big No. A guy needed to keep an eye on his weak points, rule number one, because anything that can go wrong will go wrong. We *know* that, right? Nods all round.

Felix wisely assigned those opinions as writing topics.

He avoided the romantic comedies: too frivolous for this bunch and not a good idea to get into questions of sex, which could lead to uproar. And *Hamlet* and *Lear* were off the table too, for another reason: they were too depressing. There were enough attempted suicides at Fletcher as it was, and some of them had succeeded. The three plays he'd done so far were acceptable, because although each one ended with a clutch of deaths, each also provided a new beginning in the shape of whoever it was who won. Bad behaviour and even stupid behaviour were punished and virtue was rewarded, more or less. With Shakespeare it was always more or less, as he took pains to point out.

His teaching method was the same for each play. First, everyone read the text in advance, a text shortened by him.

He also provided a summary of the plot and a set of notes, and a crib sheet for the archaic words. Those who couldn't make it through at that point would usually drop out.

Then, once he could meet with the class, he would outline the keynotes: what was the play about? There were always at least three keynotes, sometimes more, because, as he told them, Shakespeare was tricky. He had a lot of layers. He liked to hide things behind curtains, until – presto! – he'd surprise you.

His next move was important to his method: he'd limit the curse words permitted in the class. The students were allowed to choose a list of swear words, but only from the play itself. They liked that feature; also it ensured that they read the text very thoroughly. Then he'd set up a competition: points off for using the wrong swear words. You could only say "The devil damn thee black, thou cream-faced loon" if the play was *Macbeth*. Transgressors lost points. At the end there was a valuable reward consisting of cigarettes, which Felix smuggled in. That aspect was very popular.

Next in the curriculum came an in-depth study of the main characters, explored in class one by one. What made them tick? What did they want? Why did they do what they did? Hot debates would take place, alternate versions would be proposed. Was Macbeth a psycho, or what? Was Lady Macbeth always bonkers, or did she go that way out of guilt? Was Richard III a stone-cold killer by nature, or was he a product of his times and his totally depraved extended family, where you had to kill or be killed?

Very interesting, Felix would say. *Good point.* The thing about Shakespeare, he would add, is that there's never just one answer.

Next he would cast the play, assigning a backup team for each main character: prompters, understudies, costume designers. The teams could rewrite the character's parts in their own words to make them more contemporary, but they couldn't change the plot. That was the rule.

Their last assignment, the one they completed once the play had been performed, was the creation of an afterlife for their character, supposing that character was still alive. If not, then a piece about how the other characters viewed the dead person once he or she was underground and the play was over.

Having tweaked the text, they'd rehearse, work on the soundtrack, and finalize the props and costumes, which Felix would gather together for them outside and trundle into Fletcher. There were limits, of course: nothing sharp, nothing explosive, nothing you could smoke or inject. Potato guns were not allowed. Nor, he discovered, was fake blood: it might be mistaken for real blood, went the official reasoning, and act as an incitement.

Then they'd perform the play, scene by scene. They couldn't present it to a live audience: administration was leery of gathering the whole prison population in one place for fear of riots, and anyway there was no auditorium that was big enough. So they'd video each scene and then edit it digitally, allowing Felix to check off "acquired marketable skill" on the numerous forms where checking-off was required. Also, making a video meant that no actor need be embarrassed in case he fluffed a line: they could do retakes.

When the video was finished, complete with special effects and music, it was shown to everyone in Fletcher on the closed-circuit TVs in the cells. Felix – sitting in the Warden's office during the screening, along with the Warden and several higher-ups – was heartened by the cheers and applause and the comments he could hear coming from the cells over the surveillance intercom. The prisoners loved the fight scenes. Why not? Everyone loved the fight scenes: that's why Shakespeare put them in.

The performances were a little rough, maybe, but they were heartfelt. Felix wished he could have squeezed half that much emotion out of his professionals, back in the day. The limelight shone briefly and in an obscure corner, but it shone.

After the screening there would be a cast party, as in the real theatre – Felix insisted on that – with potato chips and ginger ale, and Felix would distribute the cigarettes, and there would be high-fives and fist bumps, and they might watch the last part of the video again, where the credits rolled. Everyone in the class – even the bit parts, even the understudies – got to see his stage name in lights. And, without prompting, they did what real actors did: they propped up one another's egos. "Hey Brutus – brutal!" "You aced it, Ritchie boy!" "Give us an eye of newt!" Grins, nods of thanks, shy smiles.

Watching the many faces watching their own faces as they pretended to be someone else – Felix found that strangely moving. For once in their lives, they loved themselves.

The course was offered from January to March, and during those months Felix ran on high octane. But in the summer and fall when he was back in his hovel full-time, he reverted to despondency. After a stellar career like his, what a descent – doing Shakespeare in the clink with a bunch of thieves, drug dealers, embezzlers, man-slaughterers, fraudsters, and con men. Was that how he would end his days, petering out in a backwater?

"Felix, Felix," he would say to himself. "Who are you fooling?" "It's a means to an end," he would reply. "There's a goal in sight. And at least it's theatre." "What goal?" he would respond.

Surely there was one. An unopened box, hidden somewhere under a rock, marked V for Vengeance. He didn't see clearly where he was going, but he had to trust that he was going somewhere.

9. Pearl eyes

It's now Year Four of the Fletcher Correctional Players. Today is the first class of the season. As always on first days, Felix is slightly nervous. He's done well with the program so far, but there could always be an accident, a slip-up, a rebellion. Something unforeseen. *Tip of the tongue. Seashells. No slush,* he admonishes his reflection. *Be prepared.*

Having brushed and affixed his teeth, Felix arranges his hair, which is fortunately still thick. Then he snips a few stray wisps off his beard. He's been growing it out for twelve years, and it's the right shape now: full but not bushy, eloquent but not pointed at the end. Pointed would be demonic. He's aiming for magisterial.

He dresses in his work clothes: jeans, hiking boots, the dark-green Mark's Work Wearhouse shirt, a worn tweed jacket. No tie. It's necessary to look like the version of himself that's become familiar up at Fletcher: the genial but authoritative retired teacher and theatre wonk, a little eccentric and naive but an okay guy who's generously donating his time because he believes in the possibility of betterment.

Well, not donating it exactly; he does get paid. But peanuts, so he's not doing it just for the money. His students are suspicious of ulterior motives, having so many ulterior motives themselves. They disapprove of greed in others. As for themselves, they only want what's due to them. Fair is fair, and that way many a fracas can lie, as Felix already knows.

He tries to keep out of their private arguments. Just don't bring this crap into class, he tells them. I'm not in charge of who stole your cigarettes. I'm the theatre guy. When you walk in here, you shed your daily self. You become a clean slate. Then you draw on a new face. If you're nobody, you can't be somebody unless you're somebody else, he tells them, quoting Marilyn Monroe, a name they've heard of. And in here, we all begin by being nobody. Yes, me too.

They zip it up then: they don't want to be kicked out of the class. In a world that doesn't contain much for them that they can actually choose, they're in the Shakespeare class because they chose it. It's a privilege, as they are told perhaps too often. Some folks on the outside would kill for what Felix is giving them. Felix himself never says that, but it's implied in everything he does say.

"I'm not doing it for the money," Felix says out loud. He turns: Miranda's sitting at the table, a little pensively because she won't be seeing much of him now that it's January and the spring semester is about to begin. "I never did," he adds. Miranda nods, because she knows that to be true: noble people don't do things for the money, they simply have money, and that's what allows them to be noble. They don't really have to think about it much; they sprout benevolent acts the way trees sprout leaves. And Felix, in the eyes of Miranda, is noble. It helps him to know that.

Miranda's fifteen now, a lovely girl. All grown up from

the cherub on the swing who's still enclosed in her silver frame beside his bedside. This fifteen-year-old version is slender and kind, though a little pale. She needs to get out more, run around in the fields and woods the way she used to. Bring some roses to her cheeks. Of course it's winter, there's snow, but that never used to bother her; she could skim above the drifts, light as a bird.

Miranda doesn't like it when he's away so much, during the months when he's giving the course. Also, she frets: she doesn't want him to wear himself out. When he gets back after a heavy day they share a cup of tea together and play a game of chess, then eat some macaroni and cheese and maybe a salad. Miranda has become more health-conscious, she's insisting on greenery, she's making him eat kale. When he was growing up, no one had ever heard of kale.

If she'd lived, she would have been at the awkward teenager stage: making dismissive comments, rolling her eyes at him, dying her hair, tattooing her arms. Hanging out in bars, or worse. He's heard the stories.

But none of that has happened. She remains simple, she remains innocent. She's such a comfort.

But lately she's been brooding about something. Has she fallen in love? He certainly hopes not! Anyway, who would she fall in love with? That log-toting lout of a Walter is long gone, and there's nobody else around.

"Be good till I come back," he tells her. She smiles wanly: what else can she be but good? "You can do some embroidery." She frowns at that: he's stereotyping. "Sorry," he says. "Okay. Some higher math." That gets a laugh out of her, at any rate.

She won't stray far from the house, he knows that. She can't stray far. Something constrains her.

*

Now he'll have to brave the snow outside, plunge into the cold, face the daily test: will his car start? In winter he parks it at the top of the laneway. It's not the Mustang any more, that car rusted out some years back. It's a blue second-hand Peugeot he bought through Craigslist once Mr. Duke was getting his paycheques from Fletcher. Even when the lane is ploughed, it can be treacherous, and it's muddy in spring; so he uses it only in the dry seasons, which are summer and fall. If the snowplough has gone by on the sideroad, he'll have to dig through the windrow of ice and chunks of frozen brown guck from the undersides of passing vehicles. This road has been paved since he moved into the shack, so it's become more of a route. The propane truck uses it, for one. The FedEx van. The school bus.

The school bus, full of laughing little children. When it passes, he averts his eyes. Miranda might have been on a school bus once, if she'd ever reached that age.

From the hook on the back of the door Felix takes down his winter coat, with the mitts and tuque stuffed into the sleeves. He needs a scarf, and he has one; it's plaid. He's put it somewhere, but where? In the big old armoire in the bedroom, Miranda reminds him gently. Odd: he doesn't usually keep it there.

He opens the door. There's his one-time wizard's staff, the fox-head cane. His magic garment is hanging in there too, shoved to the back. The cloak of his defeat, the dead husk of his drowned self.

No, not dead, but changed. In the gloom, in the gloaming, it's been transforming itself, slowly coming alive. He pauses to consider it. There are the pelts of the plush animals, a little dusty now, striped and tawny, grizzled and black, blue and pink and green. Rich and strange. The many pearly eyes twinkle at him from the underwater darkness.

He hasn't worn his mantle since that time of treachery and rupture a dozen years ago. But he hasn't thrown it out, either. He's kept it in waiting.

He won't put it on yet: it's not the right moment. But he's almost certain it will be the right moment soon.

II. A Brave Kingdom

10. *Auspicious star*

Monday, January 7, 2013.

Felix shovels his car out from the windrow thrown by the snowplough across the top of his laneway. Keep this up and you'll rupture, he tells himself. You're not twenty-five any more. You're not even forty-five. Maybe you should stop playing at hermits, and sublet a rundown condo, and shuffle around town with a dog on a string like other old farts your age.

After a few ulcer-making moments when the car fails to start – he should get a block heater – Felix heads off to Fletcher Correctional. Sprites and goblins, here I come, he broadcasts silently to the inside of the car. Ready or not!

And he's ready.

A month ago, in mid-December, Felix got an email from Estelle. She had some wonderful news for him, she said; she would like to convey it to him in person. How about lunch, or maybe even dinner?

Felix opted for the lunch. Over the past three years, he's confined himself to lunches where Estelle is concerned. He's worried that dinner might become prolonged, and involve alcoholic drinks, and then get intense, either on Estelle's part or on his. Yes, he's a widower, but that doesn't mean he's available. It's not that she's unattractive – indeed, she has her stellar points – but he has a dependent child, and those duties come first. Though naturally he can't tell Estelle about Miranda. He doesn't want her to think he's hallucinating.

They never have their lunches at the McDonald's near Fletcher Correctional – too many off-duty staff from Fletcher go there, says Estelle, and the walls have ears, and she wouldn't want people to start gossiping about them being an item. Instead they've fixed on a more upmarket place in Wilmot, Estelle's suggestion. *Zenith*, it's called. It goes in for seasonal cuteness. On the day of their lunch it was the leadup to Christmas, so it had a bevy of elves in the window, busy with their decorating and toy production and their painting of frost flowers on cold windowpanes. Happily, it has a liquor licence.

"Well!" said Estelle, sitting across from him in a corner booth. "You've certainly been stirring up some waves!" She was wearing a sparkly necklace Felix had never seen before: rhinestones, if he was not mistaken.

"I try to," said Felix with the appropriate hint of self-deprecation. "Though it's not me so much. As you know, the guys have been giving it their all."

"I don't know why I ever doubted," said Estelle. "You've done wonders with them!"

"Oh, scarcely wonders," said Felix, gazing down into his coffee cup. "But progress, yes; I think I could admit to that. It's been a great help to have your support," he added judiciously. "I couldn't have done it without you."

Estelle flushed at the compliment. He should be careful, he didn't want to lead her on: that could be injurious for them both. "Well, your wave-making has had results! I was in Ottawa two weeks ago, for one of those committees I sit on, and I talked to some people, and you'll never believe what I've pulled off for you," she said a little breathlessly. "I think you'll be pleased!"

She'd done him quite a few favours over the years, acting discreetly in the background. It was thanks to her influence that he'd been able to pay for the technical support he needed, and the supplies for making the costumes and props. She'd managed to free up a little extra budget money for the course; in addition, she'd smoothed his access to the Warden, which had made security matters easier for him. She wanted to please him, that was obvious. And he'd shown his pleasure; though, he hopes, not too much.

"What?" said Felix, stroking his whiskers, activating his eyebrows. "What clever thing have you done?" What clever, naughty thing? his tone implied.

"You'll be receiving . . ." She paused, lowered her voice, almost whispering. "You'll be receiving a visit from a Minister! Even better: two Ministers! That almost never happens, two at once! Maybe even three!"

"Really?" he said. "Which Ministers might those be?"

"Justice, for one," she said. "It's his jurisdiction, and I emphasized to the Deputy Minister what strides you've been making with the – with your students! It could be a model for a whole new approach, in correctional services!"

"Fantastic," said Felix. "Well done! The Justice Minister! That would be Sal O'Nally." When Sal's party had lost the provincial election he'd moved into federal politics, and dang if he didn't get elected. With his experience and connections, and, it had to be said, his fundraising capabilities, he was soon in Cabinet once more, only this time at a higher level. Now he had a mini-kingdom.

"Correct," said Estelle. "He was Heritage when they first got in, then he was over in International Affairs for a while, but he's been moved into Justice now; they like to keep shuffling them around. He's been doing that 'tough on crime' agenda kind of talking, but the mere fact that he's coming here to see your, your – what you've been doing, at first-hand, shows he has a more open mind than some people give him credit for."

"In that case I hope he'll enjoy our humble thespian offering," said Felix. "And who's the second Minister?" As if he didn't know: he'd watched as Tony had followed the example set by Sal and had slid into federal politics, where the pickings were richer and the social gatherings more prestigious.

"He's new, he just got appointed," said Estelle. "He has a background in the theatre himself! You must know him. Anthony Price. Didn't he work with you years ago, over at the Makeshiweg Festival?" She must have been rummaging around in Anthony's Wikipedia entry.

"Oh, *that* Anthony Price!" said Felix. "Yes, he did work with me once. He was very efficient. My right-hand man." Couldn't she hear his loud heartbeat, the rushing sound in his ears? He could scarcely believe his luck. His enemies, both of them! They'd be right there in Fletcher! The one place in the world where, with judicious timing, he might be able to wield more power than they could. "It'll be like a family reunion," he said.

"Oh yes, it will, won't it?" said Estelle. "To tell you the truth, there've been some questions about continuing your program, what with the budget cuts, and . . . Various of my colleagues, some of the other advisers – well, they don't entirely see the point, despite the wonderful . . . They think prisons should only be used for . . . But this is my baby, I take a personal interest, as you know. So I pushed hard, and the Ministers agreed to at least take a look; and, after all, what you've been doing has generated a lot of positive buzz!"

"Positive buzz," said Felix. "'Where the bee sucks, there suck I.' That's better than sticking your foot in a hornet's nest, I suppose." His little joke. Now that Estelle had given him this opening, he intended to cram his foot into that hornet's nest as far as it would go. Then there would be a buzz, all right.

Estelle laughed, with a tiny gasp. "Oh! Yes. We're so lucky they'll be coming to see what an amazing ... I told the Deputies it's a really wonderful example of discipline cross-fertilization, showing the way the arts can be used as a therapeutic and educational tool, in a very creative and unexpected way! I think they'll both want to at least consider building on that. Both of the Ministers. They'll want a photo op," she added. "With the whole group of ... Even the, I mean ..."

"The actors," said Felix. He refused to call them inmates, he refused to call them prisoners, not while they were in his theatre troupe. Of course, he thought: a photo op, always the main purpose of any ministerial visit.

"Yes indeed. With the actors," Estelle smiled. "They'll want that."

"And do they know that I'm the director?" he asked. This was important. "I mean, me? My real name?"

"Well, they know what's on the course description. You're Mr. Duke there. I've always kept our little secret, as promised." She twinkles.

"Thank you for that," said Felix. "I know I can depend on you. Best to keep the spotlight on the actors themselves. When are they coming? The Ministers?" he asked.

"At the end of the course, on that day you show the play on video to everyone on the closed-circuit TVs. March 13 this year, isn't it? I thought that would be the best time for them to see the finished results. They'll meet with the, with the prison . . . with the actors, it'll be almost like a real opening night, with, you know, dignitaries . . ." Two spots of colour appeared in her cheeks. She was excited about this achievement of hers. She clearly needed a word of praise, so Felix delivered one.

"You're such a star," he said. "I can't thank you enough."

Estelle smiled. "You're more than welcome," she said. "I'm happy to be able to contribute. It's such a worthwhile . . . Anything I can do to facilitate . . . You know I'd pull out all the stops to keep this going." She leaned forward, almost touched his wrist, thought better of it. "And what's your Shakespeare pick for this year?" she asked. "Don't I remember you were planning a *Henry V*? With the longbows, and . . . The wonderful speech just before the, such a stirring . . ."

"I was thinking of that, it's true," said Felix. "But I've changed my mind." In fact, he'd just changed it. He's been chewing over his revenge for twelve years – it's been in the background, a constant undercurrent like an ache. Though he's been tracking Tony and Sal on the Net, they've always been out of his reach. But now they'll be entering his space, his sphere. How to grasp them, how to enclose them, how to ambush them? Suddenly revenge is so close he can actually taste it. It tastes like steak, rare. Oh, to watch their two faces! Oh, to twist the wire! He wants to see pain. "We're doing *The Tempest*," he said.

"Oh," said Estelle, dismayed. He knew what she was thinking: Way too gay. "They've managed so well with the more warlike themes! Do you think the, the actors will relate to . . . ? All that magic, and spirits, and fairies, and . . . Your *Julius Caesar* was so *direct*!"

"Oh, the actors will relate to it, all right," said Felix. "It's about prisons."

"Really? I never thought . . . maybe you're right."

"Also," said Felix, "it's on a universal theme." What he had in mind was vengeance – that was certainly universal. He hoped she wouldn't ask him about the theme: vengeance was so negative, was what she'd say. A bad example. Especially bad, considering the captive audience.

She had other worries. "But do you think our two Ministers will . . . We wouldn't want to raise any more doubts about the . . . Perhaps if you could choose something less . . ." She twisted her hands anxiously.

"They'll relate to it as well," said Felix. "The Ministers. Both of them. Guaranteed."

11. *Meaner fellows*

The same day.

In his wheezing blue Peugeot, Felix drives up the hill, winding around it toward the two high chain-link fences topped with razor wire, one fence inside the other. The snow is falling again, more heavily now. Good thing he keeps a shovel in his car, and a bag of sand. He may have to dig himself into the top of his laneway in the evening, having just dug himself out of it. Heart attack, heart attack: one of these days he'll overdo it with the shovelling, keel over, be found frozen stiff. It's a hazard of isolation.

He stops his car at the first gate, waits for it to swing open, drives through to the second gate, rolls down the window, shows his pass.

"You're good to go, Mr. Duke," says the guard. Felix is a well-known feature by now.

"Thanks, Herb," says Felix. He drives into the chilly inner courtyard, parks in his designated parking spot. No point in locking the car, not here: it's a thievery-free zone. He crunches along the sidewalk where snow-melt crystals have already been strewn, pushes the familiar button on the intercom, announces his name.

There's a click. The door unlocks and he walks into the warmth, and that unique smell. Unfresh paint, faint mildew, unloved food eaten in boredom, and the smell of dejection, the shoulders slumping down, the head bowed, the body caving in upon itself. A meagre smell. Onion farts. Cold naked feet, damp towels, motherless years. The smell of misery, lying over everyone within like an enchantment. But for brief moments he knows he can unbind that spell.

Felix goes through the security-check machine, which everyone entering the building must pass through in case of contraband. That machine can spot a paper clip, it can spot a safety pin, it can spot a razor blade, even if you've swallowed them.

"Empty my pockets?" he says to the two guards. Dylan and Madison are their names; they've been here at Fletcher as long as he has. One is brown, one light yellow. Dylan is a Sikh and wears a turban. His real name is Dhian, but he altered it because – he told Felix – it was less hassle.

"You're clear, Mr. Duke." Grins from both of them. What could Felix possibly be suspected of smuggling, a harmless old thespian like him?

It's the words that should concern you, he thinks at them. That's the real danger. Words don't show up on scanners.

"Thanks, Dylan." Felix gives a rueful smile, signalling that all three of them know this routine is pointless in his case. Doddering ancient, a bit addled in the head. Nothing to see here, folks, move along.

"What's it going to be this year?" says Madison. "The play?" The guards have taken to watching the Fletcher Correctional performance videos along with everyone else. He gives a special talk about the play every year just for them, so they will feel included. It's always risky, the prospect that the prisoners might be having more fun than the guards. Resentments can build up, and that could cause problems for Felix. Sabotages could take place, crucial props and technical artifacts could go missing. Estelle forewarned him about that angle, so he's massaged the appropriate sensibilities. But so far nothing bad has happened.

"That *Macbeth* was great," says Madison. "The way they faked the sword fight!" It goes without saying that real swords had not been allowed, but cardboard is so versatile.

"Yeah! *There stands the usurper's cursed head*, way to go, Macduff," says Dylan. "Served the fucker right."

"It was wicked!" says Madison. "Like, *Something wicked this way comes* – that was wicked too!" He crooks his fingers into witchy claws, gives a cackle. It still astonishes Felix, the way everyone wants to get in on the act, once there is an act.

"Eye of newt," says Dylan in an equally camp-hag voice. "How about the one with the arrows? I saw a movie of that on TV. The dogs of war, I remember that part."

"Arrows would be good," says Madison. "And dogs."

"Yeah," says Dylan, "but it can't be real arrows. Or real dogs either."

"This year it'll be a little different," says Felix. "We're doing *The Tempest*."

"What's that?" says Madison. "Never heard of it." They say this every year as a way of teasing Felix; he can never tell what they really have heard of.

"It's the one with the fairies," says Dylan. "Right? Flying around and that." He doesn't sound too pleased.

"You're thinking of *Dream*," says Felix. "*A Midsummer Night's Dream.* This one doesn't have fairies. It has goblins. They're wicked." He pauses. "You'll like it," he assures them.

"Is there a fight scene?" says Madison.

"In a way," says Felix. "It's got a thunderstorm in it. And revenge. Definitely revenge."

"Awesome," says Madison. The two of them brighten up. Revenge is a known quantity: they've seen lots of it in their time. Boot in the kidneys, homemade blade in the neck, blood in the shower.

"You always do good ones. We trust you, Mr. Duke," says Dylan. Foolish lads, thinks Felix: never trust a professional ham.

Pleasantries over, it's on with the formalities. "Here's your security," says Dylan. Felix clips the alarm to his belt: it's like a pager. In case of a crisis he's supposed to press the button and summon the guards. Wearing it is mandatory, though Felix finds the thing vaguely insulting. He's in control, isn't he? The right words in the right order, that's his real security.

"Thanks," he says. "In I go. First day! Always a tough one. Wish me merde!"

"Merde, Mr. Duke." Two thumbs-up from Madison.

It's Felix who's taught them to say *merde*. An old theatre superstition, he's told them, it's like *break a leg*. The more he shares about old theatre superstitions the better: widen the circle of illuminati.

"Page us if there's trouble, Mr. Duke," says Dylan. "The guys have got your back."

There will be trouble, thinks Felix, but not of the kind you mean. "Thanks," he says. "I know I can count on you." And he's off down the hallway.

12. *Almost inaccessible*

The same day.

The hallway is in no way dungeon-like: no chains, no shackles, no bloodstains, though there are some of those backstage, as he understands. The walls are painted a medium-light green, on the theory that this shade is calming to the emotions – not like, for instance, a passion-inflaming red. If it weren't for the absence of bulletin boards and posters, this might be a university building of the more modern sort. The floor is grey, of that composition substance that wishes to look like granite but fails. It's clean, with a slight polish. The air in the corridor is static and smells of bleach.

There are doorways, with closed doors. The doors are metal but painted the same green as the walls. They have locks. This isn't a dorm wing, however. The cellblocks are over to the north: the maximum-security block, with men in it whom Felix never sees, and also the medium-security block, which is where his actors come from.

It's in this section of Fletcher that the rehabilitation for the medium-security inmates goes on, such as it is. The courses for credit, the counselling. There are a couple of psychiatrists. There's a chaplain or two. There's a visiting prisoners' rights advocate who conducts his interviews somewhere in here. They come and go.

Felix stays away from these people – the other teachers, the rights advocate, the shrinks and chaplains. He doesn't want to hear their theories. He also doesn't want to get tangled up in their judgment of him and what he's doing. He's had some brief encounters with them over the past three years, and those encounters haven't gone well. He is viewed askance, with a tut-tutting kind of moralizing that he finds obnoxious.

Is he a bad influence? They infer that he is. He has to keep reminding himself that anything he might say in return, or rather yell, will be jotted down in some notebook or other and used against him if these professionals are called upon to, as they say, evaluate his therapeutic and/or pedagogical efficacy. So he keeps his mouth shut while being bombarded with sanctimonious twaddle.

Is it really that helpful, Mr. Duke, to expose these damaged men – and let us tell you how very damaged they are, one way or another, many of them in childhood through abuse and neglect, and some of them would be better off in a mental institution or an asylum for recovering drug addicts, much more suitable for them than teaching them four-hundred-year-old words – is it helpful to expose these vulnerable men to traumatic situations that can trigger anxiety and panic and flashbacks, or, worse, dangerous aggressive behaviour? Situations such as political assassinations, civil wars, witchcraft, severed heads, and little boys being smothered by their evil uncle in a dungeon? Much of this is far too close to the lives they have already been leading. Really, Mr. Duke, do you want to run those risks and take those responsibilities upon you?

It's theatre, Felix protests now, in his head. The art of true illusions! Of course it deals in traumatic situations! It conjures up demons in order to exorcise them! Haven't you read the Greeks? Does the word *catharsis* mean anything to you?

Mr. Duke, Mr. Duke. You are being far too abstract. These are real people. They are not ciphers in your aesthetic of drama, they are not your experimental mice, they are not your playthings. Have some respect.

I do have respect, Felix answers silently. I have respect for talent: the talent that would otherwise lie hidden, and that has the power to call forth light and being from darkness and chaos. For this talent I clear a time and a space; I allow it to have a local habitation and a name, ephemeral though these may be; but then, all theatre is ephemeral. That is the only kind of respect I recognize.

Brave sentiments, he tells himself. But high-falutin', Mr. Duke, wouldn't you say?

He pauses at a closed door blocking his way, waits until it slides open, walks through. It glides shut behind him. There's a similar door at the other end of this segment of the building. Both of these doors are kept closed and locked while his classes are in session. Safer that way, Mr. Duke.

There's no audio link with Security outside, there's no video. He has insisted on that: actors should not be spied on while they are rehearsing, it's too inhibiting. The pager on his belt should be enough, is his position, and so far he's been vindicated. In three years, he's never had an occasion to use it.

There's a washroom in here, first door on the left. There are three smaller rooms that he can use as rehearsal space or dressing rooms or green rooms, according to need. There are two demonstration cells, a replica of a cell from the fifties and another one from the nineties, once used in conjunction with a Justice Administration course taught at the University of Western Ontario but uninhabited since. Each has four bunks, two upper, two lower, and an observation window in the door.

The Fletcher Correctional Players utilize them for sets during their video filmings. They've been army tents, for Brutus and Richard and their nightmares. With the aid of red blankets and paper banners, they've been throne rooms. They've been the Scottish witches' cave, they've been the Roman Senate, they've been a dungeon in the Tower, where First and Second Murderer have skulked, preparing to drown Clarence in booze. Lady Macduff and her children have been slaughtered in them. That was almost too traumatic: some of the actors had had flashbacks to their nightmare childhoods. Violent brutes, threats, bruises, screams, knives.

Felix peers through the windows of these cells on his way past. All is dingy within, although tidy, the bunks neatly made up with grey blankets. Who'd ever suspect the sorcery, the ceremony, the mayhem that has taken place in there? And what will happen in them next?

Finally there's the largest classroom, the one Felix uses for the more expositional segments of his course, prior to rehearsals. It has twenty desks; it has a whiteboard; it also, thanks to Estelle, has a computer – unconnected to the outside Internet, so no porn-site surfing is possible; it is to be used for theatre work only. Most importantly, the room has a large flatscreen. It's on this screen that the actors are able to watch the results of their endeavours.

This room has two doors, one at the front and one at the back. It has no windows. It smells faintly of salt, and of unwashed feet.

This is the extent of it, Felix muses. My island domain. My place of exile. My penance.

My theatre.

13. *Felix addresses the Players*

The same day.

Felix stands beside the whiteboard at the front of the large main room, facing this year's class. Although he's read the signup list and sent out the course packages – the playbook, the notes – he never knows ahead of time who will actually show up. There are always some dropouts, and thus some replacements from the waiting list. To his credit there's always a waiting list. There can be absences for other reasons too. Transfers to other facilities, early paroles, injuries requiring infirmary time.

He scans the room. Familiar faces, veterans of his previous plays: these nod at him, offer half-smiles. New faces, blank or apprehensive: they don't know what to expect. Lost boys all of them, though they are not boys: their ages range from nineteen to forty-five. They are many hues, from white to black through yellow, red, and brown; they are many ethnicities. The crimes for which they've been convicted are assorted. The one thing they share, apart from their imprisoned state, is a desire to be in Felix's acting troupe. Their motives, he expects, are varied.

He's read their files, obtained for him by Estelle through some mysterious process, although he pretends he hasn't; so he knows what they're in here for. Some are gang members taking the rap for a higher-up, some have been busted for semi-amateur drug-dealing. Theft, from banks to break-and-enters to cars to convenience stores. A boy-genius hacker, convicted as a for-hire purloiner of corporate information. A con man and identity-theft specialist. A renegade doctor. An accountant from a respectable firm, doing time for embezzlement. A lawyer and Ponzi scheme scammer.

Some of them are seasoned actors, having been in several of his plays. Technically they shouldn't be able to take the course more than once, but Felix has sidestepped this stricture by adding a few spinoffs to his main offering, with how-tos and plug-ins downloaded from the Net. In "Technology for the Theatre," they learn lighting, props, special effects, and digital scenery. In "Theatre Design," they learn costume, makeup, wigs, and masks. In "Video Editing for the Theatre," they learn how to make silk purses out of sows' ears. He doles out academic credits accordingly. It all looks good on paper to the powers that be. Mr. Duke is such a bargain: four courses for the price of one.

Meanwhile he's nurtured a number of skill sets he can call upon when needed. He's got costume designers, he's got video editors, he's got lighting and special-effects men, he's got tip-top disguise artists. He does sometimes wonder how the crafts he's teaching might come in handy in, for instance, a bank robbery or a kidnapping, but he backgrounds such unworthy thoughts when they appear.

He gazes around the room, already casting the roles in his head. There's his perfect Ferdinand, Prince of Naples, gazing at him with round, ingenuous eyes as if ready to fall in love: WonderBoy, the con artist. There's his Ariel, unless he's much mistaken, elemental air spirit, slender and adroit, scintillating with cool juvenile intelligence: 8Handz, genius black-hat hacker. A podgy Gonzalo, the boring, worthy councillor: Bent Pencil, the warped accountant. And Antonio, the magician Prospero's treacherous, usurping brother: SnakeEye, the Ponzi schemer and real-estate fraudster, with his slanted left eye and lopsided mouth that make him look as if he's sneering.

A moon-calf Trinculo, the fool, the jester. No obvious Stephano, the drunken butler. Various Calibans, scowling and muscular: earthy, potentially violent. He'll have a choice. But before making up his mind about any of them he'll have to hear them speak some lines.

He smiles confidently, the smile of someone who knows what he's doing. Then he launches into a version of the speech with which he begins every new season.

"Good morning," he says. "Welcome to the Fletcher Correctional Players. I don't care why you're in here or what they say you've done: for this course the past is prologue, which means we begin counting time and accomplishments right here, right now.

"As of this moment, you are actors. You will all be acting in a play; everyone will have a function, as the old hands who've done it before will tell you. The Fletcher Correctional Players only do plays by Shakespeare, because that is the best and most complete way of learning theatre. Shakespeare has something for everyone, because that's who his audience was: everyone, from high to low and back again.

"My name is Mr. Duke, and I'm the director. That means I'm in charge of the overall production, and the final say is mine.

"But we work as a team. Each man will have an essential part to perform, and if someone's having trouble it's the job of his teammates to help him out, because our play will be only as strong as the weakest link: if one of us fails, we all fail together. So if a guy on your team has trouble reading the words, you need to help him. And you need to help each other memorize the parts, and understand what the words mean and how to deliver them with force. That's your mission. We must all rise to the highest level. The Fletcher Correctional Players have a reputation to live up to, and what we create together will honour that reputation.

"You've heard me mention teams, and those of you who've been in one of my plays before know what that means. Each of the principal characters will have a team surrounding him, and everyone on that team must learn that character's speeches. That's because each main actor must have some understudies, in case of illness or any other . . . in case of unforeseen emergencies, such as early parole, for instance. Or a slip in the shower room. The play must go on despite everything: that's how it is in the theatre. In this company, we back each other up.

"You'll be doing some writing. You'll be writing about aspects of the play, but you'll also be rewriting those parts of the play you decide – we decide – could be made more understandable to a modern audience. We'll be filming a video of our production; that video gets screened for everyone in the – for everyone in Fletcher. Our video will be something to be proud of, as our previous productions have been."

He smiles reassuringly, consults a folder. "Next, you'll need to choose a stage name. Many actors in the past did that, and opera singers and magicians as well. Harry Houdini was born Erik Weisz, Bob Dylan was Robert Zimmerman, Stevie Wonder was Steveland Judkins." He's looked these names up on the Internet, searching *stage alter egos*. He knows only some of them: he adds a few younger ones each time he gives this speech. "Movie stars do it, not to mention rockers and rappers. Snoop Dog was Calvin Broadus. You see what I mean? So think up your stage name. It's like a handle."

There are nods and murmurs. The seasoned actors already have their stage names from earlier productions. They're smiling now: they welcome the return of this other self of theirs, standing there like a costume, ready for them to assume.

Felix pauses, steels himself for the hard sell. "Now. This year's play." He writes on the whiteboard, using a red marker: THE TEMPEST. "So," he says. "You've been given the playbook in advance, you've got my notes, you've had time to read up on it." For a few of them this is true only in a manner of speaking, since they're third-grade level at best. They'll improve, however: their team will improve them. They'll be hauled up the stairs of literacy step by step.

"I'll start with the keynotes," Felix continues. "These are the important things to look for when we're figuring out how to present this play."

Using the blue marker, he writes:

IT'S A MUSICAL: Has the most music + songs in Shkspr. Music used for what?

MAGIC: Used for what?

PRISONS: How many?

MONSTERS: Who is one?

REVENGE: Who wants it? Why?

Consulting their faces – stony, frowning, or blankly bewildered – he thinks: they don't get it. Not like *Julius Caesar*, not like *Macbeth*; they saw the point of those right away. Not even like *Richard III*, which had posed a challenge, since a few too many of them had sided with Richard.

He takes a deep breath. "Off the top, any questions?"

"Yeah," says Leggs. Break-and-enter, assault. He's a veteran of the Fletcher Correctional stage, having played Mark Antony in *Julius Caesar*, one of the witches in *Macbeth*, and Clarence in *Richard III*. "We read it. But why're we doing this one? There's no fight scene, and it's got, like, a fairy in it."

"I'm not being a fairy," says PPod. He'd been Lady Macbeth in *Macbeth* and Richmond in *Richard III*. He's a sweet-talker, with – according to him – a bevy of devoted beauties waiting for him once he gets out.

"Not being a girl, either." That from Shiv: he has a Somali drug-gang connection and was caught in a big bust a few years back. He looks around the room for support: truculent nods, murmurings of agreement. No one wants either of these parts: not the Ariel, not the Miranda.

Felix has a potential rebellion on his hands, but he's anticipated it. He's faced the gender issue in the other plays, but those female characters had been grown women and either ciphers or downright nasty, and thus much easier to accept. The witches in *Macbeth* had been a pushover – the guys had no objection to playing evil crones because they were monsters, not actual women – and Calpurnia was minor. Lady Macbeth was even more of a monster than the witches: PPod said she was just like his mother, and had enacted her to great effect. Lady Anne in *Richard III* was angry and a spitfire; in fact, she was a spitter. Shiv had made a meal of it.

Miranda, however, is not a monster or a grown woman. She's a girl, and a vulnerable girl. Any man playing her would lose status in a disastrous way. He'd become a butt, a target. Playing a girl, he'd risk being treated as one. It would be ruinous for the Ferdinand as well: having to pitch those swooning love speeches to a surly fellow inmate.

"Let's get the girl thing out of the way right now," says Felix. "First, nobody in this room will have to be Miranda. Miranda is a sweet, innocent fifteen-year-old. I can't see any of you being very convincing with that."

The grunts of relief are audible. "Okay, good," says Shiv. "But if nobody here's doing it, then who is?"

"I shall engage . . ." Felix pauses, rearranges his language. "I'm hiring a professional actress," he says. "An actual woman," he adds so they truly grasp the point.

"She's coming in here?" says PPod. "To be in our play?" They look at one another, incredulous. Already *The Tempest* is more appealing to some of them.

"You can get some chick to do that?"

WonderBoy, the soulful-eyed con man, speaks up. "I don't think it's right that you'd bring a young girl in here. You're putting her in a weird position. Not that I'd lay a finger myself," he says. "But. Just sayin'."

"Yeah, you fuckin' A would," says a voice from the back. Laughter.

"She'll be *acting* the part of a young girl," says Felix. "I didn't say she would *be* a young girl. Not that she'll be old," he adds to counter the expressions of dismay. "Consider her participation a privilege. Any trouble – pestering, groping, pinching, dirty talk, and so forth – and she's gone, and so are you. I expect you all to behave like the professional actors I consider you to be." Not that professional actors fail to indulge in the pinching and groping, he reminds himself. But no need to share that reflection.

"Some lucky stiff's gonna be playing Ferdie what's-his-name," says Leggs. "Gets those hot closeup scenes."

"Stiff is right," says PPod.

"Guy's gonna be so stiff he'll be frozen." Murmuring, chuckling.

"We'll deal with that when we come to it," says Felix.

"That's all very well," says Bent Pencil, the embezzling accountant. His stage name has been conferred upon him by common consent. He wasn't too pleased about it at first, he tried to insist on something more dignified, such as "Numbers." He wanted to preserve his feeling of superiority.

But he's come to accept "Bent Pencil," because what choice does he have?

Bent Pencil played Cassius in *Julius Caesar* and is a stickler on details, often tediously so. Felix finds him a trial. He always wants to show how well prepared he is. Gonzalo, he thinks: Bent Pencil is excellent for it.

"That's all very well," Bent Pencil goes on, "but you haven't addressed the issue of the, uh . . . the Ariel issue."

"Yeah, the fairy," says Leggs.

"We'll discuss that on Friday," says Felix. "Now, your first written exercise. I want you to go through the text very carefully and make a list of all the curse words in the play. Those are the only curse words we'll be using in this room. Anyone caught using those other words, the F-bomb and so on, loses a point off their total. Counting of points is by the honour system, but we are one another's witnesses. Understood?"

Grins from the veterans: Felix always sets the class a challenge like this.

"We playing for cigarettes?" asks PPod. "As usual?"

"Of course," says Felix. "Once you have your list, pick ten of those curse words and memorize them, and then learn how to spell them. Those will be your special swear words. You can apply them in this class to anyone and anything. If you don't know what they mean I'll be happy to tell you. Ready, steady, go!"

Heads are bent, notebooks are opened, playbooks are consulted, pencils busy themselves.

Your profanity, thinks Felix, has oft been your whoreson hag-born progenitor of literacy. Along with your whoreson cigarettes, may the red plague rid them.

14. *First assignment: Curse words*

Wednesday, January 9, 2013.

On the Wednesday, Felix is feeling more relaxed. He's over the first hurdle. He puts on his most avuncular face: indulgent but hoping for excellence. "Let's see how you made out with your curse words," he says. "Who's got the consolidated list?"

"Bent Pencil," says Shiv.

"And who's going to read it so we can all hear it?"

"Him," says Leggs.

"'Cause he can pronounce them," says PPod.

Bent Pencil takes the floor and reads out, gravely and impressively, in his best board-meeting voice: "Born to be hanged. A pox o'your throat. Bawling, blasphemous, incharitable dog. Whoreson. Insolent noisemaker. Wide-chapp'd rascal. Malignant thing. Blue-eyed hag. Freckled whelp hagborn. Thou earth. Thou tortoise. Thou poisonous slave, got by the devil himself. As wicked dew as e'er my mother brushed, With raven's feather from unwholesome fen, Drop on you both. A south-west blow on ye, And blister you all o'er. Toads, beetles, bats light on you. Filth as thou art. Abhorr'ed slave. The red plague rid you. Hag-seed. All the infections that the sun sucks up, From bogs, fens, flats, fall on – add name here – and make him, By inch-meal a disease. Most scurvy monster. Most perfidious and drunken monster. Moon-calf. Pied ninny. Scurvy patch. A murrain on you. The devil take your fingers. The dropsy drown this fool. Demi-devil. Thing of darkness."

"Well done," says Felix. "That sounds fairly complete. I can't think of anything you've missed. Any questions or comments?"

"I been called worse," says PPod.

"Why is *earth* such an insult?" says Leggs.

"Yeah, we live on the earth," says Red Coyote. "It grows food, right? And *tortoise*. That's like a turtle, right? It's a sacred thing for some nations. Why is it bad, a turtle?"

"Colonialism," says 8Handz, who spent a lot of time on the Internet in his former life as a hacker. "Prospero thinks he's so awesome and superior, he can put down what other people think."

Multiculturalism at its finest, thinks Felix. He's anticipated the objection to "earth," but not the one to "tortoise." He takes that jump first. " 'Tortoise' just means slowpoke," he says. "In this play."

"Like, dragging your ass," says HotWire helpfully.

"So, I vote we don't use that one, anyway," says Red Coyote.

"Your choice," says Felix. "As for 'earth,' it's the opposite of 'air,' here. It's supposed to mean low-down."

"I vote we don't use that one too," says Red Coyote.

"Again, your choice," says Felix. "More?"

"I'm putting it on record," says Red Coyote. "Anyone who calls me tortoise or earth, just sayin'."

"Okay, we hear you," says Leggs.

"I got one," says Shiv. "One question. Is 'shit' a curse word? Can we use it, or what?"

It's a fine point, thinks Felix. Technically, "shit" might

not be considered a curse word as such, only a scatological expression, but he doesn't want to hear it all the time. *Shit this, shitty that, you shit.* He could let them vote on it, but what's the point of being in charge of this motley assemblage if he refuses to take charge? "'Shit' is off bounds," he says. "Adjust your cursing accordingly."

"'Shit' was okay last year," says Leggs. "So how come?"

"I changed my mind," says Felix. "I got tired of it. Too much shit is monotonous, and monotony is anti-Shakespeare. Now, if there are no more questions, let's do the spelling quiz. No peeking at anyone else's paper. I can see everyone from here. Ready?"

15. *Oh you wonder*

Felix has already engaged the Miranda he wants. She's the girl he'd cast in the part twelve years ago for his cancelled *Tempest*: Anne-Marie Greenland, the one-time child gymnast.

Of course she'd be older now, he'd reflected, though not that much older by absolute standards since she'd been very young twelve years earlier. With her body type – slender, wiry – she could surely still get away with Miranda. Supposing she hadn't bloated.

It had taken him some ingenuity to track her down. He didn't want to go through a casting agency, since no agency would wish to place a client inside a penal institution: there might be liabilities. He'd need to contact her himself and talk her into it. He would even offer to pay her; he could use some of his tiny budget for that.

The Internet came in handy: once he started searching, he found her CV fairly quickly. She was posted on ActorHub, she was on CastingGame. After his *Tempest* had been cancelled she'd done a few minor parts at Makeshiweg: a prostitute at the bawdy house in *Pericles*, a slave girl in *Antony and Cleopatra*, a dancer in *West Side Story*. Nothing big. Playing Miranda would have done wonders for her: he could have brought out her talent, he could have taught her so much. It would have made her career. He isn't the only person whose life has been seriously damaged by Tony and Sal.

After *West Side Story* Anne-Marie had crossed over completely into dance. She'd done several seasons as an apprentice and then as a guest dancer with Kidd Pivot: he'd found an outstanding YouTube video of her in a vigorous routine with two male dancers. However, due to an injury she'd had to leave before the company's spectacular *The Tempest Replica*, and had disappeared from her own CV for eight months. Then she appeared again as the choreographer for a semi-amateur production of *Crazy for You* in Toronto. That was last year.

Hard times in the world of Anne-Marie, he'd guessed. Did she have a husband, a partner? None was mentioned.

She had a Facebook account, though she hadn't posted much on it recently. A few pictures of herself: a thin, muscular honey blonde. Big eyes. Yes, she could still do Miranda. But would she want to?

Felix asked to be her Friend on Facebook, using his real name; miraculously, he was accepted.

Next to make the pitch. Did she remember him? he queried online. Yes, she did, was the terse reply. No exclamations of joy. Was she available for theatrical work? That would depend, she replied. He'd let her down once, he assumed she was thinking, so why did he think he could waltz back into her life as if nothing had happened?

It turned out she was working as a part-time barista in a coffee emporium – Horatio's – right in Makeshiweg. Hoping to pick up something at the Festival, was his guess. He set up a meeting time, then collected her at Horatio's. He wasn't too worried about anyone from his former life recognizing him: he looked so different now, with his white beard and eyebrows, and anyway most of the old crowd had gone: he'd checked that out on the company website.

Anne-Marie was still young-looking, he noted with relief. If anything, she was thinner. Her hair was up in a dancer's bun; each of her ears held two small gold earrings. She was wearing skinny jeans and a white shirt, which seemed to be the barista uniform at Horatio's.

He steered her around the corner to one of the noisier bars, the Imp and Pig-Nut: the sign outside sported some kind of red-eyed troll, grinning like a slasher-flick trailer. Once they'd settled into a dark-wood booth, Felix ordered a local craft beer for Anne-Marie and one for himself. "Something to eat?" he asked. It was edging toward lunchtime.

"Burger and fries," she replied, watching him with her huge gamine eyes. "Medium rare." He remembered the starving actor's first rule: never pass up free food. How many green room grapes-and-cheese plates had he himself once devoured?

"So," she said. "It's been a while. You just, like, vanished. Nobody knew where you went."

"Tony got me axed," he said.

"Yeah, word went around," she said. "Some of us thought he really did axe you. Clove you through the skull. Stuck you in a hole in the ground."

"Almost," he said. "It felt like that."

"You didn't say goodbye," she said reproachfully. "To any of us."

"I know. I apologize. I couldn't," he said. "There were reasons."

She relented a little, gave him a tiny smile. "Must've been hard for you."

"I was especially sorry," he said, "that I wasn't able to direct you. In *The Tempest*. You'd have been spectacular."

"Yes, well," she said, "I was sorry about that too." She rolled up her shirtsleeves – it was hot in here among the craft beers – and he saw that she had a bee tattooed on her arm. "What's up?"

"Better late than never," he said. "I want you to play Miranda. In *The Tempest*."

"No shit," she said. "You're not joking?"

"Not in any way," he said. "It's a slightly odd situation."

"They all are," she said. "But I still remember the lines. I was working so hard on that, I could say them in my sleep. Where are you doing it?"

He paused for a breath. "In Fletcher Correctional," he said. "I teach a class there. For the, ah, the inmates. Some of them are quite good as actors, you'd be surprised."

Anne-Marie took a hefty pull at her beer. "Let me get this straight," she said. "You want me to go inside a prison with nothing in it but a lot of men criminals and do Miranda?"

"None of them was willing to be a girl," he said. "You can see why not."

"I know, right? I don't blame them," she said with a hard edge to her voice. "Being a girl is the pits, trust me."

"You'd be very welcome," he said. "In the company. They're thrilled at the prospect."

"I bet," she said.

"No, really. They'd respect you."

"Bunch of lily-white no-touchy Ferdinands, are they?"

"There's security," he said. "With tasers and guards and what-not." He paused. "Not that they'd be needed. Really." He paused again. "You'd get paid." Another pause, then his final inducement: "You'll never have another theatrical experience like it. Guaranteed."

"You couldn't get anyone else to do it, could you," she said, and he knew he was almost there.

"You're the first one I asked," he said truthfully.

"I'm too old, though," she said. "It's not twelve years ago."

"You're perfect," he said. "You have a freshness."

"Like new-laid shit," she said, and he blinked. That foul mouth of hers had always startled him. He was never ready when a slice of filth came out of her child-like mouth.

"It's because you think I look like a kid," she said. "No tits."

Scant use denying it. "Tits are overrated," said Felix – music to the ears of a small-titted woman, always – and she grinned a little.

"You're doing Prospero yourself?" she said. "Not some bank robber taking on the enchanting old fart? Because I loved it, those speeches of his. I couldn't stand to hear them fucked up."

"Correct," he said. "Wizardry in the slammer: it's a challenge for me. Acting on an ordinary stage is a walk in the park, compared. Or look at it this way: it could be my last chance to do it."

She gave him a sudden wide smile. "You're as crazy as ever," she said. "What the crap, you're inspired! Fuck, who else would try a caper like this? Okay, you're on!" She held out a hand so they could shake on it, but Felix wasn't done.

"Only two things," he said. "First, my name in there is Mr. Duke. No one knows about the Festival – that I was once . . . It's a long story, I'll tell you sometime. But 'Felix Phillips' is off bounds. It could raise questions and cause trouble."

"You're suddenly afraid of trouble?" she asks. "You?"

"This would be bad trouble. Second, no conventional swearing. It's not allowed: my rules. They can only use the curse words that are in the actual play."

She gave it a moment of thought. "Okay, I can manage that," she said. "How now, moon-calf? Kiss the book! It's a bargain!"

This time they shook on it. She had a grip like a jar-opener. Chastity won't be the only reason his Prospero will be warning the Ferdinand lad to keep away from this girl: Ferdinand wouldn't want to be a pre-mangled bridegroom.

"I like your bee," he said. "The tattoo. Any special meaning?"

She looked down at the table. "I was having a thing with the Ariel," she said. "The actor, in your play. Fun while it lasted, though he broke my heart. The bee was sort of our joke."

"A joke? What kind of joke?" As soon as he said it Felix realized he didn't want to hear the answer. Luckily the hamburger arrived, and Anne-Marie sank her small white teeth into it with a sigh of pleasure. Felix watched her devour it, trying to remember what it had been like to be that hungry.

16. *Invisible to every eyeball else*
Friday, January 11, 2013.

Felix opens the Friday class with a hook. "I've got some news about the actress," he says. "The one I said would play Miranda." He keeps his voice level, takes a few beats. Is it good news or bad news? they'll be wondering.

They're alert: not a mutter, not a grunt. "It was difficult," he says. "Only an exceptional woman would take this on." Imperceptible nodding. "She had quite a few reservations. I had to do a lot of convincing," he goes on, spinning it out. "I thought I'd failed. But finally . . ."

"Yeah!" says 8Handz. "You did it! F . . . I mean, scurvy awesome!"

"Yes. Finally, I succeeded!"

"Way to red plague go!" says PPod.

"Thank you," says Felix. He allows himself a smile, gives a little bow. They expect him to be slightly formal. Courtly, as befits an old-school gentleman like the one he imitates. "Her name is Anne-Marie Greenland," he continues, "and she's not only an actress, she's a dancer as well. A very athletic dancer," he adds. "I've brought a clip to show you."

He's downloaded the YouTube video onto a memory stick, which he plugs into the class computer. "Lights out, please."

There's Anne-Marie in her dancing days, wearing a black halter top and green satin shorts. She throws her lithe male partner to the ground, then winds her arms and legs around him like an octopus and pulls his head back in a chokehold. He fights her off, flings her into the air, swirls her around in a circle, her head barely off the floor. Now she's slithering between his legs, then she's up on her feet, into the air again, feet akimbo. Now she's got him in a vise grip and is twisting one of his elbows to a painful right angle. The muscles in her sinewy arms are clearly visible.

"Whoa," says a voice. "That's ... what the pied ninny is this?"

"She could tear a whoreson strip off you!"

"She's got a plaguey tattoo!"

"Poisonous poxy!"

"What's it scurvy about?"

"Romantic love," says Felix. "I suppose." Immediately he's ashamed of himself: such jaded cynicism has no place in the enchanted world he'll soon be asking them to believe in.

Anne-Marie pirouettes, circling her partner, who is rolling across the floor. She does a backflip, lands on her feet. A second male dancer bounces in, picks her up, and slings her over his shoulder, her feet flailing. She's on the ground again; she takes, briefly, the stance of a boxer, but then she flees and there's a chase, with both of the male dancers pursuing her. She stops, lifts a foot, flexes it, kicks with her heel. Down they go, in graceful tandem. Anne-Marie leaps into the air, higher than you'd think possible.

Blackout.

A roomful of men exhales.

"Lights, please," says Felix. Illumination: he's confronting a vista of wide-eyed faces. "That was a small sampling of our new Miranda's many talents. Anne-Marie will be joining us for a full readthrough week after next, once we've dealt with the casting process."

"Is she, like, a black belt?" Leggs wants to know.

"Man, she's . . . she's malignant, man!" This from PPod.

"She kicks you in the nuts, they shoot right out your mouth," says SnakeEye. "I bet she's a red plague dyke – one way to find out!" Nobody laughs.

"She's poxy skin and bones," says Phil the Pill. "Eating disorder."

"I like the poxy wenches curvier myself," says PPod.

"Beggars can't be choosers," says Krampus the doleful Mennonite.

"Yeah, toad-face," says Leggs. "She looks hot to me!"

"She's a very talented performer," says Felix. He's pleased to note that they're already practising their chosen curse words. "We're lucky she's agreed to work with us. But I wouldn't cross her, if I were you. You can see why."

"I bet she can kill with her scurvy thumbs," says Wonder-Boy sadly.

"Now," says Felix, "let's talk about Ariel. Who thinks he might like the part?"

"No way, man," says a voice from the back of the room. "Not playing a fairy, that's final. Like I said." SnakeEye, a man of definite opinions.

A universal sentiment: no hands go up, all faces close. He can hear what they're thinking: as with Miranda, so with Ariel. Too weak. Too gay. Out of the question.

"You're bringing in an actress for Miranda, right? So, bring in a fairy for the fairy," says Shiv. Murmurs of "Yeah," soft laughter.

Felix could ask them why they think Ariel is a fairy, but he knows why. Flies through the air, sleeps in flowers, delicate. Looks like a fairy, acts like a fairy, is a fairy. As for Ariel's song that claims he sucks like a bee, forget it: who with any sense of self-preservation would sing that? Not only is Ariel a fairy, he's a super-sucking fairy. You'd never live it down. You'd be reduced to a cipher. You'd suck, in every possible way.

It would be useless for Felix to point out that Ariel isn't a fairy, he's an elemental air-spirit. Equally useless to tell them that that "suck" in Shakespeare's time did not have the many derogatory meanings it has since acquired, because it has those meanings now, and now is when they're putting on the play.

"Let's talk about Ariel for a minute," says Felix, which means that he will talk about Ariel, because no one else in the room is going to open his mouth on that risky subject. "Maybe we're seeing this character as a fairy because we aren't thinking *widely* enough." He pauses to let this sink in. Wide thinking? What is that?

"So, before sticking on a label, let's list his qualities. What sort of a creature is he? First, he can be invisible. Second, he can fly. Third, he has superpowers, especially when it comes to thunder, wind, and fire. Fourth, he's musical. But fifth, and most important." He pauses again. "Fifth: *he's not human.*" He gazes around the room.

"What if he's not even real?" says Red Coyote. "Like, if it's Prospero talking to himself? Maybe he's shaken hands with Mr. Peyote Button. Wasted out of his mind, or maybe he's crazy?"

"Maybe it's, like, a dream he's having," says Shiv.

"Maybe that boat sinks, the one they put him in. So the whole play happens right when he's drowning." One of the newbies: VaMoose.

TimEEz: "I saw a movie like that once."

"Or he's got an imaginary friend," says PPod. "My kid had one of them."

"Nobody else sees him," says Leggs.

"They see him when he appears as the harpy," says Bent Pencil.

"They hear him," says HotWire.

"Well, yeah, okay," says Red Coyote. "Though it could be that Prospero's some kind of a ventriloquist."

"Let's suppose that Ariel is real in some way," says Felix. He's pleased: at least they're talking. "Suppose you'd never heard of this play, and all you knew about this being called Ariel was what I told you about him. What kind of a creature have I just been describing?"

Mutterings. "Like, a superhero," says Leggs. "Fantastic Four. Superman kind of thing. Except Prospero's got the kryptonite or whatever, so he's got the control."

"*Star Trek* kind of thing," says PPod. "He's an alien, like, he's had some kind of spaceship accident, he ended up on Earth. He's trapped here. He wants to take off, go up to his home planet or whatever, like in *E.T.*, remember that one? That could cover it, right?"

"Doing what Prospero says so Prospero will help him get back there." 8Handz this time. "Earning his freedom."

"Then he can be with his own people," says Red Coyote.

Murmurings of agreement. This all makes sense! An alien! Way better than a fairy.

"How do you see the costume?" says Felix. "What does he look like?" He won't mention any of the traditional ways of portraying Ariel: the bird feathers, the dragonfly outfit, the angel, the butterfly wings. He won't mention, either, that for two centuries Ariel was always played by a woman.

"He'd be, like, green," says PPod. "With those bug eyes, like aliens have those big eyes with no pupils."

"Green is for trees. Blue's better," says Leggs. "Because of air. Ariel for air. Air's blue."

"Can't eat human food. Only flowers and stuff." Red Coyote speaking. "Natural. Like, he's a vegan."

General nodding: with this theory the bee-sucking activity is covered with no loss of honour, because that's the kind of thing you expect from aliens: weird eating habits.

"Fine," says Felix. "Now: what function does he perform in the play?"

An undertone of mumbling. "What do you mean by 'function'?" says Bent Pencil. "As you suggested in your notes, he's the good servant. He does what he's told. Caliban is the bad servant."

"Yes, yes," says Felix. "But where would the play be without the tasks Ariel carries out for Prospero? Without the thunder and lightning? Without, in fact, the tempest? Ariel performs the single most important act in the whole plot, because without that tempest there's no play. So he's crucial. But he acts behind the scenes – nobody but Prospero knows that it's Ariel making the thunder and singing the songs and creating the illusions. If he were here with us now, he'd be called the special-effects guy." Felix does another of his panoramic around-the-room scans, aiming for eye contact. "So, he's like a digital expert. He's doing 3-D virtual reality."

Tentative grins. "Cool," says 8Handz. "Scurvy cool."

"In our play, then, Ariel is the character Ariel, but he's also the special effects," says Felix. "Lighting, sound, computer simulation. All of that. And Ariel needs a team, like the team of spirits he's in charge of in the play."

Light is dawning: they love fooling with computers, on the rare occasions when it's possible for them.

"Monster cool!" says Shiv.

"So who wants to be on Team Ariel?" says Felix. "Any takers?"

Every hand in the room goes up. Now that they grasp the possibilities, they all want to be on Team Ariel.

17. *The isle is full of noises*

The same day.

The sun's declining; its light is cold, pale yellow. Along the top of the inner fence two crows are perched, keeping watch. No hope for you, my friends, thinks Felix. I'm the only one coming out today and I'm not dead yet. He climbs into his frozen car. After two tries, the motor starts.

The outer gate swings open, propelled by invisible hands. My thanks, ye demi-puppets, Felix addresses them silently, ye elves of barbed wire, tasers, and strong walls, weak masters though ye be. As he drives away downhill the gate closes behind him, locking itself with a metallic thud. Already the air is darkening; behind him, the searchlights blare into life.

His car follows the highway, then turns off and snouts its way along the narrow snowy roadway toward his cave, almost as if he isn't steering it but commanding it by thought alone. He allows himself to feel relief: the first and greatest obstacles have now been overcome, the first goals achieved. He has captured his Miranda, and Ariel has been transformed and accepted. He can sense the rest of his cast emerging as if from a fog, their faces indistinct but present. So far, his charms hold good.

His car stops as if grounded. Luckily there's no new

windrow of hard-packed snow and frozen sludge to be shovelled. He parks and locks, then trudges up the lane to his hovel, snow creaking underfoot. From the field to the left comes a glassy whispering: it's the dead weed stalks that are sticking up through the drifts, glazed with ice, stirred by the wind. Tinkling like bells.

All dark within, no light at the window. Almost he knocks, but who would answer? He has a sudden cold sensation, as if from news of a boundless loss. He opens the door.

Empty. Devoid. No presence. Inside the shack it's chilly; he banked the woodstove before going off to Fletcher that morning, but he doesn't like to leave the electrical heater on when he's not there. Too risky, though surely Miranda would keep a watch on it. Wouldn't she?

Fool, he tells himself. She's not here. She was never here. It was imagination and wishful thinking, nothing but that. Resign yourself.

He can't resign himself.

He builds up the fire, switches on the heater. It won't take the place long to warm up. He'll have an egg for supper and a couple of soda crackers. A cup of tea. He's not very hungry. After the adrenalin hit of this first week he's having a let-down; surely that's all it is. But he feels a weakness within himself, a dejection, a fissure in his will, a faltering.

Lately his vengeance has seemed so close. All he had to do was wait until Tony and Sal came to Fletcher Correctional for their VIP visit, then make sure they did not view the video of the play upstairs with the Warden but in the sealed wing – where he would be expecting them, although unseen by them at first. Once the video began to run, it would split in two. One version would be the video running onscreen in the rest of the prison. The other version would suddenly have real people in it, directed and controlled by himself. Creating an illusion through doubles – it's one of the oldest theatrical gimmicks in the box.

But now his vision is blurring. Why is he so sure he can pull this off? Not the play itself; that will already exist as a finished video. But the other play, the improvised drama he has in mind for his distinguished enemies – how to arrange it? He'll need a degree of technical expertise he doesn't possess. And even if he can solve that problem, how foolhardy of him to attempt such a gambit! How risky! So much could go wrong. His actors might get carried away, especially in the presence of a tough-on-crime Minister of Justice. That situation could prove tempting for them. Someone might be hurt.

"No harm, no harm," he tells himself. But there could very well be harm. He doesn't have any obedient elementals backing him up, he has no real alchemy. He has no weapons.

Better to abdicate. Give up his plans for retribution, for restoration. Kiss his former self goodbye. Go quietly into the dark. What has he ever accomplished in his life, anyway, beyond a few gaudy hours, a few short-lived triumphs of no importance in the world where most people live? Why did he ever feel he was entitled to special consideration from the universe at large?

Miranda doesn't like it when he's depressed. It makes her anxious. Maybe that's why she's rendered herself invisible, though she's usually almost invisible anyway. Is that her, in the other room? Does he hear a humming? Or is it only the bar fridge?

The bedroom has a medicinal smell, as if someone's been ill in it. An invalid, for a long time. No, she's not in here.

Only the photo in its silver frame: the small girl on the swing, frozen in Time's jelly. Visible but not alive.

He switches on the bedside lamp, opens the door of the large armoire. There's his wizard's garment; it's been waiting for him now for a dozen years. Must it go to waste, after all? Its many eyes glint, alive, aware.

"Not yet," he tells his magic animals. "Not quite yet. It is not the hour."

Their hour will be his hour. His vengeful hour. There must be a way he can make it work. Surely he still has a few tricks left.

He moves back into the front room. "Dear one," he says out loud; and there she is, over in the corner. Luckily she's wearing white: she glimmers. What is this fretful energy he's feeling? She's picked up on his worries, and now she's worrying herself.

"There's no harm done," he says. "And there won't be, I promise. I will do nothing but in care of thee."

But what has his care amounted to? He's protected her, true, but hasn't he overdone it? There are so many things he should be able to offer her. She should have what other girls her age take for granted, not that he knows what those things are. Clothes, certainly. Pretty clothes, more clothes than she has at her disposal now. She seems to go around in makeshifts, fabricated out of cheesecloth and old bed sheets. She ought to have silks and velvets, or mini-skirts and those tall boots girls these days seem so fond of. She ought to have an iPhone, in a pastel shade. She ought to be painting her nails blue or silver or green, chattering with her friends, listening to music through her pink ear buds. Going to parties.

He's been such a failure as a parent. How can he make it

up to her? It's a wonder she isn't sulkier, cooped up here with nobody but her shabby old father; but then, she doesn't know what she's missing. Still, he's been able to teach her a lot of things that most girls her age would never have a chance of learning.

"What have you been up to all day?" he says to her. "Would you like a game of chess?"

Reluctantly – is that reluctance? – she moves to the chess board, set up as usual on the red Formica table.

Black or white? she asks him.

18. *This island's mine*

Monday, January 14, 2013.

By Monday morning Felix has recovered his confidence. He must proceed as if everything is unfolding as it usually does with a Fletcher Correctional Players production. This week he'll help the class explore the main characters, as a prelude to casting them. Now that the troublesome matter of Ariel and Miranda has been dealt with, there shouldn't be much difficulty over the others, except for Caliban. Caliban is bound to raise uncomfortable issues.

As for his other enterprise, the secret one, he must keep the thread tight in his grasp. He must follow it forward into darkness. Whatever the form the thing assumes, it will depend on exact timing. This is his last chance. It's his only chance. To vindicate himself, to restore his name, to rub their noses in it – the noses of his foes. If he misses it, his fortunes will ever after droop. They've been droopy enough as it is.

He can't back off, he can't hesitate. He needs to sustain the momentum. Everything depends on his will.

"How's it going, Mr. Duke?" Dylan asks as Felix passes through the security check.

"All's well so far," says Felix cheerfully.

"Who's playing the fairy?" says Madison.

"It's not a fairy," says Felix.

"Really?"

"Trust me on that," says Felix. "By the way, next week I'm bringing in a guest actor – a very distinguished actress, actually. Her name is Anne-Marie Greenland. She'll be playing the female part in the play. Miranda."

"Yeah, we heard," says Madison. The grapevine is highly active inside Fletcher Correctional, at least on some matters; or perhaps it's the surveillance system. Gossip spreads like the flu. "We're looking forward, eh?" He grins.

"She got clearance?" says Dylan.

"Of course," says Felix with more authority than he feels. Estelle has arranged that for him. It was a tight squeeze – there were some objections – but Estelle knows which strings to pull and which egos to massage. "I hope that everyone here – the staff – I hope you'll be welcoming to her."

"She'll need to wear a security pager," says Dylan. "The actress, or whatever. We'll show her how to use it. In case of difficulties." Their curiosity is palpable: they'd like to ask for more details about this girl, but they're not about to betray themselves by showing too much enthusiasm. Should Felix throw them a crumb, tell them about the freely available YouTube video of Anne-Marie making lasagna out of her two male dancing partners? Better not, he decides.

"There won't be any difficulties," he says, "but that's very kind of you."

"No problem, Mr. Duke," says Dylan.

"We aim to please," says Madison.

"You can count on us. Enjoy your day, Mr. Duke," says Dylan. "Merde!"

"Merde, eh?" says Madison. He gives Felix two thumbs-up.

"The whole play takes place on an island," says Felix, standing beside his whiteboard. "But what kind of island is it? Is it magic in itself? We never really know. It's different for each one of the people who's landed on it. Some of them fear it, some of them want to control it. Some of them just want to get away from it.

"The first person to set foot on it is Caliban's mother, Sycorax, said to be a loathsome witch. She dies before the play begins, but not before Caliban is born on the island. He grows up on it, and he's the only one who really likes it. When Caliban is a young boy, Prospero is kind to him, but then sex gets in the way and Caliban loses it and gets locked up. After that he's afraid of Prospero and his imps and goblins because they torment him. But he's never afraid of the island. In turn, it sometimes plays sweet music to him."

He writes CALIBAN on the whiteboard.

"There's another character who's been there as long as Sycorax, but he's not a human. That would be Ariel. What does he think about the island? We don't know. He's in charge of creating illusions on it, but he's only doing what he's told."

Under CALIBAN he writes ARIEL.

"The next ones to come to the island are Prospero, the rightful Duke of Milan, and baby Miranda, who have been set adrift in a leaky boat by Prospero's wicked brother, Antonio. They're lucky they landed there because otherwise they would have starved or drowned. But they have to live in a cave and there aren't any other people, except Caliban, so Prospero's main aim is to get himself and Miranda off the island and back to Milan as fast as possible. He wants his old position back, he wants his daughter well married, and he can't have any of that if he stays on the island. Miranda herself is neutral on the subject. She hasn't known anything else, so she's fine with the island until an alternative arrives."

PROS & MIR, he writes.

"Then, after twelve years have passed, a number of others wash up as the result of a tempest staged by Prospero and Ariel. The tempest is an illusion, but they're convinced by it: they think they've been shipwrecked. For Alonso, the King of Naples, the island is a place of sorrow and loss, because he believes his son, Ferdinand, has been drowned offshore.

"For King Alonso's brother, Sebastian, and Prospero's evil brother, Antonio, the island is a place of opportunity: it seems to give them the occasion to murder Alonso and his councillor, Gonzalo, after which Sebastian would inherit the kingdom of Naples – not that he has the least idea about how he's going to get himself back there. These two think the island is a barren place, without any charm.

"Gonzalo, the elderly, well-meaning councillor, thinks the island is rich and fertile. He amuses himself by describing the ideal kingdom he'd set up on it, in which all the citizens would be equal and virtuous, and none would have to do any work. The others make fun of his vision.

"All of these men are thinking mostly about ruling and rulers. Who should rule, and how. Who should have power, how they should get it, and how they should use it."

Felix writes ALON, GON, ANT, SEB, and draws a line under them.

"The next character is very different. He's Ferdinand, son of Alonso. Since he swam ashore to a different part of the island, he believes his father has drowned. As he's mourning his loss, Ariel lures him away with music. At first he thinks the island is magic; then, when he sees Miranda, he initially thinks she's a goddess. When he hears that she's a human girl and unmarried into the bargain, he falls in love with her at first sight and proposes to marry her. So his island is a place of wonder, and then of romantic love." Felix writes FERD, draws another line.

"At the bottom of the heap come Stephano and Trinculo," he says. "They're fools. Also they're drunk. Like Antonio and Sebastian, they see the island as a place of opportunity. They want to exploit the gullible Caliban by making him their servant; they even consider exhibiting him as a freak or selling him, once they get back to civilization. But they're quite ready to add theft, murder, and rape to their repertoire. Get rid of Prospero, Caliban tells them, and the island will be their kingdom, with Miranda thrown in as a bonus.

"They too are concerned with who should rule, and how; they're comic versions of Antonio and Sebastian. Or you might say that Antonio and Sebastian are fools in better clothing."

STEPH & TRINC, he writes.

He pauses, looks out over the room: no hostility, but no real enthusiasm either. They're watching him. "Maybe the island really is magic," he says. "Maybe it's a kind of mirror: each one sees in it a reflection of his inner self. Maybe it brings out who you really are. Maybe it's a place where you're supposed to learn something. But what is each one of these people supposed to learn? And do they learn it?"

He draws a double line under his list. "So," he says. "Those are the main characters. Write them down in that order, all except Prospero and Miranda – I'll be playing Prospero, and you know who's playing Miranda. Then write a number beside each of those names, from zero to ten. Ten means you'd really like to play that character; zero means you have zero interest in it. Consider whether you think you can do a good job of the part. For instance, it would help for Ferdinand to be reasonably young, just as Gonzalo should be reasonably old.

"Between now and the time I cast the parts, we'll be reading some speeches. After we've done that, you might change your mind about your preferred character. If so, feel free to scratch the number out and write a new one in." They all set to work; there's the laborious creaking of pencils.

Is the island magic? Felix asks himself. The island is many things, but among them is something he hasn't mentioned: the island is a theatre. Prospero is a director. He's putting on a play, within which there's another play. If his magic holds and his play is successful, he'll get his heart's desire. But if he fails . . .

"He won't fail," Felix says. A few heads come up, a few stares are directed his way. Has he said that out loud? Is he talking to himself?

Watch that tendency, he tells himself. You don't want them to think you're on drugs.

19. *Most scurvy monster*

Tuesday, January 15, 2013.

On Tuesday morning Felix counts the votes. Of the twenty members of his acting company, only one wants to play the worthy Gonzalo. Happily it's Bent Pencil, the warped accountant. Felix writes him in.

King Alonso and his brother, Sebastian, don't have any takers; they're well down the list for everyone, but they don't get any zeros.

Antonio, Prospero's evil brother, is more popular: five list him as a nine.

Stephano and Trinculo: two each. That makes four who see themselves as jokers.

Eight of them fancy themselves as Ferdinand, of which six are wishful thinkers: no way they could be convincing as the romantic lead. But two are possible.

Ariel, twelve. Many, it seems, are seriously interested in aliens and special effects.

And Caliban, an astonishing fifteen.

Hard choices to be made on Wednesday, thinks Felix. He'll start with Caliban. Caliban is secretly poetic. By the time they've talked that aspect through, some of the contenders will surely have dropped out. There's more to Caliban, he'll tell them, than just an ugly face.

*

In preparation for the stern task ahead, Felix takes his weekly bath in the tin washtub. It's a production. First he has to heat the water, on the hotplate and also in the electric kettle. Then he has to mix the hot with cold from the hand pump. Then he has to disrobe. Then he has to get in. It's a chilly, slippery business at this time of year, with a draft coming in under the door and – right now – ice pellets pattering against the window. Matters are not helped by the threadbare towel. He ought to get another one; what holds him back? His sense of design, that's what. A new towel would not fit the sparse, monkish decor.

As befits modesty, Miranda is never present when he's performing this ritual. Where does she go? Somewhere else. Wise lass. Nothing would diminish an adolescent girl's respect for her sagacious male parent more than a glimpse of his spindle shanks and puckering, wizened flesh.

How exactly did Prospero and Miranda bathe themselves when on the island? Felix ponders this question while gingerly soaping himself under the arms. Did they have a tub? Unlikely. Perhaps there was a waterfall. But every time she used it, wouldn't Miranda have risked predation by the lustful Caliban? Certainly; but Prospero must have penned him up in his rocky cell at such moments.

All very well, but what about Prospero himself? In order to keep his charms going, didn't he need to be wearing his magic garment? Didn't he require his books, his staff? He wouldn't have been able to keep his magic garment on while having a shower in the waterfall. So maybe he didn't take showers. The old boy must have been fairly rank, after twelve years with no showers.

But he's forgetting: Ariel would have stood guard. Ariel in harpy wings, and Prospero's praetorian guard of obedient goblins. "Bath attendant" wasn't a function mentioned for Ariel in the text, but it must have been understood.

It's an omission in much literature of the theatre, Felix decides: nobody bathes or even thinks about it, nobody eats, nobody defecates. Except in Beckett, of course. You can always count on Beckett. Radishes, carrots, pissing, stinky feet: it's all there, the entire human corpus at its most mundane and abject level.

He rises up from the tin tub, feet squeaking, and steps out onto the cold floorboards, then briskly towels himself off. Into his flannel nightshirt. Fill the hot water bottle. Teeth in a glass of water, effervescent tablet sizzling. Vitamin pill, cocoa. He can't face the outhouse in a blizzard, so he pees into a Mason jar he keeps for the purpose and pours the effluent down the sink. Prospero never had to deal with snow: he wouldn't have needed a jar.

And so to bed.

Once he's tucked in and turned out the light, Miranda coalesces in the darkness. "Goodnight," he says to her. Does she brush the air above his forehead lightly with her hand? Surely she does.

Wednesday morning is bright and clear. After a boiled egg for breakfast Felix drives past the snow-covered fields and glittering trees, then up the hill to Fletcher Correctional, whistling a silent tune. *Ban, ban, Ca caliban.* An excellent moment for a musical number, that scene. He'll tell them the Caliban chant is an early example of rap, which it kind of is.

"We have a problem," he begins after positioning himself beside the whiteboard. "Fifteen of you want to play Caliban. We need to talk about it." He picks up his marker. "What kind of being is Caliban?" Blank stares.

"So," he tries again, "we agreed that Ariel wasn't human – that he's some kind of an alien. What about Caliban? He had a human mother, we know that anyway. So – human or not human?"

"Yeah, human," says HotWire.

"Too human," says WonderBoy, looking around for support. "How he wanted to jump into Miranda." Some rueful laughter, murmurs of "Yeah."

Getting somewhere, thinks Felix. "Off the top of your head," he says, "what's the one word that best describes Caliban?"

"Monster," says PPod. "Lots of them call him a monster."

"Evil." "Stupid." "Ugly." "Fish. They say he stinks like a fish."

"Sort of a cannibal. Like, a savage."

"Earth," says Phil the Pill.

"Slave," says Red Coyote. "Poisonous slave," he adds.

"Hag-seed," says 8Handz, the hacker from the dark side. "That's the best one."

Felix writes down the words in sequence. "Not a very nice guy," he says. "So why do you want to play him?"

Grins. "He's poxy awesome."

"We *get* him."

"Everyone kicks him around but he don't let it break him, he says what he thinks." This from Leggs.

"He's mean," says Shiv. "Wicked mean! Everyone who's dissing him, he wants to get them back!"

Felix draws a line under the words. "We hear a lot of bad words about him from other people," he says. "But nobody's just the sum total of what other people say. Everyone has another layer." Nods: they're buying it. "What about these other layers?" He answers himself, as often:

"First, He loves music. He can sing and dance." MUSICAL, he writes. "So he's sort of like Ariel."

"Not in a fairy way, though," says Shiv. "No cowslips."

Felix ignores this. "He knows the island – where to find everything on it, such as what to eat." LOCAL KNOWLEDGE, he writes. "He has the most poetic speech about the island in the whole play – the one about his beautiful dreams." ROMANTIC, he writes. "And he feels that his birthright – the island – has been stolen from him by Prospero, and he wants it restored." VENGEFUL, he writes.

"In a way he has a case," says SnakeEye.

"So he's like Prospero," says 8Handz. "He's full of these ideas to get vengeance. And he wants to be King Shit."

"Point off, you said *shit*," says WonderBoy.

"Wasn't a curse," says 8Handz. "Just a name."

"What I'm trying to tell you," says Felix, "is that Caliban is a difficult part. You need to think about it. Playing him is hard work." He pauses to let this sink in. There are some sub-vocal noises. Are some of the fifteen Caliban aspirants reconsidering? Possibly.

"And yes, he's partly like Prospero," Felix continues. "But Prospero never wants to be king of the island and set up a colony on it. On the contrary, he wishes to see the last of it. But Caliban thinks he should be its king, and he wants to populate it with replicas of himself, which he'd like to do by raping Miranda. When he can't have that, he throws in his lot with Stephano and Trinculo and urges them to murder Prospero."

"Not a bad plan," says Leggs. Murmurs of agreement.

"Okay, you don't like Prospero," says Felix. "And there are some reasons why you wouldn't. We'll talk about that later. Meanwhile, here's your assignment. On our first day, I said that one of the keynotes of this play is Prisons." PRISONS, he writes at the top of the whiteboard. "Now, I want you to go through and find all the prisons, including those in the backstory – the part that happened before the play begins.

"What kinds of prisons are they? Who's been put in each of them? And who's the jailer – who's put them in, who's keeping them there?" PRISONER. PRISON. JAILER, he writes. "I found at least seven prisons. Maybe you can find more." There are actually nine, but let them outdo him.

"If it's the same actual place, such as the island, but a different part of it, does that make two prisons?" says Bent Pencil. "Or one?"

"Let's call them unique incarceration events," says Felix.

"Unique incarceration events?" says Leggs. "Yeah, when I get out, I'm gonna say, I had a four-year poxy, suckin' *unique incarceration event*." Laughter from the company.

"Least it's not a unique *dead* event," says PPod.

"Unique smash your face in event."

"Unique totally wasted event."

"Right," says Felix. "You know what I mean." They call him out when he talks too much like a social worker.

"What exactly counts?" says 8Handz. "Like, that pine tree Ariel was stuck in?"

"Let's say a prison is any place or situation that you've been put in against your will, that you don't want to be in, and that you can't get out of," says Felix. "So, yes: the pine tree counts."

"Whoreson!" says HotWire. "Doing solitary in a pine!"

"Whoreson *awesome*," says 8Handz.

"The oak would be worse," says Red Coyote. "Oak's harder wood."

"Is there a score for the most prisons? We get cigarettes for this?" says Leggs.

III. These Our Actors

20. *Second assignment: Prisoners and jailers*

Consolidated Class Results

Prisoner	Prison	Jailer
Sycorax	Island	Government of Algiers
Ariel	Pine tree	Sycorax
Prospero and Miranda	Leaky boat	Antonio and Alonso
Prospero and Miranda	Island	Antonio and Alonso
Caliban	Hole in the rocks	Prospero
Ferdinand	Enchantment, chains	Prospero
Antonio, Alonso, and Sebastian	Island, Enchantment, Madness	Prospero
Stephano and Trinculo	Muddy pond	Ariel and Goblin Dogs, by order of Prospero

21. *Prospero's Goblins*

Wednesday, January 16, 2013.

In block letters, red, Felix covers his whiteboard with the class findings. "You've done well," he says. "You've spotted eight . . ." He pauses. "Eight unique incarceration events." Let them swallow the phrase this time, he thinks, and they do: there are no scoffing comments. "There's a ninth prison, however." Puzzled looks. Skepticism from 8Handz: "No plaguey way!"

Felix waits. Watches them counting, pondering.

"You gonna tell us?" PPod asks at last.

"After we've done the play," says Felix. "Once our revels are ended. Unless, of course, someone guesses it before then." They won't guess, is his bet, but he's been wrong before. "Now, let's look at the jailers. Three characters are imprisoned by someone who isn't Prospero: Sycorax, on the island, by the officials of Algiers; Ariel, in a pine, by Sycorax, and Prospero himself, by Antonio, with an assist from Alonso, first in the leaky boat and then on the island itself. Four characters if you count Miranda, but she was only three years old when she landed so she grows up on the island without feeling imprisoned by it. Then, seven individuals are imprisoned in events in which the jailer is Prospero. He would seem to be the top jailer in this play."

"Plus he's a slave-driver," says Red Coyote.

"Not just with Caliban, he's got his foot on Ariel too," says 8Handz. "He threatens him with that oak tree. Permanent solitary. It's inhuman."

"Plus he's a land stealer," adds Red Coyote. "Suckin' old white guy. He should be called Prospero Corp. Next thing he'll discover oil on it, develop it, machine-gun everyone to keep them off it."

"You're such a poxy communist," says SnakeEye.

"Shove it, freckled whelp," says Red Coyote.

"No whoreson dissin', we're a team," says Leggs.

Calm is called for. "I know you hold those things against Prospero," says Felix. "Especially his treatment of Caliban." He looks around the room: frowns. Jaw-tightenings. Definite hostility toward Prospero. "But what are his options?"

"Options!" says Shiv. "We don't give a – we don't give an *earth* about his suckin' options!"

"Watch it with the *earth*," says Red Coyote. "Just sayin'."

"Not everything's about you," says Shiv.

"Give Prospero a chance. Let's hear about the options," says Bent Pencil mildly. He likes to play the man of reason.

"I'll spell it out," says Felix. "Suppose the ship with King Alonso and Antonio and Ferdinand and Gonzalo had never showed up. It was blind luck that it sailed near the island on the way back from the wedding of Alonso's daughter. Or, in the language of Prospero, it was the action of an auspicious star and Lady Fortune. But suppose that ship never arrived. There was Prospero, trapped on the island, with a young daughter and a young, stronger male who tries to have sex with her against her will. Even though Prospero has been kind to the wild-child Caliban, the grown-up Caliban turns against him.

"Nobody has a gun. Nobody has a sword. In a match of

strength, Caliban could easily have killed Prospero. In fact, that's what he wants to do as soon as he sees the chance. So, does Prospero have the right of self-defence?"

Mutters. Scowls.

"Let's vote on it," says Felix. "Yes?"

Most hands go up, reluctantly. Red Coyote holds out.

"Red Coyote?" says Felix. "He should allow Caliban to run loose and run the risk of being murdered by him?"

"Shouldn't have been there in the first place," says Red Coyote. "It's not his island."

"Did he choose to land there?" says Felix. "He's hardly an invader, he's a castaway."

"He's still a slave-driver," says Red Coyote.

"He could keep Caliban penned up all the time," says Felix. "He could kill him."

"Says it himself, he wants the work out of him," says Red Coyote. "Picking up the firewood, washing the dishes. All of that. Plus, he does the same thing to Ariel. Makes him work, against his will. Won't give him liberty."

"Granted," says Felix. "But he still has the right to defend himself, no? And the single way he can do that is through his magic, which is effective only as long as he has Ariel running errands for him. If tethering Ariel on a magic string – a temporary magic string – was the only weapon you had, you'd do the same. Yes?"

This time there's general agreement. "Okay," says Wonder-Boy, "but why put the others through all that? The harpy scene, the craziness. Why doesn't he just kill the enemies and take their ship? Leave Caliban on the island, sail back to Milan or whatever?"

Because there wouldn't be a play, thinks Felix. Or it would be a very different play. But if he wants the characters to stay real for them, he can't use that ploy.

"I'm sure he was tempted," he says. "He probably felt like bashing their brains in. Who wouldn't, after what they did to him?" Widespread nodding. "However, if he enacted that kind of revenge he might get his dukedom back, but since Antonio made a deal with King Alonso whereby Milan is under the rule of Naples, then whoever inherits the kingdom of Naples will naturally bear a grudge. They wouldn't take kindly to their King and his son mysteriously disappearing, and the sailors would talk. The new ruler of Naples would kick Prospero out again or else kill him, and bring in someone else as the Duke of Milan. Failing that, Naples would go to war against Milan. Naples is bigger. Milan risks losing. What's Prospero's best plan?"

"Ferdinand marries Miranda," says Bent Pencil. "That makes Miranda the Queen of Naples, and she brings the dukedom into a union with Naples. Peace with honour. It's what was called a dynastic marriage," he explains to the others.

"Got it in one," says Felix. "But Prospero isn't a tyrant: he doesn't want to enforce a marriage for political reasons, the way Alonso has with his own daughter. He doesn't want to marry Miranda off as part of a cold-hearted flesh-trade deal. Instead, he wants the young folks – Ferdinand and Miranda – to fall in love, genuinely. So he uses his magic to arrange it. Or at least to help it along." Nods: they approve.

"I wouldn't do that to my kid either," says Leggs. "Marry her off. Sucks."

Felix smiles. "Prospero also needs to create a situation in which Alonso will accept this marriage," he says. "Ordinarily he wouldn't, because Naples is a kingdom and Milan is only a dukedom. Alonso doubtless wanted to marry his son, Ferdinand, into a big, rich kingdom. He'd be more powerful that way. And Ferdinand would have had to marry whoever his father picked."

"It was the law, in those times," says Bent Pencil. "You had to go along."

"Poxy law," says VaMoose.

"So Prospero makes Alonso think Ferdinand is drowned, and then he does the big reveal," says 8Handz. "*Look! He's alive!* Cool."

"And the King's so blissed out he'd let Ferdinand marry a frog if that's what he wanted," says SnakeEye.

"Exactly," says Felix. "On the one hand, Ferdinand's pretend death is a punishment for Alonso – it's revenge, it causes anguish – but on the other hand, it's a calculated stratagem."

"Two birds with one stone," says Krampus the Mennonite.

"Not too dumb," says SnakeEye. "Good con."

"So, is Prospero justified in what he does, considering his narrow range of options? Let's vote again," says Felix. "Who's for yes?"

This time all hands go up. Felix unclenches his shoulders: relief. Prospero is absolved, at least for the time being. "We're agreed, then," he says. "Now let's talk about the enforcers."

"Enforcers?" says Bent Pencil.

"All authority ultimately rests on force," says Felix. "The island is a prison, and where there are prisons there have to be enforcers. Otherwise everyone inside would simply get out and run away." Emphatic nodding.

"But there are no enforcers listed in the cast," says Bent Pencil. "In 'The Persons of the Play.'" He opens his text to the page, consults it.

"They're present nonetheless," says Felix. "They do the pinching and the cramping when Caliban has been mouthy, and the hunting of Stephano and Trinculo, disguised as spirit hounds."

"That's not Ariel?" says 8Handz. "I thought it was him."

"Look again. Ariel commands them," says Felix. "It's right here. *My goblins.* That's who they are: Prospero's goblins. They aren't listed in the cast because they were played by whoever wasn't already onstage in that scene. You put on a mask and, bingo, you're a goblin. So everyone in our play will have two roles: their own role and one of Prospero's goblins. They're the agents of control, but also they're the enablers of vengeance and retribution. They do the hands-on dirty work."

Ah yes. He can see how it could unfold: Tony and Sal, surrounded by goblins. Herded by them. Menaced by them. Reduced to a quivering jelly. *Hark, they roar,* he thinks. *Let them be hunted soundly. At this hour / lies at my mercy all mine enemies.* He looks around the classroom, smiling benevolently.

"Neat," says 8Handz. "I get it. Goblins 'R' Us."

22. The Persons of the Play

Thursday, January 17, 2013.

So far Anne-Marie hasn't met with the class. She's been learning her lines on her own, or rather refreshing them. Her first session inside Fletcher Correctional will be on Friday, the day Felix announces his casting, but he's arranged to have lunch with her first. He wants to prepare her, give her some idea of what she'll be walking into. Who, for instance, will be her Ferdinand? She has a right to know, in advance.

As he eats his solitary morning egg – solitary because Miranda's off somewhere in her special private space, and like all teenage girls she's being cagey about where that is – he reviews the choices he has all but made.

He's given much thought to these choices. There are the stated preferences of the actors themselves, but through long experience Felix has learned to disregard these. What natural Romeo has not longed to play Iago, and vice versa?

Should he cast by type or against type? Uglies in parts that call for beauty, a gorgeous hunk as Caliban? Put them into roles that will force them to explore their hidden depths, or are those depths better left unexplored? Challenge the audience by showing them well-known characters in surprising and possibly disagreeable guises?

During his past life at the Festival he'd been known for in-your-face envelope-pushing. In retrospect, he may on occasion have taken things too far. To be fair, more than *on occasion*; taking things too far had been his trademark. But this time, better not force it. He'll give the men parts they have a chance of performing well: he is after all a director, first and foremost. The play's the thing. His job is to help the actors help him execute it.

He's made a set of notes, partly for his own use, but also to share with Anne-Marie. These notes must never go any further than the two of them, he will emphasize to her. After his fine speech to the class – "I don't care what you've done" and so forth – it would be disillusioning for his actors to find their criminal convictions spelled out in so much detail.

He runs down his tentative list:

The Persons of the Play

PROSPERO, THE DEPOSED DUKE OF MILAN: Mr. Duke, Director and Producer.

MIRANDA, HIS DAUGHTER: Anne-Marie Greenland, Actress, Dancer, Choreographer.

ARIEL: 8Handz. Slight build. East Indian family background. About twenty-three. Very bright. Agile with a keyboard. Highly knowledgeable in tech matters. *Conviction:* Hacker, identity theft, impersonation. Forgery. Feels justified in his activities, as he believes he was playing a benevolent Robin Hood versus the evil King John capitalists of this world. Betrayed by an older colleague when he wouldn't hack refugee charities. Played Rivers in *Richard III*.

CALIBAN: Leggs. About thirty. Mixed background, Irish and black. Red hair, freckles, heavy build, works out a lot. A vet, was in Afghanistan. Veterans Affairs failed to pay for

PTSD treatment. *Conviction:* Break-and-enter, assault. Drugs- and booze-related. Was in addiction treatment but the program's been cancelled. Played Brutus, Second Witch, Clarence. Excellent actor but touchy.

FERDINAND, SON TO ALONSO: WonderBoy. Looks twenty-five, probably older. Scandinavian name. Appealing, clean-cut, handsome, plausible; can seem very sincere. *Conviction:* Fraud; sold fake life insurance to gullible seniors. Was especially effective with immigrants. Played Macduff, and Hastings in *Richard III.*

ALONSO, KING OF NAPLES: Krampus. Maybe forty-five. Mennonite background. Long horse-face. Member of a Mennonite ring ferrying drugs from Mexico through the US in farm machinery, under a cloak of piety. Depressive. Played Banquo in *Macbeth,* Brutus in *JC.*

SEBASTIAN, BROTHER TO ALONSO: Phil the Pill. Vietnamese refugee background; extended family sacrificed to get him through medical school. About forty. Feels he was wrongfully charged. *Conviction:* Manslaughter in connection with the deaths by overdose of three young college students for whom he repeatedly prescribed addictive painkillers. Says they begged him to help them. Easily manipulated. Played Buckingham in *Richard III.*

ADRIAN AND FRANCISCO, THE TWO COURTIERS. *Note: Many productions cut these parts and assign some of their speeches to Gonzalo or Sebastian. A good plan and I've followed it.*

GONZALO, ELDERLY COUNCILLOR TO ALONSO: Bent Pencil. Overweight, balding. In his fifties. WASP background. Accountant. *Conviction:* Embezzlement. Intelligent, with a philosophical turn. Feels his sentence was undeserved. Respected by the others, who think he can help them work the system once outside. Played Cassius in *Julius Caesar,* Duncan in *Macbeth.*

ANTONIO, USURPING BROTHER TO PROSPERO: Snake-Eye. Italian background. Slim, works out. Has a squint. About thirty-five. Law degree, which when traced proved a forgery. *Conviction*: Real-estate scammer; falsified deeds, then sold properties he didn't own. Also ran a minor Ponzi scheme. Persuasive, but only for those who want to be persuaded. Sense of entitlement. Thinks others are credulous and therefore deserve to be fleeced; feels he was only caught on a legal technicality. Played Macbeth. Played Richard III. Good villain.

STEPHANO, A DRUNKEN BUTLER: Red Coyote. In his twenties. Native-Canadian background. *Conviction*: Bootlegging, drug-pushing. Doesn't think he was doing wrong because the legal system is illegitimate anyway. Played Mark Antony in *JC*. Played First Witch in *Macbeth*.

TRINCULO, A JESTER: TimEEz. Chinese family background on one side. Round-faced, pale. Took his stage name from the Timmy's doughnut chain because he claims to have nothing in the middle of his head. Acts stupider than he is. Advanced pickpocket skills. *Conviction*: Running a retail shoplifting ring. Claims he was pressured into it. Soothsayer in *Julius Caesar*, doorkeeper in *Macbeth*. Natural clown.

ANNOUNCER: We have always used an announcer, who provides capsule versions of each scene so the audience can follow the plot. Considering Shiv the Mex for this part. New Mexican family background. *Conviction*: Assault. Was acting as enforcer for a local gang. Outgoing personality, good voice. Played Lord Grey in *Richard III*.

BOATSWAIN: PPod. African Canadian. Musical talent, and yes, I know about the clichés. A dancer, not as good as he thinks, but good. *Conviction*: Drugs, extortion, assault, gang-related. Would have been a fine Caliban but is needed in other capacities.

IRIS, CERES, JUNO: *A problem,* Felix has written. *None of the men will agree to impersonate these goddessess. But Prospero calls them puppets, so why not use puppets? Or dolls, with digital voices. Give them an edge of strangeness. On video it could work.*

There are a number of other roles and duties that Felix needs to assign: tech special effects, prompters, understudies. Costumes and props. He'll need a photographer for the publicity stills; there won't be any real publicity, of course, but the guys get a kick out of pictures of themselves in costume. The class has already decided they'll be altering some of the musical numbers and adding others, so singers and dancers will be required. Rap singers, break dancers, is Felix's guess. Anne-Marie can help them with the choreography.

He's roughed out the crew, but things can be switched around as he discovers the capacities and limits of each.

Provisional lineup

SPECIAL EFFECTS: 8Handz, lead tech; WonderBoy, Shiv, PPod, HotWire.

PROPS AND COSTUMES: Assign as project to each principal, with suggestions by their team.

PUBLICITY STILLS: WonderBoy. He has a sense of what looks glamorous.

MUSIC DJS: Leggs, Red Coyote, Paleface Lee, Riceball. 8Handz will do the sound editing.

INSTRUMENTALS: Leggs, Shiv the Mex, PPod, Red Coyote, Col.Deth.

CHORUS AND DANCERS: PPod, Leggs, TimEEz, VaMoose, Riceball, and Members of the Company, as required.

CHOREOGRAPHY: Anne-Marie Greenland, Leggs, PPod.

CHIEF GOBLINS: Riceball, Col.Deth, VaMoose. *Convictions:* Arson for insurance; armed robbery; drug charges. All first-time actors who can learn much from the others.

Two of them have been bouncers.

BACKUP GOBLINS: Members of the Company, as required.

The Goblins, thinks Felix. The ultimate weapon. For the kernel of his secret project, his nugget of revenge, everything hinges on the Goblins. What should they wear? Black ski masks, or is that too close to bank robbers and terrorists? If so, he thinks, all the better: fear can be very motivating. Sea-changing, you might say.

23. Admired Miranda

The same day.

Felix meets Anne-Marie for lunch at the Imp and Pig-Nut in Makeshiweg. She's a little less scrawny, but she's tense. Wired. Percolating with energy. At the same time her eyes look bigger, her expression more open: she looks ten years younger. She's wearing a simple long-sleeved shirt, white. In the play, Miranda traditionally wears white. Beige, at the very least.

Excellent, thinks Felix. She's melding into the role. Next thing you know she'll be going barefoot even though it's winter. "Beer?" he says. "Burger and fries?"

"I think I'll just have the walnut and cranberry salad and a cup of green tea," she says. "I've sort of gone off meat." Young girls are doing that now, thinks Felix: his own Miranda is the same. They eat quinoa, flax seeds, almond-milk shakes. Nuts. Berries. Zucchini pasta.

"Don't go overboard," he says.

"Overboard?"

"On the innocence and purity," he says. "You know. The salads." She laughs.

"Okay, I'll have a beer," she says. "And fries with the salad."

Felix orders a burger for himself. It's been a while since he's had one. What did they do for protein on that island? he wonders. Oh yes. Fish. That's why Caliban smells like a fish! He's not only the digger in the earth for pig-nuts with his long nails, he's also the fish-catcher. *No more dams I'll build for fish.* Why has Felix never put that together before?

"How're you getting on with it?" he asks. "Your part?"

"It's all there," she says. "From before. In my head. It was just waiting – stored in, you know, the dark backward and abysm of time. One of my roomie's hearing my lines for me. I'm almost word-perfect."

"I look forward to doing that scene with you," says Felix. "The *dark backward* scene. The whole play, actually. You're going to ace it!"

She gives a rueful smile. "Yeah, I know, right? It'll make my career, doing Miranda with a bunch of crims. You're talking as if it's real. A real production."

"It is real," he says. "More than real. Hyper-real. You'll see."

The food arrives, miraculously not late, and there's an interlude of chewing. When he judges the time is right, Felix says, "I've cast the show. Provisionally. There could still be changes. I've brought the list so you'll know who you're playing with, before you meet them. I've made some notes on them for you."

He hands the paper-clipped pages across the table; she studies them. "So you put their crimes in," she says reproachfully. "Thoughtful of you, but is that fair? You wouldn't do that for normal actors. You used to say we should come to it naked. No preconceptions about each other."

"Normal actors are on Wikipedia," he says. "Their crimes are their bad reviews. Public knowledge. Anyway, these aren't crimes as such, they're convictions. Different thing. We don't know if they actually *did* whatever."

"Okay, wink, nudge, fair enough," she says. She runs her finger down the list. "Assault, embezzlement, fraud. Nice. At least there's no serial killers or baby-fuckers."

"Those are in the maximum wing," says Felix. "Under special surveillance. For their own protection. My guys don't approve of that kind of thing."

"Good," says Anne-Marie. "So Caliban won't really try to rape me?"

"Not a hope," says Felix. "The other guys would stop him. One of them's an accountant." He indicates Gonzalo. "And here's your Ferdinand."

"Cute," says Miranda. "WonderBoy. He pick that stage name himself?"

"Not sure," says Felix. "He's got the right face for it though. The fifties after-shave look. Earnest." He's dated himself with *fifties after-shave*, but she doesn't tease him.

"So, a fraudster. Ripping off oldies," she says. "That's not pleasant."

"He didn't injure anyone," says Felix defensively. "Not physically. He was selling fake life insurance to seniors, doing very well at it. They never found out until after they were dead."

"Say that again?" says Anne-Marie, smirking.

"All right, it's the beneficiaries who'd find out, but since none of his targets had died yet, that hadn't happened. It was a dumped girlfriend who spilled the beans on him, as I understand."

"And how many of those were there? Dumped girl-friends?" Already she's sounding possessive: of an unreal actor playing Ferdinand, the facsimile of a non-existent swain.

"'Full many a lady,'" says Felix, quoting, "but not a patch on you. You're perfect and peerless, remember?"

"I know, right?" She laughs again. He'll ask her during rehearsals to reprise that laugh, turn it from a laugh of self-mockery to a laugh of delight.

"He's obviously a sweet-talker," says Felix. "Some of the seniors came to his trial. They wanted him to get a reduced sentence, be given another chance. They loved him; they thought of him as a son. If anyone can make those flowery love speeches convincing, it'll be WonderBoy."

"You're telling me something?" says Anne-Marie.

"Forewarned is forearmed," says Felix. "This kid could talk the pants off a statue of Queen Victoria. He'll want you to be his girlfriend on the outside, smuggle stuff in for him, who knows? Just don't get involved. He's probably already married. To more than one woman," he adds for greater effect.

"You think I'll fall in love with him, right?" says Anne-Marie. "You think I'm that easy?" She clenches her jaw.

"No, no," says Felix. "Heaven forefend. But you'll need your wits about you once you're in character. Even a hard-shelled little nut like you."

"You're in character already," says Anne-Marie, grinning. "Playing my overprotective dad. But you know teenage girls, they desert their adored daddies the minute some young ripped stud heaves into view. Don't blame me, blame my fucking hormones."

"Okay, truce," says Felix. "You're doing well, only quench the swearing. It's off-limits, remember; especially for Miranda."

"Agreed," says Anne-Marie. "I'll try." She continues down the list. "I see you're having the song-and-dance."

"Well, *The Tempest* spent the whole eighteenth century as an opera," says Felix. "So I pitched it to the guys as a musical. Puts it in more of a context for them. They were having trouble with the fairies and the bee-sucking song and so forth."

"Yeah, I get that," says Anne-Marie, grinning.

"I was wondering if you could help out with the choreography. Give them some pointers."

"Could do," she says. "I take it no ballet. We'll have to see what their bodies can handle." Felix smiles: he likes the word *we*. "What'll you do about that bee-sucking? It could be a deal-breaker."

"Remains to be seen," says Felix. "They could redo the wording. In the other plays we've put on, they've written some new material for sequences they felt needed some updating. Using the, ah, the contemporary vernacular."

"The contemporary vernacular," says Anne-Marie. "You mean trash talk. How now, grave sir?"

"It's the literacy part of the course," he says a little apologetically. "Writing things. Anyway, judging from the texts we have, Shakespeare's troupes must have done some improvising."

"You always pushed the boundaries," says Anne-Marie. "What about Iris, Ceres, and Juno? The engagement-party masque. That's a weird scene. It's got a lot of words, it could get boring. I see here you're thinking of dolls?"

"I can't ask the men to dress up like goddesses. We can montage . . ."

"What kind of dolls?"

"I was hoping you'd help me out," Felix says. "I'm not proficient in that area. Grown-up dolls."

"You mean, with tits."

"Well, not babies, or, you know, animals. What would you suggest?" His Miranda hadn't made it past the teddy-bear stage: dolls are a pain point for him.

"Disney Princesses," says Anne-Marie decisively. "They'd be perfect."

"Disney Princesses? Such as . . ."

"Oh, you know. Snow White, Cinderella, Beauty as in Sleeping, Jasmine from *Aladdin* in those campy pants, Ariel from *The Little Mermaid*, Pocahontas in the leather fringes . . . I had the whole set, once. Not Merida from *Brave*, though – that was since my time."

This is a foreign language to Felix. What is Merida from *Brave*? "It can't be Ariel," he says. "We already have an Ariel."

"Okay, I'll noodle on it. Could work really well! Who wouldn't want three Disney Princesses to turn up at their engagement party and shower them with blessings? And maybe some glitter confetti," she adds slyly, Felix being notorious for the glitter.

"I'll be counselled by you," says Felix at his most courtly. "Miss Nonpareil."

"Save it for the fans," she says, laughing. But he has what he wants: now they're allies.

Or are they? Maybe her eyes aren't wide because of innocence. Maybe it's fear. He has a split instant of seeing Prospero through the gaze of Miranda – a petrified Miranda who's suddenly realized that her adored father is a full-blown maniac, and paranoid into the bargain. He thinks she's asleep when he's talking out loud to someone who isn't there, but she's heard him doing it, and it scares her. He says he can command spirits, raise storms, uproot trees, open tombs, and cause the dead to walk, but what's that in real life? It's sheer craziness. The poor girl is trapped in the middle of the ocean with a testosterone-sodden thug who wants to rape her and an ancient dad who's totally off his gourd. No wonder she throws herself into the arms of the first sane-looking youth who bumbles her way. *Get me out of here!* is what she's really saying to Ferdinand. Isn't it?

No, Felix, it isn't, he tells himself firmly. Prospero is not crazy. Ariel exists. People other than Prospero see him and hear him. The enchantments are real. Hold on to that. Trust the play.

But is the play trustworthy?

24. *To the present business*

Friday, January 18, 2013.

At the Print Pro shop in Wilmot, Felix makes copies of his revised cast list – just the character names and the actors, no descriptions – to hand out to the actors. Then he drives into Makeshiweg and picks Anne-Marie up outside the house she shares with her three roommates. He gives her the Fletcher Correctional pass Estelle has arranged for behind the scenes, and she follows him in her own car – a dented silver-grey Ford – up the hill and through the outer gate to the parking lot.

She clambers out of her car, sets a tentative boot upon the ice. Should he extend a helping hand? No, he should not, he'd be slapped down with a quip. She surveys the chain-link fence, the barbed-wire topping, the searchlights. "This is grim," she says.

"Yes, it's a prison," he says. "Though 'Stone walls do not a prison make, Nor iron bars a cage.' But they do contribute to a cage-like ambience."

"What play is that in?" says Anne-Marie.

"Not a play," he says. "A poem. The man who wrote it actually was in prison – he chose the wrong political side. It does say in *The Tempest*, 'Thought is free,' but unfortunately that's in a song sung by three idiots."

"What a downer," says Anne-Marie. "Dwelling on the dark side these days? Winter getting to you? Cold enough for you?"

"It's over this way," says Felix. "The entrance. Watch out. Icy."

"This is Anne-Marie Greenland," he says to Madison and Dylan at Security. "She's a very well-known actress," he lies, "who has kindly agreed to join our acting company. She'll be helping us out with the play. She's got a pass."

"Nice to meet you," says Dylan to Anne-Marie. "Anything, any trouble, you can call on us."

"Thanks," says Anne-Marie curtly in her I-can-take-care-of-myself voice.

"This is like a pager," says Madison to her. "You push this button. Can I clip it onto your – "

"Got it," says Anne-Marie. "I'll clip it on myself."

"Then you put your bag through here, and you walk through here. What's that in the bag? The sharp things?"

"Knitting needles," says Anne-Marie. "For my knitting."

Felix is taken aback – knitting and Anne-Marie don't seem a fit – but Dylan and Madison smile indulgently: it's a womanly occupation. "Ma'am, sorry, but those have to stay with us," says Dylan.

"Oh for god's sakes," says Anne-Marie. "I'm going to knit someone to death?"

"Those needles could be used against you," Madison says in a patient voice. "Anything sharp can. You'd be surprised, ma'am. There are dangerous men in there. You can pick up the bag on the way out."

"Right," says Anne-Marie. "Just don't mess with my wool while I'm gone." They grin at that, or maybe just at her, because evidently she delights them. Why not? thinks Felix.

Despite her razor edge she's a bright light in a dim space. She breaks up the monotones.

Felix steers her down the hallway of his dedicated wing, indicating the various empty rooms. "We've got the use of these, plus the two demonstration cells, for green rooms and backstage. And rehearsal space," he adds.

"Good," she says. "I'll be needing one of those. For the dance numbers."

The men are already in the classroom. Felix introduces Anne-Marie. She's slipped off her coat: she's dressed conservatively, white shirt, black cardigan, black pants. Her hair is up in a prim honey-coloured bun; in each of her ears there's only a single earring. She smiles non-committally in the direction of the rear wall, then sits down at the front of the room in the desk Felix has indicated. Her spine is straight, her head balanced on the top end of it, a dancer's posture. No inviting slouches.

"Ms. Greenland's just sitting in for now," says Felix. "Getting to know you. She'll pitch in once we start rehearsing."

Dead silence. The men to either side of her try not to stare: their eyes veer sideways. Those behind are gazing spellbound, though none of her is visible to them except her back. Be alert, Felix tells himself. Keep an eye out for her. Don't assume you know them. Try to remember what you were like when you were that age. You may be a fading ember now, but you weren't always.

"Now, the casting," he proceeds as if all is as usual. "I'm the director, and these choices are mine. Maybe you won't get the role you want, but that's life. No pressuring, no horse-trading, no complaints. The theatre isn't a republic, it's a monarchy."

"Thought you said we're a team," says VaMoose in a surly tone.

"You are," says Felix. "You are a team. But I'm the king of it. All decisions final. The seasoned actors know that, right?" There are some nods from his veterans.

Next, he passes out the cast lists. There's a suppressed grumbling.

"You want me to play a drunken Indian," says Red Coyote, who's down for Stephano.

"No," says Felix. "I want you to play a drunken white man."

"Yay, I'm the fool," says TimEEz. "I can do that!"

"Ferdinand," says WonderBoy. "I'm up for this." He smiles in the direction of Anne-Marie's back, showing his perfect teeth.

"I'm not," says Krampus the Mennonite. "Up for this. The King part – all he does is moan. I should be Caliban."

"I know a lot of you wanted Caliban," says Felix, "but there's only one slot for that."

"Caliban should be First Nations," says Red Coyote. "It's obvious. Got his land stole."

"No way," says PPod. "He's African. Where's Algiers anyway? North Africa, right? That's where his mother came from. Look on the map, pox brain."

"So, he's a Muslim? I don't whoreson think so." VaMoose, another Caliban aspirant.

"No way that he's smelly-fish white trash, anyways," says Shiv, glaring at Leggs. "Even part white."

"I score," says Leggs. "You heard the man, fen head, it's final. So suck it."

"Points off, you swore," says PPod.

"*Suck it*'s not a swear word," says Leggs. "It's only a diss. Everyone knows that, and the devil take your fingers!"

Anne-Marie laughs.

*

Their next task is to study their scenes: what's going on in them, how should they be played, what are the problems? Felix has been careful to include one or two of his seasoned actors in each team: they can provide guidance. Or that's the theory.

The men move off into the rooms assigned. Anne-Marie stands up, stretches, bends a leg behind her, pulls it into a right angle. "They don't seem that bad," she says.

"Did I say they were?" says Felix.

"No, not exactly. But –" She must be remembering their convictions.

"Are you still all right with this?" says Felix.

"Yeah, of course," she says, though her voice is tentative. "So what do I do next? Where's my cute Ferdinand? Should I go start rehearsing the mushy stuff with him?"

"He's licking his lips, but don't start today," says Felix. "They need to work into their roles, figure things out for themselves. Then I spend time with them on each scene in turn. Because the final version's a video, we can shoot the scenes when the guys are ready, and once we have the costumes and so forth, then stick it together like a mosaic. But the two of us can run through Act I, Scene 2, now if you like."

So Miranda weeps and implores, and Prospero hushes and comforts and reassures her, and then expounds. Just as he's launching into the story of Antonio's brotherly treachery that's landed them on the island, 8Handz appears in the doorway.

"So who do I rehearse with?" he says. "Ferdinand's practising how to sit on a rock looking gloomy and then I'm supposed to come in and lure him away with music, but we don't have the music yet. Anyway my first speech is with you, Mr. Duke."

"Ah, my Ariel," says Felix. "There's a few tech issues I need to discuss with you. We'll take a break," he says to Anne-Marie. "Go have a look, see what the boys are up to."

"Plotting, are you?" she says with a smile for 8Handz. "Cooking up the illusions? You got to watch the old enchanter, he'll charm you silly."

"I know, right," says 8Handz, grinning. "He already did that."

Felix waits till she's gone. He lowers his voice. "What exactly do you know about surveillance systems?" he asks.

8Handz smiles. "I'm cool," he says. "If I've got what I need; like, the tools. Something in mind?"

"I want to see without being seen," says Felix. "In all the rooms, plus the hallway."

"You and every secret service on the planet," says 8Handz. "I'll make you a shopping list. Get me the stuff and it's a done deal."

"If you can fix up what I have in mind," says Felix, "I'm pretty sure I can get you early parole."

"Really?" says 8Handz. "I've already applied, but it's taking time. How'll you swing that?"

"Influence," says Felix enigmatically.

Foes in high places, he thinks to himself.

25. *Evil Bro Antonio*

Wednesday, February 6, 2013.

The time has whipped by, and now there's little of it left. Only five weeks to zero hour, the hour at which the hated dignitaries will enter his domain, and his plan, now in bud, will burst into full flower. Anticipation sharpens Felix's wits, brightens his eyes, tenses his muscles. The readiness is all.

Tony and Sal draw closer, attending banquets, appearing at galas, dispensing interviews to the press like thrown roses, leaving a spoor of photo ops wherever they go. He follows them through the vibrations of the Web, playing spider to their butterflies; he ransacks the ether for their images. All unsuspecting they wend their carefree way, with never a thought in their otherwise scheming heads for him, Felix Phillips – exiled by their unjust hands, lying in wait for them, preparing his ambush. It's taken a while, but revenge is a dish best eaten cold, he reminds himself.

He checks off the days, he counts the hours remaining. They'll arrive at Fletcher Correctional in mid-March, ready to see the show.

But the show isn't ready for them. The company is nowhere close yet. Felix is in an agony of impatience: what can he do to speed things up, get this video filmed, cut and polished, rendered into a gem? In time for the scheduled arrival.

Gremlins conspire against him. There have been two defections among the minor Goblins, though he talked one of them back. Another Goblin's in the infirmary with an unspecified injury: some sort of payback involving a nail file, Leggs told him, "nothing to do with any of us." There has been name-calling at rehearsals, a scuffle when his back was turned. This thing could fall apart very easily; but then, he's thought that about any play he's ever directed.

All he's got on video is a few preliminary scenes: rough, very rough. He's ordered an electronic keyboard from the rental agency he uses, but it hasn't come yet, and how can they do the music without it? they say. They want him to arrange Internet access for them so they can download MP3s, but that's a bridge too far: even Estelle is unable to swing it, since Management raises the usual objections. The inmates will abuse it, they'll use it to watch porn and make escape plans. No point in Felix saying that they're far too wrapped up in the play to bother with escaping: he wouldn't be believed. Also, he might well be wrong. He's doing his best, bringing in music clips for them and running them on the class computer, but no, no, this isn't the version they asked for, they say, rolling their eyes. Doesn't he know the Monkees suck?

Frustration awaits him at every turn. WonderBoy and Anne-Marie have hit a snag. Their first rehearsal was excellent, but the next one was lacklustre: WonderBoy wasn't producing. He was going through the motions only.

"What happened?" Felix asked Anne-Marie over coffee on a Thursday.

"He proposed to me," said Anne-Marie.

"He's supposed to do that. It's in the scene," Felix said, keeping neutral.

"No, I mean he really proposed to me," said Anne-Marie. "He said it was love at first sight. I said it was only a play, it wasn't real."

"Then what?" Felix asked. She was fiddling with her spoon: he knew there was more.

"He sort of grabbed me. He tried the mouth mash."

"And?"

"I didn't want to cripple him," said Anne-Marie.

"But you did?"

"Only temporarily," she said. "His feelings were hurt, more than anything. Once he stopped writhing around on the floor and got up. I did apologize."

That would explain his lack of passion, thought Felix. "I'll have a word with him," he said.

"Don't do that, you'd inhibit him," she said.

Even his Ariel, 8Handz, is messing up. At their second Act I rehearsal together he began his speech with "Sieg heil, great monster!" and then broke into embarrassed sniggering because something that had been in his mind had sprung unbidden out of his mouth.

They goof around behind his back, they have their own disparaging names for him and for Prospero too, they make fun of the play – that's normal – but 8Handz has to remember who he's supposed to be. Granted, Ariel has a lot of tasks to keep track of – he's Prospero's secret sharer – but still. 8Handz needs to sober up.

Is it always so hard at this stage? Felix asks himself. Yes, it is. No, it isn't. It's harder this time because he's gambling so much on it.

Fourteen more sessions, then the big day. They're still

dithering over their costume choices, they're fluffing their lines, they mumble. "Tip of the tongue, top of the teeth," he reminds them. "Crisp! E-NUN-ciate! It doesn't matter what you're saying if we can't hear you! She sells seashells by the seashore! No slush!"

If it were an ordinary company in the old days he'd have been yelling at them by now, calling them shit-for-brains, ordering them to reach deep, find the character, torquing their emotions to the breaking point and telling them to use the resulting blood and pain, *use it!* But these are fragile egos. Some have taken anger management therapy, so yelling by him would set a bad example. For others, depression is never far. Push them too much and they'll collapse. They'll give up, even his key players. They'll walk out. It's happened before.

"You've got the talent," he tells them. Shrugs, passive defiance. "You're better than this!" What's he supposed to do, threaten them with prison? That won't work, they're already in prison. He has no leverage.

Where's the energy? Where's the spark that will ignite this pile of inert damp wood? What am I doing wrong? Felix frets.

He's insisted on coffee, quality coffee, not the abominable powdered stuff – he's paid for the beans, he's had them ground, he's brought it in himself, taking care to share some with Dylan and Madison. During this morning's quality coffee break, he's approached by SnakeEye. Anne-Marie is behind him, standing ready to back him up with whatever it is, Felix guesses. She's in one of her dance rehearsal outfits: the knitted leg warmers, the peacock-blue sweatpants, the long-sleeved black T. The tap shoes, he notes: there will be percussion.

"We put together a thing," says SnakeEye. "My team. The Antonio team."

"Go ahead," says Felix.

"You know that place where you, I mean Prospero, you tell the backstory? To Miranda? About how come, what with the brother –"

"Act I, Scene 2," says Felix. "Yes?"

"That's the one."

"What about it?" says Felix.

"It's too long," says SnakeEye. "Plus it's boring. Even Miranda finds it boring. She almost goes to sleep."

He's right, thinks Felix. That scene's been a challenge for every actor who's ever played Prospero: how to get through the Act I, Scene 2, narration of Prospero's doleful history while at the same time making it compelling. The thing is too static. "But the audience needs to know the information," he says. "Otherwise they can't follow the plot. They need to hear about the wrongs he's suffered, and his reason for wanting revenge."

"Yeah, we get that," says SnakeEye. "So we thought, Why not do it as a flashback?"

"It already is a flashback," says Felix.

"Yeah, but you know how you're always saying, Show, don't tell, move it, get some energy?"

"Yes," says Felix. "And?"

"And, so, we can do it as a flashback number, only with Antonio telling it. We've been rehearsing."

Ha. He's cutting me out, thinks Felix. Elbowing me aside. Making a bigger part for himself. How appropriate for Antonio. But isn't this what he's asked them to do? Rethink, reframe? "Great, let's hear it," he says.

"The boys are doing backup for me," says SnakeEye. "Team Antonio. We call this 'Evil Bro Antonio.'"

"Okay," says Felix. "Showtime."

"Remember to count," says Anne-Marie as they arrange themselves, SnakeEye in front, his backups in a line behind: Phil the Pill, VaMoose, and, more improbably, Krampus the Mennonite. If Anne-Marie has wrung anything like dancing out of Krampus it will be a miracle.

"I'm all ears and eyes," says Felix.

"Beginning on three!" says Anne-Marie. She counts, *One-two-three*, then claps once, and away they go.

SnakeEye is aiming for the essence of Antonio: ruthless; full of himself. He puffs himself up, he rubs his hands together, he squints with his slanty left eye, he sneers with his lopsided mouth. If he had a moustache he'd be twirling it. He prances fit to kill. His team sets the rhythm: stamping, clapping, finger-snapping. A cappella breath-work.

They're good, they're much better than Felix expected. Is it all due to Anne-Marie, or do they get this stuff from music videos? Maybe both. *Stamp stamp clap, stamp stamp clap, clap clap stamp stamp snap*, go the backups. SnakeEye launches in:

I'm the man, I'm the Duke, I'm the Duke of Milan,
You want to get pay, gotta do what I say.
Wasn't always this way, no, no,
I was once this dude called Antonio,
I was no big deal and it made me feel so bad, so mad,
Got under my skin, 'cause I couldn't ever win,
Got no respect, I was second in line,
But I just kept smilin', just kept lyin', said everything's
   fine.

It was my bro called Prospero,
He was the real man,

He was the Duke, he was the Duke, he was the Duke of Milan.
Ooo-ah hah! Ooo-ah hah! Stamp clap, clap stamp, snapsnap stamp.

But he was a fool, not cool, he didn't look,
Didn't look around, take care of his stuff,
Didn't watch his back, stuck his head in a book,
Said Bro, you know
How all of this works, so put on a good show,
Say I say you're the boss, the boss of Milan,
They'll do whatever you command,
Send 'em here, send 'em there, send 'em far and near,
Rake in the loot for me, get a new suit, whatever.

He was stuck in his book, doin' his magic,
Wavin' his wand around and all that shit,
I took what I like, and that was fine,
Whatever I wanted, it was mine,
I got so used to it.
But he didn't look, he was slack, didn't watch his
    back,
What a fool, not cool, laid out the temptation,
I was bossin' around the whole Milan nation,
He didn't see what I took, it turned me into a crook,
Turned me into his evil twin, I went the way of sin,
Only way I could win.

Ooo-ah hah! Ooo-ah hah! Stamp clap, clap stamp, snapsnap stamp.

So I went to the King, the Naples King,
He wanted control of that Milan thing,
So we made a deal,
He'd help me steal it, I'd pay him back,
And we grabbed my Bro, that Pros-per-o,

In the dead of night,
We paid off his guards so they didn't put up a fight,

We tossed him into a leaky boat,
No chance in a million that thing would float,
Along with his kid, got rid of her too,
Towed them out onto the ocean blue,
Told the folks he went away, took a break, took a
    vay-cay-shun
On a tropical isle, that made 'em smile, but after a while
When he didn't come back, said he must've drowned.

Ooo-ah hah! Ooo-ah hah! Stamp clap, clap stamp, snapsnap stamp.

Oh no! Oh no more Prospero,
Too bad, how sad, that's what they said:
He must be dead.
So now I'm the man, the man, the big man,
I'm the Duke, I'm the Duke, I'm the Duke of Milan.

Yeah!
He's the Duke, he's the Duke, he's the Duke of Milan.
Stampity stamp, stampity stamp, stampity stampity stamp!
Clap clap. Hah!

On their final "Hah!" they all look at Felix. He knows that look. *Love me, don't reject me, say I'm in!*

"What d'you think?" SnakeEye asks. He's gone all out on the prancing, he's breathing hard.

"It has something," says Felix, who in fact would like to throttle him. Scene-stealer! But he tamps down on that emotion: it's their show, he scolds himself.

"Better than something! Come on, it's terrific!" says

Anne-Marie, who's been watching from the back of the room. "Tells us what happened, sums it up! It's a keeper!"

"Snazzy foot-stamping," says Felix.

"That's what I'm here for," says Anne-Marie, grinning. "Miss Helpful. Log-carrying, dance numbers, whatever."

"Thank you," says Felix.

"Jealous, Mr. Duke?" Anne-Marie whispers impishly. She sees into him, too far. "You want to be in the backup, right?"

"Don't be a brat," he whispers back.

"Then, we think," says SnakeEye, pushing on through, "so, after that, we cut to the boat, the leaky boat they're in, and we can show that on the video, while he's saying, I mean you – he's saying that part where Miranda tells him what a trouble she must have been, a three-year-old kid in that boat, and he says she was like an angel that preserved him? A cherubin. That part."

"I know that part," says Felix. His heart twists within him.

"So some of the guys have kids," he says. "They've got photos of them, you're allowed to have those kinds of photos. Of your family, suppose you've got one. So we video the boat – we can use, like, a toy boat, bang it around, fix it so it looks falling apart; and it's dark, wind's blowing, it's night, and then in the sky we show the pictures of their kids. That's how the guys feel about it, with their kids: it's a cherubin type of thing that helps them get through the rough parts."

How can Felix say no? "Let's give it a try," he says.

"8Handz says he can cut photos like that in easy," says SnakeEye. "Into a video. He says he can make them flash, each one, just for a second. Like stars."

"That sounds nice," says Felix. His throat is closing up on him. Why is a cornball idea like this wrecking him so completely? Sentimental sludge! Is he going to cry?

Careful, he tells himself. Hold it together. Prospero's always in control. More or less.

SnakeEye has more to say: he's shifting from foot to foot. Spit it out, Felix wants to snap. Let's have the second barrel. Finish me off.

"We thought maybe you might like to add something of your own, Mr. Duke." His voice is shy. "If you've got a special photo like that. You could add it in to the sky thing too. Sort of like a guest cameo. The guys say you'd be welcome."

His lost Miranda, three years old, on her swing, up in the sky, in her silver frame. Laughing with joy. *That did preserve me.*

"No," Felix almost shouts. "No, I don't have anything suitable! But thank you all the same. Excuse me." They're not doing this to get at him. They can't possibly know anything about him, him and his remorse, his self-castigation, his endless grief.

Half blinded, choking, he blunders down to the fifties-period demonstration cell and collapses onto a bottom bunk. Scratchy grey blankets. Arms crossed on knees, head bowed. Lost at sea, drifting here, drifting there. In a rotten carcass the very rats have quit.

26. Quaint devices

Saturday, February 9, 2013.

Moods pass. Things look up. Bustling around is always a help.

On the weekend, Felix makes a trip into Toronto in search of costumes and props. He goes on the train, leaving his car in the Makeshiweg station lot because he can't face the traffic and the ordeal of trying to park. He's no longer used to urban crowds.

The guys have made their lists of what they think is needed. He hasn't promised them certainty, but he's vowed to do his best for them. Anne-Marie has added the three Disney Princess dolls. She would have ordered them online, she said, but her credit cards are maxed out.

He gets off the train at Union Station and begins his quest. Anne-Marie, after a search on her smartphone, has made him a map, with likely locations marked on it.

His first stop is a toy store a few subway stops away. He can contemplate these kinds of stores now: Miranda is no longer at the age for toys. He walks past the front window, walks past again: it's only plastic in there, it's only cardboard. Surely he can risk going in.

He takes a deep breath, plunges across the threshold into that world of damaged wishes, forlorn hopes. So bright, so shining, so out of reach for him. There's a fluttering in his chest, but he holds firm.

Once safely inside, he heads for the beach-toy section: anything that might float is likely to be there. As he ponders the many primary-coloured items on offer, a salesgirl comes up to him. "May I help you?" she says.

"Thank you," says Felix. "I'd like two boats. One more like a rowboat, the other maybe bigger, more like a sailboat." No, he doesn't want a model kit. Something that can actually handle water, like a bath toy, or –

"Ah," says the girl. "Grandchildren?"

"Not exactly," says Felix. "I'm more like an uncle." Together they select the boats. The small one can be covered with patches, the big one will look good in the tempest.

"Anything else?" the girl asks. "Can I interest you in some flotation devices for the little ones? Water wings – they're decorated like butterflies, cute for girls – and the noodles are very popular. Swim noodles," she adds, seeing his blank look.

"Actually," says Felix, "do you have any, ah, Disney Princesses?"

"Oh yes," says the girl, laughing. "We've got a surfeit of them!" She's a history major or something like that, because who else would say *surfeit*? "Over there." She's finding him droll. That's fine, he tells himself: droll can work for me.

"Would you help me pick them out?" he asks, putting on his helpless face. "I need three."

"What lucky nieces!" she says with an ironic quirk of her eyebrow. "Did you have any particular princesses in mind?"

Felix consults his list. "Snow White," he reads. "Jasmine. Pocahontas."

"My," says the girl. "How knowledgeable you are! About the tastes of girls. I bet you have daughters as well as the nieces!"

Felix winces. Why, this is hell, he thinks, nor am I out of it. Damn Anne-Marie, I should have made her come with me and buy these things herself. He negotiates the purchase process, then asks that the future goddesses be deboxed, wrapped in tissue, and crammed into a single bag. Humiliating for them, but their apotheosis awaits.

Carrying his two shopping bags, he locates the costume and joke emporium on Yonge Street that Anne-Marie has marked down for him. In the window is an almost-naked mannequin in stiletto heels, a sequined mask, and leather bondage gear, wielding a whip. Inside, he scopes through the vampire teeth, Batman capes, and zombie masks, trying not to look like a fetishist. Behind the counter is a heavily muscled young man with an array of chrome ornaments in his ears and a skull tattooed on his forearm.

"Anything special?" he says with a demi-leer. "We've got some new leather, very nice. We do custom-fitted. Muzzles, shackles." He's spotted Felix for a masochist; not so far from the mark, thinks Felix.

"Got any black wings?" he says. "Or any colour really, except white."

"Fallen angel, are we?" says the guy. "Sure. We've got some blue ones. Those do?".

"Even better," says Felix. He buys the wings, a jar of blue face paint, a jar of muddy-green face paint, a clown makeup kit, a scaly green Godzilla hat with lizard eyes on top and upper teeth that frame the forehead, a pair of snakeskin-patterned leotards – these last three items for Caliban – and some were-wolf masks, which is the closest he can get to spirit dogs.

The shop doesn't have any ruffs, but there are four short velvet capes, so he adds them to the pile for the aristocrats. A handful of fake gold medallions on chains, with lions and dragons on them. Two cheap gold-sequinned wraparounds and a silver one: glisterwear, to allure the fools. A couple of packages of blue glitter confetti, several sheets of temporary tattoos: spiders, scorpions, snakes, the usual.

The wings are hard to carry. He stops at a luggage place, buys a large wheeled suitcase, and stows the wings, the boats, the Disney Princesses, the werewolf masks, and the glistering trash. It all fits in with room to spare, which is good, because there's more to come.

Next, a sports shop. He wants some ski goggles, he tells the healthy-looking young sales clerk: the iridescent kind of goggles. "These are our top sellers," says the youth. "Plutonite." There's a purple-blue sheen to the lenses, which are enormous and wraparound: a bug-eye effect. "For yourself?" says the clerk, raising his eyebrows; evidently the image of Felix on skis is a stretch for him.

"No," says Felix. "A juvenile relative."

"Good skier?"

"Let's hope so," says Felix. "And I want fifteen black ski masks."

"Fifteen?"

"If you've got them. It's for a party."

They only have eight in stock, but there's a Mark's Work Wearhouse in the Wilmot mall where he can doubtless pick up the rest of them, plus fifteen pairs of stretchy black gloves. He's unsure of how many Goblins he will finally need, but it's best to be well prepared.

In a corner knick-knack shop that sells umbrellas and handbags he picks up a semi-opaque women's raincoat in aqua, with a cheerful pattern of ladybugs, bees, and butterflies. "The biggest one you've got," he tells the clerk. It's a Large, woman's size, but despite that it may still be a tight squeeze for 8Handz. They can always cut it up the back and pin the two sides to his shirt: only the front needs to show.

In a Canadian Tire outlet he buys a blue shower curtain, a stapler, a clothesline, some plastic clothes pegs – these last two for Stephano and Trinculo's clothes-stealing scene – and a green plastic bowl for the feast that's offered, then snatched away.

Next he goes to a nearby Staples and scores a large pack of construction paper in various colours, a roll of brown wrapping paper, and some felt markers: cactuses, palm trees, those kinds of things, for the island sets. All you need is a few items: the brain completes the illusion.

His last stop is at a women's swimwear boutique. "I'd like a bathing cap," he says to the elegant middle-aged woman who's presiding. "Blue, if you have one."

"For your wife?" says the woman, smiling. "Going on a cruise?" Felix is tempted to tell her it's for a convicted criminal inside a prison who's playing the part of a magic flying blue alien, but he thinks better of it.

"Yes," he says. "In March. To the Caribbean," he elaborates.

"That sounds lovely," says the woman a little wistfully. It's her fate to provide for cruises but never to go on one.

He views and rejects several bathing caps: one with daisies, one with a pattern of pink roses on aqua, one with waterproof bows. "She likes them really plain," he says. The best he can do is an impish cap with overlapping rubber scale-shaped scallops on it. "Do you have a larger size?" he asks. "The largest. She has a big head and a lot of hair," he feels compelled to explain.

"She must be quite tall," says the clerk.

"Statuesque," says Felix.

Maybe there will be some way of stretching the cap, he hopes. He doesn't want 8Handz to look ridiculous, with a tiny blue cap perched on his head like a mushroom.

27. Ignorant of what thou art

The same day.

Felix returns to Makeshiweg on the train, then wheels his big suitcase through the station parking lot to his car. More snow is falling; once he's back at the laneway leading to his hovel, it's a struggle to lug the suitcase through the fresh drifts to his door.

Despite the local flurries the sun is setting, far to the southwest, in clouds the colour of apricot. On the edge of the drifted field the shadows cast by the trees are bluish. Once, not so long ago, Miranda would have been outside at this time, taking advantage of the last rays of light to play in the snow, throwing handfuls of it into the air or making snow angels. He looks for footprints: no, she hasn't gone out recently. But he reminds himself that she doesn't leave footprints, so lightly does she tread.

There's an earthy, ashen smell inside the house, as often when the fire's gone out. He turns on the heater. It whirs; there's the ping of warming metal. "Miranda?" he says.

At first he thinks she isn't there, and his heart plummets. Then he detects her: she's over by their table, in the gathering shadows. She's waiting by the chess set, ready to resume their lesson. He's been teaching her some mid-game developments. When he opens the new suitcase, however, she leaves the table and comes over to look wonderingly at what he's brought.

Such riches – the gold fabric, the blue rubber bathing cap, the little boats! The three Disney Princesses in their tawdry finery: she finds them enchanting.

What is each thing? she wants to know. Where did it come from, what is it for? A bathing cap? Ski goggles? What is bathing, what is skiing? Of course these items are unknown to her: she knows so little about the outside world.

"They're for the play," Felix tells her. Then he has to explain what a play is, what acting is, why people pretend to be someone they're not. He's never talked to her about the theatre; in fact, up until this time she has shown scant interest in where he goes when he's not in their two shoddy rooms, but now she listens attentively.

When he gets back from Fletcher Correctional on the Monday, exhausted after six hours of thrashing through Act II scene by scene, he finds she's read *The Tempest*. He shouldn't have left his spare playbook lying around so carelessly. Now that she's seen it, she's been seized by it. He should have known.

He's never wanted her to go into the theatre. It's too hard a life, it's too rough on the ego. There are so many rejections, so many disappointments, so many failures. You need a heart of iron, a skin of steel, the willpower of a tiger, and more of these as a woman. It would be an especially difficult vocation for a girl like her: she's so tender-hearted, so sensitive. She's been protected from the worst in human nature: how would she cope, once brought face to face with that worst? She ought to choose a safer career path, such as medicine, or perhaps dentistry. And marry a stable and loving husband eventually, of course. She shouldn't fritter herself away on a world of illusions – of vanishing rainbows, of bursting bubbles, of cloud-capped towers – the way he himself has done.

But the theatre must be in her blood, because now she's determined. She insists on being in the production. Worse, she wants to play Miranda. She feels the part is right for her, she tells him. It makes her so happy to think about it! She can hardly wait to meet the person who'll be playing Ferdinand. She knows they'll be spectacular together.

"You can't play Miranda," he says as firmly as he can. "It's not possible." This is the first time he's opposed her directly in anything. How to tell her that no one but he himself would be able to see her? She'd never believe it. And if she did believe it, if she were forced to believe it, what would become of her then?

Why not? she persists. Why can't she be Miranda? He's being so mean! He doesn't understand! He's treating her as if –

"What, moody?" he says to her.

Is that a pout? Her arms crossed in defiance? But why? she wants to know. Why can't I?

"Because I already have an actress for Miranda," he says. "I'm sorry."

She's sad about that, which makes him sad as well. He hates to hurt her feelings; it wrings his heart.

She disappears – is she outside, walking in the dark, in the snow? Is she in her room, sulking on her bed, as teenage girls do?

But she doesn't have a room, he reminds himself. She has no bed. She never sleeps.

28. Hag-Seed

Monday, February 25, 2013.

Now that they have costumes to try on the cast has become more energized. The play's becoming real for them. They spend a lot of time in front of the mirrors in Room Two, now renamed the Green Room, looking at themselves from various angles, making faces, trying out their lines. Doing the warmup exercises he's taught them.

Tip of the tongue, top of the teeth, he can hear them saying. *Ar, ar, ar: Repentance! El, el, el: Loss! Liberty! Ess, ess, ess: Sweet sprites! Pee, pee, pee: Perfection!* Those who are to sing warm up their voices, chanting as Anne-Marie has taught them: *Om Om Om! Bones! Gone! Ding dong hell!*

The keyboard arrives; after some wrangling, it's allowed past Security. Felix designates Room Four as the Music Room. Anne-Marie is working with the dancers. Before every session they warm up: she has them doing pushups and floor exercises. Patrolling the hallway of his little kingdom, eavesdropping, Felix can hear her:

"Keep the beat! One-two, hit it on the *two*! Shake it! Shake it! Shake it or break it! From the core! Count! Move that pelvis! Yes!"

One day 8Handz is elbows-deep in cables, the next it's mini-cameras. After that he's installing some tiny microphones and speakers, wireless ones: it would be contraindicated to drill holes in the walls.

Felix has set up a folding screen in the corner of the main room, the one they'll use for the video viewing. Behind the screen are a desk with a computer screen and keyboard, and two chairs, one for 8Handz, one for himself. Felix can now snoop on any point in his domain.

"Green Room," says 8Handz, calling it up onscreen. "Music Room. Demonstration holding cell, the old one. Now the other one. I've got them all labelled here, see? There's audio and video, and recording for both of those."

"Exactly what I need," says Felix. "My brave spirit!"

"You sure you got permission for all this?" says 8Handz a little anxiously. He doesn't want to incur any penalties: that might delay his parole.

"You're in the clear," says Felix. "Everything's part of the play. I take full responsibility. I've explained it to the authorities, they know what we're doing." Half true, but half will do. "Any questions, just refer them to me."

"Cool," says 8Handz.

Anne-Marie and WonderBoy have been rehearsing their scenes, creditably for both. She's virginal and spontaneous, he's puppy-eyed and doting. He's puppy-eyed and doting offstage too, but Anne-Marie is affecting not to notice. She's settled on a den-mother act, aiming to inspire filial devotion rather than lust among her fellow cast members. To that effect she's taken up baking: she arrives with pans of caramel brownies, with chocolate-chip cookies, with cinnamon buns, and hands them around during coffee breaks. Dylan and Madison are awarded samples and make jokes about there being drugs in the goodies, isn't that what theatre people are into? Wild, crazed orgies? Anne-Marie smiles indulgently at them, as if they are clever nine-year-olds.

Astonishing, thinks Felix, how someone so slender and girlish can appear so matronly. He wasn't wrong about her those many years ago: she's a fine actress.

She's also taken charge of the goddesses. Snow White will be Iris, the messenger, she's decreed; Pocahontas will be Ceres, goddess of fertility; and Jasmine will play Juno, patroness of marriage. "But they can't wear this shit," she'd told Felix when he'd handed them over. She'd begun to peel off their finery.

"I can see that," Felix said, "but where will we get . . ."

"My knitting group can do it as a project."

"I still can't see you in a knitting group." Knitting groups used to be for missionary aunts and World War One matrons turning out socks for the boys in the trenches, not for hip young actresses.

"It calms the nerves. Knitting. You should try it. Guys are doing it too."

"I'll pass," said Felix. "You think your group will want to take this on? Doll-dressing?"

"They're pretty rad," she'd said. "They'll love it. Rainbow colours for Iris; fruit and tomatoes and, you know, wheat sheaves and stuff for Ceres; a peacock-feather design for Juno."

"Goddesses in wool?" Felix asked. "Won't that make them look fat?" There was bad taste lurking somewhere in the vicinity, but not the kind of bad taste he favoured.

"You'll be surprised," said Anne-Marie. "They won't look fat, though. Promise."

"The thing is," he said, "my best speech in the entire play comes right after these goddesses do their thing. 'Our revels now are ended,'" he can't resist declaiming.

"These our actors
As I foretold you, were all spirits, and
Are melted into air, into thin air,
And, like the baseless fabric of this vision,
The cloud-capped towers, the gorgeous palaces,
The solemn temples, the great globe itself,
Yea, all which it inherit, shall dissolve,
And, like this insubstantial pageant faded,
Leave not a wrack behind. We are such stuff
As dreams are made on, and our little life
Is rounded with a sleep."

"Damn, you can still do it," said Anne-Marie when he'd finished. "That's why I always wanted to work with you. You're the maestro. You almost made me cry."

"Thank you," said Felix, making a small bow. "It is rather good, isn't it?"

"Rather? Fuck," said Anne-Marie. She wiped at an eye.

"All right, skip the rather," said Felix. "But don't you think these wool-covered Disney Princesses might be somehow ..." What was the word he wanted? "Might be somehow undercutting? To the speech? Don't they risk the merely ridiculous?"

"I've searched online, plus I've seen three productions, and the goddess thing always risks the ridiculous even when they're people," said Anne-Marie. "They've used back-screen projections, they've used inflatables, they did it on stilts a few years ago. But ours won't look like Disney Princesses once we get there. I'm face-painting them. Glo in the Dark, I thought, and some glitter. Give them a mask look. And since they're sort of Ariel's puppets anyway, why don't we use that Japanese Bunraku technique, or black light – have them moved around by some of the guys in ski masks and black gloves? You've got those anyway. Do the voices with a voice-changer; sort of a weird spirit type of thing."

"It's worth a try," said Felix.

Wednesday, February 27, 2013.

Two weeks to go before the day the planets converge and the tempest is unleashed. They've now recorded the initial tempest scene, with the sinking boat and 8Handz in the bathing cap and goggles: it filmed surprisingly well. Felix will do his own first scene with Ariel next week. 8Handz has been so busy with the tech that he needs more time on the lines.

Today they're shooting Caliban. They'll do the closeups of his speeches, add the far shots later. This is the first day Leggs has been in full costume: the scaly Godzilla headgear, its eyes and teeth obliterated, its edges altered to hang in tatters around his face; his face itself mudded with makeup; lizard-skin patterns on his legs, temporary tattoos of spiders and scorpions covering his arms. It's no worse than some other Caliban outfits Felix has seen, and better than some.

"Ready?" says Felix.

"Yeah," says Leggs. "Um, we added something. Anne-Marie helped us with it."

Felix turns to Anne-Marie. "Is this any good? We can't fool around, we're running out of time, we need to get on with it." He did encourage them to write their own extra material, so he's not entitled to be grumpy.

"Three and a half minutes," she says. "I timed it. And yes, it's terrific! Would I lie to you?"

"I won't answer that," says Felix.

"Take One," says TimEEz. "Hag-Seed. By Caliban and the Hag-Seeds. First there's an Announcer bit, we can shoot that later. 'Here comes Caliban, From his prison in a stone, Kept in slavery, Made to groan, But come what may, He got to have his own say!' Like that."

Felix nods. "Fine," he says.

"Don't forget to breathe," Anne-Marie says to Leggs. "From the diaphragm. Remember what I said about anger. It's like fuel – find it, use it! This is your chance to roar! Take off like a rocket! One, two, go!"

Leggs rears up, crouches, shakes a fist. TimEEz, PPod, VaMoose, and Red Coyote stand off to the side, clapping out the beat, adding a soft Uh-oh, Uh-oh in syncopation, while Leggs does his chant, his rant.

My name's Caliban, got scales and long nails,
I smell like a fish and not like a man –
But my other name's Hag-Seed, or that's what he call me;
He call me a lotta names, he play me a lotta games:
He call me a poison, a filth, a slave,
He prison me up to make me behave,
But I'm Hag-Seed!

My mom's name was Sycorax, they call her a witch,
A blue-eyed hag and real bad bitch;
My daddy was the devil, or that's their story,
So I'm two times evil and I ain't never sorry,
'Cause I'm Hag-Seed!

They dump her on an island, 'cause she was up the spout,
They leave her there to croak, wasn't no joke,
I get born, she gets dead, so the island is *my* land,
This place was my kingdom! And I was the king!
I was the king of everything:
King Hag-Seed!

Then along come Prospero, his little baby bitch,
He think he something 'cause he once was rich;
At first it was good,
I showed him all the food,
He made me a pet, now this is what I get,
'Cause I tried to jump that girl, no other man to do it,
Would'a done her a favour, made a whole population,
An island nation, all Hag-Seeds!

So he pinch me black and he pinch me blue,
I got to do the work while he lies around snorin',
Or talkin' his magic, he is so borin',
I curse him back but he pinch me more,
I one big cramp, I am so sore,
But I'm Hag-Seed!

So if I get the chance I'll rip up his book,
Break his magic staff, that would be a laugh,
Bash in his brains, pay him back for my pains,
Make that girl be my Hag-Seed queen,
No matter how she scream,
The more she scream, she askin' for it,
Down on her knees, I'll make her adore it,
No matter how she whine, I'll hump her blind,
'Cause I'm Hag-Seed!

Just keep it in mind:
I'm Hag-Seed!

He's done. He's breathing heavily.

"Wow, you killed it!" says Anne-Marie. She claps, and so
do the backups; and then so does Felix.

"Yeah, I remembered it all," says Leggs modestly.

"More than that! Best runthrough yet," says Anne-Marie. "We'll put it up on the screen so you can see it, and then let's do a final, next shooting day! We need costumes for the backups, they should be in those lizard hats, matching." To Felix she says, "Bet you've never seen it done like that before!"

"Correct," says Felix. "I haven't." He feels a little choked: Leggs has come through for him. No, not for him: Leggs has come through for Anne-Marie. And the play, of course. Leggs has come through for the play. "'O brave new world, that has such people in it!'" he says.

"'Tis new to thee,'" she laughs. "Poor old Felix! Are we crapping up your play?"

"It's not my play," says Felix. "It's our play." Does he believe this? Yes. No. Not really.

Yes.

29. Approach

Saturday, March 2, 2013.

When Felix wakes up on Saturday at noon he's got a bad hangover, which is strange because he hasn't been drinking. It's the brain drain, it's the energy drain. Too much thinking, too much coaching, too much watching. Too much output, too much uttering, too much outering. He's slept for fourteen hours, but that hasn't begun to recharge him.

In his disgraceful nightshirt, worn thin by the years, he stumbles into the front room. Light is pouring through the window, doubled by its reflection from the snow outside. He blinks, recoils like a vampire: why are there no curtains? He's never bothered with curtains, because who would want to look in?

Apart from Miranda when she's outside, peeping through the glass to make sure he's all right. Where is she? Mornings are not her time, and especially not twelve o'clock noon when the sun's at its highest. The brightness fades her; she needs the twilight to glow.

Idiot, he tells himself. How long will you keep yourself on this intravenous drip? Just enough illusion to keep you alive. Pull the plug, why don't you? Give up your tinsel stickers, your paper cutouts, your coloured crayons. Face the plain, unvarnished grime of real life.

But real life is brilliantly coloured, says another part of his brain. It's made up of every possible hue, including those we can't see. All nature is a fire: everything forms, everything blossoms, everything fades. We are slow clouds . . .

He shakes himself, scratches his head. Blood flow, blood flow, to revive the shrivelling walnut inside his skull. Coffee is what he needs. He boils water in his electric kettle, steeps the ground-up beans, filters the potion, then gulps it down like an alky gulping rum. Neurons begin to spark.

Clothes on, jeans and a sweatshirt. He makes himself a gruel of mushed-up breakfast cereals, the dregs of what's left at the bottoms of three boxes. It's time to go shopping for food, replenish the cupboard. He can't let himself turn into one of those desiccated recluses discovered months after they've died of starvation because they forgot to eat, so compelling were their visions.

Right. Now he's restored. Now he's prepared.

He turns on his computer, does a search for Tony and Sal. There they are, them and their sound bites, three hundred miles away. They've got another of their ilk in tow: Sebert Stanley, Minister of Veterans Affairs, a weak-spined yes-man from way back, though his voters trust him because they knew his uncle and they've always elected a Stanley.

They'll be here in a twink, and how delicious that will be for Felix! Will they recognize him? Not at first, because he'll stay out of sight while the Goblins are doing their work. How will they react when they think their lives are dangling by a thread? Will there be anguish? Yes, there will be anguish. Double-twisted anguish. No doubt about that.

On the calendar he previews the week ahead: his own scenes in the play, upcoming. There's time for only one take on the video camera, two at the most: he'll have to be as good as possible the first time through. He's been cocksure about his lines – surely they're engraved on his bones by now – but is that wise? What about the stances, the gestures, the rubberizing of the face? The force, the precision. He should rehearse. *Tip of the tongue, top of the teeth. She sells sea-shells by the seashore.*

He opens the large armoire. There's his magic garment, its many eyes catching the light. He takes it out, brushes off the dust and a few filmy cobwebs. For the first time in twelve years, he slips it on.

It's like stepping back into a shed skin; as if the cloak is wearing him and not the other way around. In the small mirror, he preens. Shoulders back, lift the diaphragm, expand the lower belly, make room for the lungs. *Mi-mi-mi, mo-mo-mo, mu-mu-mu. Sagacious. Preposterous. Tempestuous.*

Malicious sprite. Don't spit.

Next for his staff. The cane with its silver fox head leaps into his hand. He raises it into the air: his wrist's electric.

"Approach, my Ariel. Come," he intones.

His voice sounds fraudulent. Where is the authentic pitch, the true note? Why did he ever think he could play this impossible part? So many contradictions to Prospero! Entitled aristocrat, modest hermit? Wise old mage, revenge-ful old poop? Irritable and unreasonable, kindly and caring? Sadistic, forgiving? Too suspicious, too trusting? How to convey each delicate shade of meaning and intention? It can't be done.

They cheated for centuries when presenting this play. They cut speeches, they edited sentences, trying to confine Prospero within their calculated perimeters. Trying to make him one thing or the other. Trying to make him fit.

Don't quit now, he tells himself. There's too much at stake.

He'll try the line again. Should it be more like an order or more like an invitation? How far away does he think Ariel is when he's saying this? Or calling it? A sibillant or a shout? He's imagined himself in the scene so often he hardly knows how to play it. He can never match his own exalted conception of it.

"Approach, my Ariel." He leans forward, as if listening. "Come!"

Right next to his ear he hears his Miranda's voice. It's barely a whisper, but he hears it.

All hail, great master, grave sir, hail! I come
To answer thy best pleasure, be't to fly,
To swim, to dive into the fire, to ride
On the curled clouds; to thy strong bidding, task
Ariel and all his quality.

Felix drops his staff as if it's burning him. Did that really happen? Yes, it did! He heard it!

Miranda's made a decision: she'll be understudying Ariel – surely he can't raise any objections to that.

How clever of her, how perfect! She's found the one part that will let her blend in seamlessly at rehearsals. Only he will be able to see her, from time to time. Only he will hear her. She'll be invisible to every eyeball else.

"My brave spirit!" he cries. He'd like to give her a hug, but that's not possible. Prospero and Ariel never touch: how can you touch a spirit? Right now he can't even see her. He'll have to be content with the voice.

IV. Rough Magic

30. *Some vanity of mine art*

Monday, March 4, 2013.

On Monday morning Felix wakes early, his dream still haunting him. What was it? There was music in it, and someone moving away from him into the trees. He wanted to call out, ask them to wait, but he couldn't speak or move.

DREAMS, he should have written on his whiteboard. It's surely a main keynote. *My spirits as in a dream are all bound up.* How many people in the play fall asleep suddenly or talk about dreaming? *We are such stuff as dreams are made of.* But what are dreams made of? *Rounded with a sleep.* Rounded. It chimes so exactly with *the great globe itself.* Did Shakespeare always know what he was doing, or was he sleepwalking part of the time? In the flow? Writing in a trance? Enacting an enchantment he himself was under? Is Ariel a Muse figure? Felix can picture a whole different *Tempest,* one in which . . .

Shut up, he tells himself. Don't add anything more to the mix. The guys have got their hands full as it is.

Drinking his first coffee, he peers out the window. It's overcast and freezing cold: the pane is scrolled with his gelid breath. A front must be moving through. There's been sleet during the night; maybe there will be power lines down. There will also be black ice, treacherous because invisible.

The sanders must have been along the road, though, so he should be fine if he drives slowly.

Today they'll be shooting his first Act I scene with Ariel, in full costume. He stuffs his animal cloak into a green garbage bag, adds the fox-head cane. Then he inserts himself into his outerwear: quilted coat, fleece-lined boots, heavy gloves, red and white faux-wool tuque with a bobble on top, two bucks at the Value Village in Makeshiweg, said Anne-Marie, who presented it to him because she didn't want his head to get cold. "We need the junk in your skull," she said, which was her gruff way of putting it. She claims to disdain sentiment.

"Have you made peace with WonderBoy?" he asked her, keeping his voice neutral. "Is he still bothering you?"

"He wants to be my pen pal," she said. "Write me letters, once we've done the play."

"That's a terrible idea!" he said too vigorously. "Then he'll know your address, and when he gets out, he'll try to – I trust you said no."

"Just let me get through this," she said.

"You're leading him on," said Felix. "Is that fair?"

"We haven't shot the big love scene yet," she said. "You're the director. You want an *Ooo* scene or a *Meh* scene? Because if I say a definite no, it'll be *Meh*."

"You're ruthless! That's unethical," he said.

"Don't preach, I learned from the best. Everything for the play, right? That's how you put it twelve years ago. As I recall."

That was then, Felix thought. Would I say it today? "I'll talk to him," said Felix. "Straighten things out."

"You're not my real dad," she said. "I can deal with this. It'll be all right. Trust me."

Dressing for the shot, she'd taken her hair out of its

bun, given it a windblown look, and stuck in a few paper flowers. She'd made the dress herself: white, but raggedy at the hems, with a sash of knitted twine. One sleeve was off the shoulder. Bare feet, of course. A little bronzer, a little blusher, not too much. Altogether dewy.

The scene was everything Felix could have wished: wide-eyed innocence on her part, rapt enchantment. WonderBoy was impeccable: respectful but imploring, the embodiment of yearning desire. When he said, "Oh you wonder!" and reached out as if to touch her, then let his hand hover as if restrained by glass, he would have melted steel. He was more than convincing.

I hope she won't destroy him, thought Felix. But he's a con man, don't forget. A con man playing an actor. A double unreality.

He does one last check in the mirror. He's lost weight over the past weeks, he's slightly gaunt. His eyes have the intent stare of a caged hawk, but he can make that work for him during his scenes: the stare, the glare. Bent on his prey, but also agitated, distracted. He turns his head sideways, eyes his profile. Add a pinch of scariness, a dollop of Dracula? No, better not.

He winds his scarf around his neck, then follows the white plume of his breath out to his car. The car, miraculously, starts. This is a good omen. He is fond of good omens right now.

Miranda hasn't forgotten her decision: she's determined to be in the play. She accompanies him to the car – he can feel her there, behind his left shoulder – but at first she won't get into it. Is she afraid of it? Is she remembering the last time she was in a car, on that trip to the hospital when she was three, wrapped in blankets and running a high fever? He hopes not.

Too late, too late. Why hadn't he noticed, earlier, the flushed cheeks, the quick breathing, the drowsiness? Because he wasn't there, or else he was there but immersed in some arcane scheme or other. *Cymbeline* – was that the project that had triggered his absence? That he'd found more precious than his loved darling? His fault, his most grievous fault.

He explains the car to her, slowly and carefully. It's a magic flying machine, he tells her, something like a ship except that it runs along the ground on wheels. He shows her the wheels. The smoke coming out of it doesn't mean it's on fire, it's from the engine. The engine is what makes it go. He will be in charge of the car, so there's nothing to fear. She can ride in the back, right behind him. If she wants to be in the play that's how they have to get there. It will be almost like flying through the air.

Luckily there's no one around watching him talk out loud, or to see him opening the back door of the car for a person who isn't there.

Once they get going she appears to enjoy the experience. Trees, farmhouses, and barns whizz by; she's curious about them all. People live in the houses? Yes, people. So many people! So many trees! "You like this, my bird?" he asks her. Yes, she does like it. But where is the play?

"We're getting closer to it," Felix tells her.

They pass a gas station, then the mall near Fletcher Correctional: so colourful, with its holiday decorations still in place! So many other flying machines! Then they're going up the hill, then through the gates. He explains that the fences are to keep people inside, and also to keep other people outside. There are guards, he says. She doesn't ask why but wonders if the guards will want to stop her from entering. "They won't see you," he tells her, "invisible as thou art," and she thinks this is a great joke.

At Security she goes through the scanner with him and doesn't even cause a blip. *That's my tricksy spirit,* he beams at her silently. Silently, she laughs. Such a pleasure to him that she's so happy!

"How's it going, Mr. Duke?" Dylan asks him.

"We're ironing out the kinks," says Felix. "I'll be in tomorrow, by the way, even though it's not a program day. I'll be delivering some equipment. Can you put it in a locker or something until we need it?"

"Sure thing, Mr. Duke," says Madison. Felix has to explain the uses of everything he brings in, or the purported uses: the other, secret uses he'll keep to himself. They'd questioned, for instance, all those black outfits: the sweatshirts, the pants, the ski masks, the gloves. Puppetry, he'd said. The Japanese method. Black light. He'd told them how it worked. Like Bunraku.

"No shit," Madison had said, marvelling. They think Felix knows so much neat theatrical stuff.

Now Dylan says, "What's this in the bag? You been trapping, Mr. Duke?"

"Just my costume," says Felix. "Magic cloak. Magic staff."

"Like in *Harry Potter,*" says Dylan. "Cool."

He thought they might veto the cane, but they don't. The luck of Felix is holding.

Everyone's already in the main room, awaiting directions. Anne-Marie has brought the three goddesses with her in her large purple tapestry knitting bag, dressed in their new woollen outfits. "Will these do?" she asks Felix.

"What's the verdict?" Felix asks the assembled cast. He holds up Iris, who's wearing a rainbow gown made of long braids of wool with beads along their lengths. Her face has been painted orange, and she has a headdress of cotton-wool clouds.

"Pox, it's the Rainbow Nation," says Leggs, and everyone laughs.

"I assume that's a Like," says Felix. Ceres is next, in a dress of vine leaves and a knobby headdress of what are supposed to be – he guesses – woollen apples and pears. Her face is green, and she has a bee sticker on her forehead.

"I saw a stripper like that once." Leggs again. More laughter, growls of "Take it off!"

"This one is Juno, patron goddess of marriage," says Felix. Juno's wearing a knitted nurse uniform and carrying a miniature knitted bottle of blood. She has a painted frown, and tiny fangs have been added to her mouth. She's wearing a necklace of skulls.

The cast is not so favourable to Juno. "Red plague, she looks like my wife," says Shiv. Murmurs of agreement.

"Whoreson ugly," says Leggs.

"Back to the drawing board," SnakeEye adds.

"Suck it up, dickhead," says Anne-Marie, "or you can make your own fuckin' goddesses, plus no cookies."

Chuckles. "Swearing! Swearing! Points off!" says Leggs.

"I'm not collecting points, so you can suck that too," says Anne-Marie. They all laugh.

"What kind of red plague cookies?" says PPod. "Is it okay to suck *them*?"

"All right, order!" says Felix. "Puppeteers, off to your rehearsal room to practise. Caliban and the Hag-Seeds, we're reshooting your number again today to see if we can get better angles. First up, Act I, Scene 2, my scene with Ariel. We'll shoot it now."

8Handz is in his Ariel gear. His face is already blue. He tweaks the raincoat, adjusts his scalloped bathing cap, lowers his goggles, puts on his blue rubber gloves. They go through the scene once, from "All hail, great master." 8Handz is word-perfect, but he's nervous.

"Can we do it again?" he asks. "I was hearing this weird feedback thing. Like someone was saying the lines at the same time as me. It, like, got in the way. Maybe it's the recording mic."

Felix's heart lurches: his Miranda, doing her prompting. "Male voice or female voice?"

"Just a voice. Probably only mine. I'll check the mic."

"Could be that. Some actors hear their own voices, anyway," says Felix. "When they're keyed up. Relax, deep breaths. We'll shoot another take."

To Miranda he says, *sotto voce*, "Not so loud. And only if he misses."

"What?" asks 8Handz. "You want me to pull it back?"

"No, no. Sorry," says Felix. "Talking to myself."

31. *Bountiful Fortune, now my dear lady*

Thursday, March 7, 2013.

The clock ticks inexorably. The planets are converging.

Palm trees and cactuses have been cut from paper, using kids' safety scissors. The plastic rowboat and the sailing ship have been defaced, drenched in water, sailed on the shower-curtain sea. Songs have been sung, discarded, rewritten, sung again. Insults about the singing voices of others have been exchanged.

Chants have been chanted, feet have been stomped. Minor injuries have been sustained by dancers, due to the use of muscles long dormant. Crises of confidence have been surmounted, grudges incurred, hurt feelings soothed. Felix has berated himself for his own lunacy in undertaking such a hopeless enterprise, then congratulated himself on his judgment. His spirits plunge, then soar, then plunge again.

Normal life.

Almost all of the play has now been filmed. There are a few scenes to go, and more edits to be done and effects to be added, and some retakes and voiceovers where the quality's not clear. The three goddesses are spectacular on video, and the black-clad puppeteers add a dimension: it's clear that the goddesses are merely apparitions, acting out someone else's script. PPod has composed a musical background for them, some eerie whistling noises with chimes and flute notes. For the moment when they vanish in confusion, 8Handz has used a multiplying effect: the image is doubled and redoubled and also slowed down, so it looks as if the goddesses are disintegrating in mid-air. Altogether a fine effect, and Felix congratulates 8Handz on it.

Less than a week before zero hour. If this were an ordinary occasion he'd be relaxing by now – they have enough time left for polishing – but as it is, there's more to do.

Felix has taken another train into Toronto. He needed to get the costumes for Stephano the drunken butler and Trinculo the jester: a battered dinner jacket for the first, red long johns with a bowler hat for the second, whiteface for both. He sourced the red long johns for Trinculo at Winners, in men's underwear, and the dinner jacket for Stephano at Oxfam. He also picked up some more Godzilla headdresses, for the Hag-Seeds.

Those purchases complete, he met with a mild-mannered, bespectacled forty-year-old who was possibly Korean in a discreet corner of Union Station. This was risky – what if this man was being followed? – but in the crowd of commuters they were surely inconspicuous. The contact was courtesy 8Handz: each side could trust the other like a brother, he assured the contact via a recorded message smuggled out by Felix on a memory stick.

Money was exchanged, and Felix received a packet of gel-cap pills, a packet of powder, a hypodermic needle, and some very precise instructions.

"Don't overdo it," the contact said. "You don't want to kill anyone or drive them batshit permanently. These gel caps are the Mr. Sandmans. Break them open, empty them into the cup, you'll get a fast dissolve in the ginger ale. It's a quick out even if they only drink half. Doesn't last long, you get maybe ten minutes. That enough?"

"We'll find out," said Felix.

"The other one's the magic pixie dust. Quarter of a teaspoon in a teaspoon of water. Don't overload the grapes."

"I'll be careful," said Felix. "What exactly is the result?"

"Like you say, let's find out. But it's gonna be some trip," said the contact.

"Not harmful though?" said Felix. "Permanently?" He was nervous: what would happen if he was caught with this stuff, and what was it exactly? Was he being reckless? Yes, but the whole operation was reckless.

"If anything happens, this never happened," said the contact in a soft but convincing voice.

Today Felix is working from home. He has his boiled egg for breakfast, then turns on his computer. He's tracking the royal progress of Tony and Sal as they eat their way through one rubber chicken dinner after another in the small-town sticks, promising favours, pocketing contributions, marking down rabble-rousers and dissenters for later banishment. He has a map on the wall into which he's been sticking red push pins, charting their course. It pleases him to see his enemies drawing ever nearer, as if they're being sucked into a vortex of his own creation.

But before his daily Google he checks his emails. He's still running the two email addresses, one under Felix Phillips for taxes and other such functions, and the other for F. Duke. The second is the address he's given to the Fletcher Correctional office for use in emergencies – not that there have ever been any – and he's given it also to Estelle, even though she knows his real name.

She's been keeping him posted. A true star, he tells her: his Lady Luck. She loves such compliments: she loves to feel that both he and the program genuinely need her. She gets a huge kick out of being an unseen but crucial part of the theatrical action.

Today she's sent him a message: *Need to see you soonest. Something's come up suddenly. Lunch?*

It would be my pleasure, he emails back.

They meet at their regular place: Zenith, in Wilmot. Estelle has dolled herself up for him, even more than usual; but why does he assume it's for him? Maybe she dolls herself up every day. Her hair is newly gilded, as are her nails, and she's sporting globe-shaped earrings like miniature disco balls, shocking pink and rhinestone-studded. Her suit is equally pink, and she's wearing an Hermès scarf with a design of racehorses and playing cards, held with a gold pin in a cornucopia design. She's applied perhaps too much mascara. Felix holds her chair for her as she sits down.

"So," he says. "Martini?" They've taken to beginning their rendezvous with martinis. She enjoys the implied glamour.

"Oh, you shouldn't tempt me," she says roguishly, "you reprobate!"

"I adore tempting you," Felix risks. He'll see her reprobate and raise her one. "And you adore being tempted. What's the news?"

She leans forward conspiratorially. Her perfume is flower-filled, fruit-laden. She places her right hand on his wrist. "I don't want you to be upset," she says.

"Oh. Is it bad?"

"I have it through my sources on the inside that Heritage Minister Price and Justice Minister O'Nally are pulling the plug on the Fletcher Correctional literacy program," she says.

"They got together on it and agreed. In their announcement, they're going to call it an indulgence, a raid on the taxpayer wallet, a pandering to the liberal elites, and a reward for criminality."

"I see," says Felix. "Harsh of them. But they're still coming to Fletcher? For this year's production? As previously confirmed?"

"Absolutely," says Estelle. "They'll say they saw the thing in action, they gave it every chance, but on balance it was not worth the – Also, their visit will play well within the criminal justice system. It will show they're paying attention to the correctional officers, and, and – They want the photo op."

"Excellent," says Felix. "As long as they're coming."

"You're not disappointed? By the cancellation?"

In fact, Felix is elated by it. It's exactly the ammunition he needs to rally the troops. Just wait till the Goblins hear that their theatrical troupe is about to be annihilated! It will be very motivating.

"I'm mad enough to spit, myself," says Estelle. "After all our work!"

"There might be a way to save it," he says cautiously. "I think. But I'll need your help."

"You know you can ask me anything," she says. "If I can do it, I will."

"Who exactly will be in their party?" he says. "Besides the two of them. Do you know?"

"I hoped you'd ask that." She reaches into her purse, a svelte design in silver lamé. "As it happens, I've got the list right here. I'm not supposed to have it, but I called in some favours. Cone of silence!" She winks as slyly as she can, considering the thickness of her eyelashes.

Felix isn't about to ask what kind of favours: as long as

she continues to shower positive rays on him personally, it's all good. Greedily he scans the page. Sal O'Nally, check. Tony Price, check. And what do you know, here's old Lonnie Gordon, still the Chair of the Makeshiweg Festival, but also, it seems, running a consulting business and heading up the local party fundraising initiative. "I notice that Sebert Stanley's cut himself in on this," he says. "Why would he bother?"

"Rumour has it – actually, more than a rumour – that he wants to run for party leader. At the upcoming convention in June. He has a dependable pedigree, and a lot of money."

"Sal's running as well," says Felix. "He was always ambitious. I knew him at school, he was a prick then too. Therefore, a rivalry between the two of them?"

"That's the word," says Estelle. "Though the insider nickname for Sebert is 'limp dick.' The back-roomers don't think he's got the, excuse me, balls." She chuckles at her own naughtiness. "On the other hand, Sal O'Nally's made a lot of enemies. His reputation is that he tosses people under the bus when he's got no more use for them."

"I've noticed," says Felix.

"But a lot of the people he's squashed have got friends in the party. They resent that kind of behaviour. So, handicaps either way. I'd say the two of them are running neck and neck."

"And Phony Tony Baloney?" Felix asks. "Tony the Fixer. Who's he backing?" Because of course Tony will be looking out for the main chance. He'll throw his weight where it will sink one contender and float the other, then collect his reward from the floater.

"Jury's out," says Estelle. "Both of their shoes have been thoroughly licked by him. According to my sources."

"He's got a wet tongue," says Felix. He runs his finger

down the page. "Who's this Frederick O'Nally? Any relative of the Minister?"

"Son of Sal," says Estelle. "Disappointing son. Postgrad of the National Theatre School, currently interning at Makeshiweg. Sal had Lonnie pull strings to get him in, because he has a hard time saying no. The boy wants a life in theatre, which a lot of my sources in the Department of Heritage think is pretty hilarious considering his dad's so anti-arts. It's getting right up Sal's – it's getting up his nose."

"He thinks he can act?" says Felix. "This kid?" Outrageous! A snot-nosed, silver-spooned brat who thinks he can politic his way into the theatre, fly in on Daddy's coattails. Wish upon a star and the Blue Fairy will turn him into a real actor. Most likely he has the talent of a beet.

"Directing," says Estelle. "That's his ambition. He really pushed to come on this visit. By the way, he's seen the previous videos you've made – I know they're not supposed to be generally circulated, but I showed them to him on the sly – and he thinks they're, and I quote, sheer genius. He says the program here is radically innovative, cutting edge, and a stellar example of theatre for the people."

Felix's opinion of the lad improves. "But he doesn't know I'm me?" he asks. "He doesn't know I'm, you know – Felix Phillips?" He wants to say *the* Felix Phillips, but perhaps he no longer rates a *the*.

Estelle smiles. "My lips have been sealed," she says. "All these years. I've kept your secret, and I've even added some camouflage for you. As far as they're concerned – our distinguished visitors – you're just this broken-down failure of an old teacher called Mr. Duke. I've sprinkled that story around and they've bought it, because who but a broken-down old failure of a teacher would be doing theatre in a no-hope place like Fletcher? Care to join me in another martini?"

"Absolutely! Let's get some deep-fried calamari," says Felix. "Live it up!" How many martinis is that? Felix is feeling terrific: the presence of Son of Sal will round things out in a very satisfying way, or that is his fervent hope. "You're the best," he tells Estelle. Somehow they're holding hands. Is he drunk? "The best Lady Luck I could ever have."

"I'm stickin' with you," she says. "You're the guy that I came in with, to coin a phrase. That was such a good *Guys and Dolls* they did at Makeshiweg, oh, fifteen years ago, remember it?"

"Before my time," says Felix, "but I was in it once, when I was young."

"You're still young," she breathes. "Young at heart."

"But you're younger," he says. "Younger than springtime." Yes, he is drunk. "Lady Luck can be a nice dame." They clink glasses.

"A very nice dame," she says, "if you stay on my good side." She takes a sip of her martini. More than a sip. "I don't know what you're up to, but you've got that rascally look. If it's about saving the Players, I'm backing you all the way."

32. *Felix addresses the Goblins*
Wednesday, March 13, 2013.

This is the day. He stands on the cliff's edge. Very soon it will be thunder time. But first, the pre-battle speech.

In the dressing room, he adjusts his magic stuffed-animal robe. It isn't everything he'd once had in mind, but a dusting of gold spray paint has brought it back to life. He takes his fox-head cane in his left hand, then switches it to his right. He peers at himself in the mirror: not too bad. *Magisterial* might be the adjective that comes to mind, given a well-disposed viewer. He smooths his beard, roughens his hair, tweaks the set of his garment, checks his teeth: they're firmly cemented in place. "Tip of the tongue," he says to his reflection.

Then he proceeds along the hallway, peering into the Green Room to make sure the grapes are standing ready. Before leaving his shack for Fletcher he'd spent the early morning carefully injecting each one with the hypodermic. The grapes had made it through Security without raising an eyebrow: after all, they contain no metal. Similarly with the mysterious pixie dust pills, stowed in a plastic bottle of painkillers. He slips his hand into the crucial pocket, just to make sure. All is in order.

*

In the main room the full cast is assembled. Anne-Marie's in her Miranda outfit: the simple white off-shoulder dress, the bare feet, the paper daisies and roses in her hair. PPod, Shiv, TimEEz, Leggs, and Red Coyote are dressed as sailors, with their black ski masks rolled into cap mode. Otherwise they're in black, as is everyone else in the room.

8Handz is behind the folding screen that hides the computer screen, the control panel, the central microphone, and the two sets of headphones – one for himself, one for Felix.

There's a tension, familiar to Felix from dozens of opening nights. Dancers, waiting in the wings, first foot already poised. Divers, on their springboards, bending their knees, raising their arms. Football players before the whistle. Racehorses before the pistol shot. He smiles encouragingly.

"This is it," he tells them. "We'll never be more ready." There's a gentle clapping. "To remind you," he continues, "these are the politicos who want to destroy our Fletcher Correctional Players." Soft boos.

"Shame," says Bent Pencil.

"Yes," says Felix. "They think it's a waste of time. They think *you're* a waste of time. They don't care about your education, they want you to stay ignorant. They aren't interested in the life of the imagination, and they have failed to grasp the redemptive power of art. Worst of all: they think *Shakespeare* is a waste of time. They think he has nothing to teach."

"Double shame," says Phil the Pill. The secret directions Felix has been rehearsing with all of them over the past week have made Phil nervous. He's been raising objections to it – isn't it illegal, what they intend to do? – but the majority of the class is in favour of it, so now he's going along.

Felix hasn't stationed Phil among the lead Goblins, however: he might lose his nerve and break the charm.

"But together we can stop their cancellation plan," says Felix. "We can set things right! What we're doing today – we're giving them some excellent reasons for why they need to reconsider. We'll be showing them that theatre is a powerful educational tool. Yes?"

Assenting murmurs, nods. "Right on, dude," says Leggs. "Beetles light on them! Blister them all o'er!"

PPod says, "They'll be thinking poxy twice, after we get through."

"We're on it," says Red Coyote. "Moon-calfs won't know what hit them."

"Thank you," says Felix. "Okay, ready to roll. First part, they're escorted here by the sailors, they come in and sit down, you serve the refreshments. Blue cups, green cups. Don't get the colours mixed up! Green for O'Nally Senior, and also for Lonnie Gordon. Blue for Tony Price and Sebert Stanley. Popcorn for all of them. Remember that!"

"The chalice with the palace is the potion with the poison," says Bent Pencil. Nobody gets it.

"The clear cups are for the rest of us, and Freddie. You've got your black gloves?" says Felix. "Great. Your ear buds? Keep them out of sight. As soon as the screen goes dark, stick in the ear buds, roll down the ski masks, put on the gloves. Then you'll be virtually invisible. Watch for the marks on the floor, you'll see them as soon as 8Handz turns on the black light. TimEEz, we're counting on you to remove their security alarms."

"Be not afeard, the isle is full of fingers," says TimEEz.

"It'll be exactly the way we've been rehearsing it," says Felix. "I'll be with 8Handz, behind the screen. Listen for our cues. We'll be able to hear you, so if you run into trouble we'll send a backup. The password for trouble is 'scurvy monster.' Got that?"

Nods all round. "I hope nobody's going to get hurt," says Bent Pencil. He's been fussing over this: snatch-and-grab is not his modus operandi.

"Not so much as a hair," says Felix. "Unless they try to fight. Which they won't. But PPod and Leggs and Red Coyote are ready to keep them under control, if necessary. They'll use a bouncer hug, not a wallop. No excessive use of force, no matter how tempting. Promise?"

"You got it," says PPod.

"There's ways," says Red Coyote.

"Now, locations," says Felix. "In half an hour, the dressing room will no longer be the dressing room: it will be Prospero's cave. The fifties demonstration cell will be Ferdinand's rock-and-log ordeal site, so young O'Nally will be placed in there. It's the one with the older toilet. Anne-Marie will babysit him for us: she's well prepared."

"Are you sure this is ethical?" says Anne-Marie. " I know you've got some scores to settle, I get it, but the O'Nally son never did anything to you."

"We discussed this," says Felix. "He won't be injured. Remember, it's partly his dad who crapped up your career twelve years ago. The palm trees are already on location, correct?"

"Correct," says WonderBoy. "Plus the mermaid." He's looking sulky: Anne-Marie in a locked cell with another man doesn't sit well with him.

"The other demonstration cell, the nineties one, will be the nap-time location for Alonso and Gonzalo – sorry, for O'Nally and Lonnie Gordon," says Felix. "It's the one with the cactuses. It's important to slot the right people into the right rooms. When they're all in the main screening room, and just before we push the Start button, Shiv will be outside in the hall, sticking up the signs on the doors: palm tree, cactus."

"Got it," says PPod.

"Excellent. Timing is everything. Goblins, we're depending on you: nothing in this play can work without the Goblins."

"We gonna get away with this?" says TimEEz. "What about Security?"

"No problem, they won't have a clue," says Felix. "The key is that we got cleared to have the dignitaries in our wing, unescorted. A friend of mind with a lot of influence swung that for us. We've got the video cued so that while we're doing our interactive theatre here with the politicos, everyone else in the place will be watching our show just the way they usually do. If they hear screams – which they won't – they'll think it's part of the play."

"Fuckin' genius, man," says Leggs. No one rebukes him for the swear word.

"I couldn't have done it without Ariel," says Felix. "Without 8Handz. He's been – he's been awesome. As have all of you." He checks his watch. "Now, here we go. Curtain's going up. Merde, everyone."

"Merde, merde, merde," they say to one another. "Merde, bro. Merde, dude." Fist bumps.

"*The Tempest*, Act I, Scene 1," says Felix. "From the top."

33. *The hour's now come*

The same day.

The group of visitors is posed outside the main entranceway, with the Fletcher name clearly visible. The two potential federal leadership candidates, chests out, teeth on display, jostle for the most prominent position in the frame. The others group around them.

The Honourable Sal O'Nally, Minister of Justice; the Honourable Anthony Price, Minister of Heritage; the Honourable Sebert Stanley, Minister of Veterans Affairs; and Mr. Lonnie Gordon of Gordon Strategy, Chair of the Board for the Makeshiweg Festival. Accompanying them is Minister O'Nally's son, Frederick O'Nally.

Sal is paunchier by the year; Tony's ultra-tailored in his sleek suit, with still a good head of hair. Sebert Stanley has always looked like a scal – small head, hardly any ears, small eyes, pear-shaped body – and he still looks like one. The boy – Freddie O'Nally – is handsome enough – dark hair, white smile – but he's looking off to the side. It's as if he doesn't like the company he's keeping, even though one of that company is his father.

Flanking the central group is a clutch of government minions and gofers, and some of the Fletcher higher-ups, who are most likely wetting themselves because it's not often they've had a ministerial visit. In fact, it's not ever.

Estelle is in the background, half obscured: she doesn't like to be too obvious on such occasions, she'd told Felix, but she'd promised to run interference for him: reassure, distract, just in case the Warden's group got nervous. She'd synchronize her watch and make sure the two videos played at the same time. "Think of me as lubricant," she'd said. "I'll make things run smoothly, guaranteed."

"How can I thank you?" Felix had said.

"We'll talk." She'd smiled.

The main doors open. The group enters. The main doors close.

In the viewing room, Felix settles himself behind the folding screen. "Take us to PPod's mic," he says. He puts on his headphones.

There's a murmur of voices. The ministerial group is being run through Security one by one, just like anyone else, no exceptions, as Dylan and Madison explain politely. Quite right, says the voice of Sal O'Nally, glad to know you boys are doing your job, haha.

All is joviality. As Felix knows from Estelle, they've just come from a local political bunfest; they must have been well received, and he assumes they've had a few drinks. A quick stop at this holding pen for bottom-feeding social misfits and they'll be on their way, and the quicker the better because it's supposed to snow. There may even be a blizzard. Already some of the lower-downs whose function it is to attend to such details must be nervously checking their watches.

Sal's feeling mellow. They'll go through the charade of seeing this play or whatever it is, mostly because Freddie has insisted on it and he, Sal, thinks the sun shines out of

Freddie's ass, even though he wants him to be a lawyer and not some fruity actor. But he'll humour the boy, and then, after they're back in Ottawa, Sal will announce the cancellation of this frill, this so-called literacy thing, whatever it is. Prisons are for incarceration and punishment, not for spurious attempts to educate those who cannot, by their very natures, be educated. What's the quote? Nature versus nurture, something like that. Is it from a play? Sal makes a mental note: ask Tony, he used to be in theatre.

Better still, ask Freddie. The kid will be disappointed when Sal puts it to him that it's law school or no more monthly allowance because he's had his playtime. It may seem severe, but Sal wants only the best, and the boy would be wasted in the arts, it's a dead end and about to become deader under Tony's stewardship, as Sal happens to know.

"Can't take your cellphone in there," says Dylan to Sal. "Sir. Sorry. We'll keep it safe for you here."

"Oh, surely," Sal begins, "I'm the Minister of . . ." but he sees Freddie looking at him. The boy doesn't like it when Sal pulls rank; though what's the use of having rank if you can't pull it? Nonetheless, he hands over his phone.

Tony has other things on his mind. Here he is with two potential leadership candidates, Sal and Sebert, and both of them want his backing. Sal feels Tony owes him, considering the help he's given Tony with his career. Supplanting Felix Phillips was just the first step: Tony's risen like a gas balloon ever since. From the life of theatre to the theatre of life, you could say, and Sal was his ladder. But once you've climbed a ladder, what use is it? You kick it away, if you don't intend to go down it again. Surely it would be better for Tony to back a candidate to whom he owes nothing; who owes a debt to Tony, instead. How to shake off Sal and tip the scales for Sebert? What's the long game?

Having sacrificed his phone, Sal turns out his pockets, gives up his Leatherman pocket knife, also his nail file. "Clean as a baby," he tells the two security guards. Much reciprocal grinning. A security pager is clipped to his belt: not that there will be any use for it, says Dylan, but no exceptions, everyone must be issued with one. Sir.

Tony sails through the X-ray with his hands in the air, affably clowning it up. Sebert does it straight-faced, smoothing down the hair on his little head after he's gone through the scanner. Lonnie proceeds through sadly, as if he's sorry there has to be such a thing as a security checkpoint, in such a thing as a prison. Freddie is awkward, wide-eyed: this is a whole other world, one he's never thought much about.

Now they're all through, and, as if on cue, around the corner comes a group of men dressed as – what? Pirates?

"Welcome, gentlemen all," says the one in the lead. "Welcome to the good ship *Tempest*, which you are now aboard. I'm the Boatswain and these are my sailors. We're sailing you across the sea to a desert isle. Don't be worried if there's some strange noises, it's part of the play. And this is an interactive piece of theatre, experimental in nature; we're alerting you of that fact in advance." He leers ingratiatingly. "Right this way."

"Lead on," says Sal. Might as well be a good sport. It hasn't escaped him that these men are inmates, but the Warden and several guards are right there in the background, smiling, and the Warden says, "See you after the show, enjoy it, we'll be watching it too, from upstairs." "Have a good time," says Estelle what's-her-name: her grandfather was a Senator, he's seen her at a lot of parties, she's on committees or something. Now she smiles and waves at them as if seeing them off on a ship. So it's all fine, and he follows the Boat-swain down the corridor to the left.

Tony and Sebert are right behind him, and Lonnie and Freddie are right behind them. Right behind Lonnie and Freddie are three of the sailors, tossing – what's this? – hand-fuls of blue, glittering confetti. "It's water drops," says the Boatswain. "There's a storm, right?"

"Oh, right," says Sal. What are shenanigans like this doing inside a prison? These men are having way too much fun.

To the rear of the party a door slides shut, locking with a clunk. Only to be expected, thinks Sal. Of course. It's the security. He feels safer.

In the distance there's a rumble of thunder.

"Right in here," says the Boatswain. "Gentlemen." He ushers them through the door into the main screening room.

"Well done, PPod," Felix whispers into his mic. He checks his watch again.

There's a large flatscreen at the front of the room. More black-clad sailors escort the visitors to their places, indicat-ing with bows and flourishes where they are to sit. Four of the sailors hand around soft drinks, in blue and green plas-tic cups, and little bags of popcorn, a homey touch. The three Ministers and Lonnie are in the front row; there's a row of sailors behind them.

Felix, looking at the screen, sees that TimEEz is in the middle of the second row, his round moon face smiling vacantly, his nimble fingers hidden in his sleeves, poised to lift the security pagers as soon as the lights go out.

Where's the rest of the party? Sal wonders. Oh, right. Upstairs with the Warden and what-not. That nice-looking woman, Estelle: a bit flashy but obviously well connected. He should take her to lunch sometime. He sits back in his desk chair. He's feeling the drink from that bunfest they went to.

"Let's get this show on the road," he says to Tony. He checks the time. "At least they didn't take my watch," he grins. He digs into his popcorn bag: lots of salt, he likes that. He takes another hefty swig of ginger ale, from the green plastic cup. He's thirsty. Nice idea, this ginger ale. Too bad there's no booze in it.

Freddie's beside Anne-Marie, in the third row. "Hi," he says to her. "I'm Fred O'Nally. I guess you're the Miranda? In the play?"

"Yes. Anne-Marie Greenland," she says.

"Really?" says Freddie. "Are you *that* Anne-Marie – Aren't you – weren't you dancing with Kidd Pivot?"

"You got it," says Anne-Marie.

"That's awesome! I must've watched your video, like, a hundred times! As a director, I want to integrate, like, more movement, and some crossover –"

"You're directing?" says Anne-Marie. "Cool!"

"Well, not exactly," says Freddie, "I mean, not my whole own productions yet. I'm more like an apprentice. But I'm getting there."

"Here's to getting there," says Anne-Marie, raising her clear plastic cup. Freddie raises his. He's gazing deeply into her wide blue eyes.

"Fabulous dress," he says. "It's got the right . . ." Now he's looking at her one bare shoulder.

"Thanks," she says, pulling her sleeve up a little but not enough to hide the shoulder. "I made it myself."

*

There are three sharp raps from behind the folding screen at the front of the room: Felix, with his fox-head cane, on the floor. 8Handz' index finger hovers over the Play button. In the light from the computer his thin face is impish.

Felix glances anxiously around the dark space: where is his own Miranda? There she is, a glimmer behind 8Handz' left shoulder.

The hour's now come, she whispers to him.

34. *Tempest*

The house lights dim. The audience quiets.

ON THE BIG FLATSCREEN: *Jagged yellow lettering on black:*

THE TEMPEST
By William Shakespeare
With
The Fletcher Correctional Players

ONSCREEN: *A hand-printed sign, held up to the camera by Announcer, wearing a short purple velvet cloak. In his other hand, a quill.*

SIGN: A SUDDEN TEMPEST

ANNOUNCER: What you're gonna see, is a storm at sea:
Winds are howlin', sailors yowlin',
Passengers cursin' 'em, 'cause it gettin' worse:
Gonna hear screams, just like a ba-a-d dream,
But not all here is what it seem,
Just sayin'.
Grins.
Now we gonna start the playin'.

*He gestures with the quill. Cut to: Thunder and lightning, in funnel
cloud, screengrab from the Tornado Channel. Stock shot of ocean
waves. Stock shot of rain. Sound of howling wind.*

*Camera zooms in on a bathtub-toy sailboat, tossing up and down
on a blue plastic shower curtain with fish on it, the waves made
by hands underneath.*

*Closeup of Boatswain in a black knitted tuque. Water is thrown on
him from offscreen. He is drenched.*

BOATSWAIN: Fall to't yarely, or we run ourselves aground!
   Bestir, bestir!
   Yare! Yare! Beware! Beware!
   Let's just do it,
   Better get to it,
   Trim the sails,
   Fight the gales,
   Unless you wantin' to swim with the whales!

VOICES OFF: We're all gonna drown!

BOATSWAIN: Get outta tha' way! No time for play!

A bucketful of water hits him in the face.

VOICES OFF: Listen to me! Listen to me!
   Don't you know we're royalty?

BOATSWAIN: Yare! Yare! The waves don't care!
   The wind is roarin', the rain is pourin',
   All you do is stand and stare!

VOICES OFF: You're drunk!

BOATSWAIN: You're a idiot!

VOICES OFF: We're doomed!

VOICES OFF: We're sunk!

*Closeup of Ariel, in a blue bathing cap and iridescent ski goggles,
   blue makeup on the lower half of his face. He's wearing a*

translucent plastic raincoat with ladybugs, bees, and butterflies on it. Behind his left shoulder there's an odd shadow. He laughs soundlessly, points upward with his right hand, which is encased in a blue rubber glove. Lightning flash, thunderclap.

VOICES OFF: Let's pray!
BOATSWAIN: What's that you say?
VOICES OFF: We're goin' down! We're gonna drown!
    Ain't gonna see the King no more!
    Jump offa the ship, swim for the shore!

Ariel throws his head back and laughs with delight. In each of his blue rubber hands he's holding a high-powered flashlight, in flicker mode.
The screen goes black.

A VOICE FROM THE AUDIENCE: What?
ANOTHER VOICE: Power's off.
ANOTHER VOICE: Must be the blizzard. A line down somewhere.

Total darkness. Confused noise from outside the room. Yelling. Shots are fired.

A VOICE FROM THE AUDIENCE: What's going on?
VOICES, FROM OUTSIDE THE ROOM: Lockdown! Lockdown!
A VOICE FROM THE AUDIENCE: Who's in charge here?

Three more shots.

A VOICE, FROM INSIDE THE ROOM: Don't move! Quiet! Keep your heads down! Stay right where you are.

35. *Rich and strange*

A black wool hand claps over Freddie's eyes, then a hood slips over his head and he's lifted out of his scat. "What the fuck?" he yells. "Let go!"

"You're goin' overboard," says a voice. "Hell is empty, and all the devils are here!"

"It's a prison riot." The voice of Tony. "Keep calm. Don't provoke them. Hit the button on your pager. Wait –"

"What pager?" The voice of Sebert. "It's gone!"

"Wait! Wait!" shouts Freddie. "Let go! Why are you pinching me? Ow!" His voice recedes toward the back of the room.

"Freddie!" The voice of Sal, shouting. "What're you doing? He's my son! I'll kill you! Bring him back!"

"Shut up." A voice in the darkness. "A plague upon this howling! Heads on the desk, hands clasped behind your neck! Now!"

Door opening, closing.

"They're taking him hostage!" Sal yells. "Freddie!"

A shot. "They've killed him!" wails Sal.

"You're coming with us," says a voice. "On your feet. Now. You too."

Scuffling sounds. "I can't see!" Sal, panicking.

"You'll pay for this!" Tony, his voice cold and level.

Sound of roaring waves and wind, rising to a crescendo. The voices are drowned out. Enormous thunderclap. Confused shouts:

"We split!" "Mercy on us!" "We split, we split, we split!"

Freddie lurches along in the dark, his arms held forcibly behind his back; there's someone on either side, propelling him. "You're making a mistake," he says. "Can't we talk about this? My dad's the Minister of –" A hand clamps across his mouth, outside the hood.

"Yeah, we know who your dad is. Justice Minister. A pox on him! May the red plague rid him! He's a dead duck by now."

"Dead as shit."

"Right. He's done and dusted."

Freddie tries to speak, but his mouth is blocked by cloth.

Sound of a door opening. Freddie is pushed inside. A hand on each shoulder forces him into a sitting position.

Sound of the door closing. Can he remove the hood? He can: his hands are free. Off comes the headgear.

He's in a prison cell, lit by a single bulb. He's sitting on one of the bunks, on a scratchy grey woollen blanket. The walls are decorated with amateurish cardboard palm trees, seashells, a squid. There's a box of plastic Lego blocks in the corner. An awful painting of the seashore, with some kind of horrible mermaid on it. Pinup pose, enormous tits, green seaweed hair. NYMPH O'THE SEA is printed underneath it.

What is this? It's a riot, they've killed his dad, they're holding him as a bargaining chip? In a room full of paper palm trees and Lego? What?

More importantly, has he pissed himself? Barely not, for

which he's grateful. Good thing there's a toilet. He's just finished emptying his bladder into it when a musical selection begins playing through a tiny speaker: there it is, up near the sprinkler on the ceiling. Two singers, or are there three?

> Full fathom five thy father lies,
> Of his bones are coral made,
> Those are pearls that were his eyes.
> Nothing of him that doth fade,
> But doth suffer a sea change
> Into something rich and strange.
> Lies, lies, lies, lies,
> Suffer, suffer, suffer, suffer,
> Rich, rich, rich, rich,
> Strange, strange, strange, strange . . .

Drums, flute sounds. Cripes, thinks Freddie. The song from *The Tempest*. Is this some kind of weird joke? Are they going to play this thing on an endless tape loop 24/7 to drive him crazy? He's heard of that, it wrecks the mind. Are they trying to break down his morale? But why?

The music fades, the door opens, and Anne-Marie Greenland slips into the room, still in her luscious off-one-shoulder Miranda dress. She beckons him over into a corner, motions him to stoop so she can whisper into his ear.

"Sorry about this," she says. "Are you okay?"

"Yes, but –"

"Shh! This place is bugged," she whispers. "Mic's up by the lightbulb. Do what I say and you won't get hurt."

"What *is* this?" says Freddie. "Is it a riot? Where's my dad? Did they kill him?"

"I don't know," she says. "There's someone in here who's crazy. Crazy as a full-moon dog. Thinks he's Prospero. No,

I mean really. He's re-enacting *The Tempest*, and you're Ferdinand."

"No shit," says Freddie. "That is fucking –"

"Shhh! What you need to do is stick to the script. I've brought your lines, they're highlighted in the playbook. Here, just do the speeches, over by the light fixture so he can hear you. Otherwise he might lose it. He's prone to tantrums."

"Are you *in* on this? Why would you –"

"I'm just trying to help you," says Anne-Marie.

"Like, who is this guy?" says Freddie. "Oh, thanks, by the way. I hope you won't get in trouble."

"No more than usual," says Anne-Marie. "He's a lunatic, that's the important thing right now. You need to humour him. Start here."

Freddie reads:

"My spirits, as in a dream, are all bound up,
My father's loss, the weakness that I feel,
The wreck of all my friends, are but light to me,
Might I but through my prison once a day
Behold this maid. All corners else o' th'earth
Let liberty make use of – space enough
Have I in such a prison."

"That's not bad," says Anne-Marie. "Maybe with more feeling. Pretend you're falling in love with me."

"But," says Freddie. "Maybe I *am* falling in love with you. O you wonder!"

"Well done," says Anne-Marie. "Keep it up."

"No, seriously," says Freddie. "Have you got, like, a boyfriend?"

Anne-Marie gives a small giggle. "Is that your idea of

asking me whether I'm a virgin? Which is what he does in the play, right?"

"This isn't the play. So, boyfriend or not?"

"Not," she says. Level gaze. "Really not."

"So would you mind if I did fall in love with you?"

"I don't think so," says Anne-Marie.

"Because I think I really am!" He takes hold of her two arms.

"Careful," she whispers. She detaches his hands. "Now we need to get back to the lines." She moves them over to the lightbulb, clasps her hands, gazes at him with adoration, projects her voice. "Nothing natural I ever saw so noble!"

"Foolish wench!" booms a voice from the speaker. "To the most of men this is a Caliban!"

"What did I tell you?" Anne-Marie whispers. "Crazy as a coot! By the way, can you play chess?"

36. *A maze trod*

Justice Minister O'Nally, Heritage Minister Price, Veterans Affairs Minister Stanley, and Lonnie Gordon of Gordon Strategy find themselves being frog-marched in an undignified manner down what seems to be a corridor. They can't see where they're going: it's pitch-dark, except for some glimmering white marks on the floor.

Who's frog-marching them? They can't tell: the figures are all in black. Around them winds whistle, waves roar, and thunder crashes, so they can't hear themselves speak. What would they be saying if they could hear? Would they be cursing, pleading, bemoaning their fate? All of the above, thinks Felix, listening to the din through his headphones.

The procession turns a corner. It turns another corner. Then a third corner. Are they going back the way they came?

The storm sounds increase. Then, suddenly, silence.

There's the sound of a door opening; they are shoved through it. Dark in here too, wherever here is. Then the overhead light goes on: they're in a four-bunk jail cell, two up, two down. The walls are decorated with silhouettes of cactuses, cut from brown wrapping paper.

They look at one another. Ashen-faced, shaken. "At least we're alive," says Lonnie. "We should be grateful for that!"

"Right," says Tony, rolling his eyes. Sebert Stanley tries the door: it's locked. He smooths down his small head, then looks out through the barred window that gives onto the corridor.

"It's dark out there," he says.

"I heard them shoot. They've shot Freddie," Sal says. He sits down despondently on one of the lower bunks. "I heard it. I heard the shot. It's the end of my life!" He's hugging himself, swaying the upper part of his body from side to side.

"Oh, I'm sure they haven't," says Lonnie. "Why would they do that?"

"Because they're animals!" Sal almost shouts. "They should all be in cages! They should all be fucking dead!"

"Instead of being indulged with literacy programs," says Tony in his cool voice. "For instance."

"They could have been shooting someone else," says Lonnie. "Or just, well, shooting. I think we should look on the bright side. Until we know for sure."

"Why?" says Sal. "There is no bright side! I've lost Freddie! I've lost my boy!" He buries his head in his hands. There are muffled noises that might be sobs.

"What happens next?" Sebert says to Tony in a low voice.

"We wait," says Tony. "Not that we have much choice."

"He better pull himself together. This is embarrassing," says Sebert. "Let's hope the proper authorities get here soon." He leans against the wall, examines his fingers.

"Whoever they are," says Tony. He's pacing the room, ten steps one way, ten steps the other. "If they've really shot his kid, heads will roll."

"Cheer up, Minister O'Nally," says Lonnie to Sal. "It could be worse! We're uninjured, we're in a nice warm room, we –"

"He's going to go on like that for hours," says Tony to Sebert, *sotto voce*. "He'll bore us to death, as usual."

"If I were redesigning the prison system," Lonnie continues, "I'd try giving the inmates more freedom, not less. They could vote on things, they could make their own decisions. Design their own menus, for instance; that could be a useful skill they could develop."

"Dream on," says Tony. "They'd poison the soup, first chance."

"Please," says Sal. "At a time like this! No more talking!"

"I was just trying to take your mind off it," says Lonnie, aggrieved.

"I'm tired," says Sal. His voice is thick, muzzy. He stretches out on the bunk.

"Funny thing," says Lonnie. "I'm drowsy too. Might as well get some rest while there's time." He lies down on the other bottom bunk. Now the two of them are fast asleep.

"Something odd about this," says Sebert. "I'm not tired at all."

"Nor I," says Tony. He checks the two sleepers. "Out cold. That being the case" – he lowers his voice – "how do you see your leadership prospects? As of now?"

"Sal's ahead in the polls," says Sebert. "Not sure how I can even the odds."

"You know I'm backing you," says Tony.

"Yeah. Thanks," says Sebert. "Appreciate it."

"And if Sal weren't in the race, it would be you, right?"

"Right. What's your point?"

"When someone gets in my way," says Tony, "I just remove them. That's how I got my own leg up. I kicked Felix Phillips out of my path, back when I was at the Makeshiweg Festival. That was the first solid rung on my ladder."

"Okay, I get that," says Sebert. "But I can't just remove Sal.

There's nothing on him, no secret scandals, no leverage. Believe me, I've turned over the stones, I've looked everywhere. Nothing that can be proven, anyway. And now, if his son's been killed in this riot – think of the sympathy vote!"

"That's a key word," says Tony. "Riot."

"What are you getting at?"

"What happens in riots? People die, who knows how?"

"I don't grasp – are you saying –" Sebert is fiddling with his tiny earlobe, twisting it this way and that.

"Let me spell it out," says Tony. "A couple of hundred years ago we would take advantage of the chaos and dispose of Sal, and blame it on the rioters. Oh, and we'd have to dispose of Lonnie too: no witnesses. But today, character assassination will double the effect."

"Such as?"

"What do you want in a leader?" says Tony. "Leadership. We can describe – reluctantly, of course – how Sal went all to jelly in a crisis. Before he died. They drowned him in the toilet. A tough-on-crime Minister of Justice, at their mercy. Kind of thing they'd do."

"But he didn't," says Sebert. "Go all to jelly. Or not entirely. And they didn't drown him in the toilet."

"Suppose we were the only survivors," says Tony. "Who would know?"

"You're not honestly suggesting this?" says Sebert, alarmed.

"Consider it as a theory," says Tony, fixing Sebert with a direct stare. "A thought experiment."

"Okay, I get it, a thought experiment," says Sebert. "In the thought experiment, what about Lonnie?" He's wavering. "We can't just –"

"In the thought experiment, Lonnie would have a heart attack," says Tony. "He's overdue for one. We could use, for instance, this thought-experiment pillow. Any questions about smothering, we'd say the rioters did it. Shame, but what can you expect, considering who they are? They're impulsive, they've got no anger-management skills. It's their nature to do things like that."

"That's some thought experiment," says Sebert.

"Did we record all of that?" says Felix behind the main-room folding screen. "It's much better than I could have hoped for!" Tony's running true to course. He must have been pondering such a betrayal for some time, and now chance has handed him an opening. This might turn fatal.

"Clear as a bell," says 8Handz. "Video and audio both."

"Excellent," says Felix. "Time to move it along before they snuff old Lonnie with the pillow. Hit the button, play the wakeup call. What've you chosen?" He's left the choice of magic-island music up to 8Handz, as Prospero seems to have done with Ariel, though he's supplied the requested selection of MP3s.

"Metallica. 'Ride the Lightning.' It's really loud."

"That's my tricksy spirit!" says Felix.

"My god!" says Sal, sitting bolt upright, wide awake. "What's that infernal racket?"

"What's going on?" says Lonnie, rubbing his eyes.

"I heard a roaring," says Tony. "The rioters – they must be on the rampage again! Stand ready! Grab a pillow, hold it in front of you in case they shoot!"

"My head feels funny," says Sal. "Like, a hangover. I didn't hear a thing."

"I only heard a kind of buzzing," says Lonnie.

37. *Charms crack not*

The door swings open. The lights in the corridor outside go on.

"Now what?" says Tony.

"It's a trap," says Sal.

Lonnie goes cautiously to the doorway, peers out. "Nobody there," he says.

"Now for the solemn music," says Felix to 8Handz. "Beaming from the Green Room. Is the fruit bowl still in there, with the grapes?"

"Should be. Checking," says 8Handz, peering at the screen. "Yup, I see it."

"Well done, Goblins," says Felix. "I hope the trapdoor under it is in working order."

"We double-checked it. So, for this I picked a Leonard Cohen tune," says 8Handz. "'Bird on a Wire.' Slowed to half-time. I recorded it myself on the keyboard."

"Highly appropriate," says Felix.

"I used the cello, with a sort of Theremin backup," says 8Handz. "The woo woo sound."

"Woo woo is good," says Felix. "I'm looking forward. Hit the button."

*

"It's coming from down the hallway," says Sebert.

"Is that 'Bird on a Wire'?" says Tony.

"They're having us on," says Sal.

" 'I have tried in my way to be free,'" says Lonnie. "Maybe it's a message, from someone trying to help us. We might as well go and see. Otherwise we'll just sit in here."

"Why not?" says Sebert, nibbling on his index finger.

"Let them go first," Tony whispers to him. "In case of bullets."

"They're out the door," says 8Handz. "All four of them. The video in the hall's not too good, but look, there they are. Going along the hall. Into the Green Room."

"I feel guilty about putting Lonnie through all this," says Felix, "but there's nothing to be done. Anyway, he's been keeping bad company. Did they plant the little speaker on him?"

"Yeah," says 8Handz. "It's on his collar, it's working. When you need it turned on, scroll to here and hit Return."

On the screen, they watch the four men as they approach the Green Room door. To either side of it, taped to the wall, there's a cutout – a T-rex, a space creature – ushering them in.

"Excellent dumb discourse," Felix murmurs to himself.

"What is this, a kindergarten?" says Sebert. "First palm trees, now this!"

"Who's running this place?" says Sal. "There needs to be some changes!" He feels his forehead. "Is that a dinosaur? I feel weird. I think I've got a fever." But they all go in through the doorway.

"What's this?" says Tony. "It's like a theatre green room! There's even a freaking fruit bowl! Though it's only grapes. There ought to be some crackers and cheese, on a plate."

"What lovely music!" says Lonnie. "Is that from *The Magic Flute?*"

"Whatever. I'm hungry," says Sal. He's swaying on his feet.

"We might as well eat as not eat," says Sebert. "Have a grape."

"Don't touch the grapes," says a small voice next to Lonnie's ear. It's a man's voice, one he almost recognizes.

"What?" says Lonnie. "Who is this?" He touches his collar, feels the little speaker. Then he stands back while the other three munch.

"These taste odd," says Sal. "We shouldn't eat them."

"We already ate them," says Sebert.

"I feel strange," says Tony. "I need to sit down."

"That's enough grapes," says Felix. "It seems to be working. Do you know what was in that stuff? That I injected?"

"Little of this, little of that," says 8Handz. "Eye of newt. Ketamine. Salvia. Mushrooms. Awesome stuff, if they put it together right. Quick as a twink they'll be buzzed out of their minds. It's fast-acting, but it doesn't last long. I wouldn't mind having a hit of it right now myself."

"Cue the thunder," says Felix.

There's a roar, a blackout. Then the lights come on: the fruit bowl has vanished. On the wall there's a terrifying shadow: a huge bird, its wings opening and closing.

"Looking good," says Felix to 8Handz.

"Yeah, you chose fabulous wings."

A voice begins to sing, somewhat offtune:

You are three men of sin
Where'm I gonna begin?
You've been so bad

It makes me sad,
As a result, you're going mad!
Felix was ruined by you,
Exiled into the blue;
Sal's lost his son,
That's no fun,
And your woes have just begun!
You must repent and say you're sorry
If you want a good end to this story:
This . . . means . . . you!

"Where did it go?" says Tony. "That thing with wings! That demon! It's over there!"

"What have I done?" says Sal. He begins to weep. "I might as well die! You heard that! They've killed Freddie and it's all my fault! Because of what we did to Felix!"

"This is awful," says Sebert. "We've been poisoned! Where's my body? I'm vaporizing!"

"What's gotten into you all?" says Lonnie.

"Fairly terrible poem, but it did the trick," says Felix. "That, plus the grapes."

"Wow, awesome," says 8Handz. "They are like totally freaked! Gotta find out what else went into that mix!"

"We'll leave them to their bad trip and look in on Ferdinand and Miranda," says Felix. "Pull up their video feed recording. What've they been up to?"

"Let me rewind," says 8Handz. "Okay, so they made a log pile out of the Lego, as per your directions. Then they said those mushy speeches to each other. Now they're playing chess. She's saying – "

"Good," says Felix. "They're right on script. They look very handsome together."

"It's almost like they meant it," says 8Handz. "The true love and all that. It's kind of elegant. Though not a very clear image," he adds.

"Clear enough," says Felix. "Let's go back to the Green Room."

38. *Not a frown further*

In the Green Room, things are not peaceful.

Sal is curled up in a corner of the room, clutching his knees. Tears are running down his cheeks; he's a diagram of woe. He seems to be having an interactive experience with the floor. "It's dark, it's all dark down there," he's saying. "Why's it so dark? I need to go there, where it's all dark, I need to find him!"

Tony's batting at the air. "Back! Back!" he's shouting. "Stay away from me!"

Sebert appears to believe he's covered with insects, or some other form of many-legged life. "Get them off me!" he's babbling. "Spiders!"

Sensible Lonnie has barricaded himself behind the table and is keeping out of their way.

"You sure you maybe didn't overdo it?" says 8Handz. "With the grapes? This is, like, over the top."

"I followed the instructions," says Felix. He wanted anguish, and he's got it. But should drug-induced anguish really count? And what are the side effects, and how long do they last? "How many minutes left to go on our official video?" he says. "The one playing in the cells, and for the Warden's party?"

8Handz consults the time. "Should be about two-thirds through," he says.

"We need to speed this thing along," says Felix. "Cue Stephano and Trinculo."

"They're ready and waiting," says 8Handz.

The Green Room door opens, and in prance Red Coyote and TimEEz, in full costume. Their faces are painted white, with clown mouths. Coyote's wearing his frowzy Oxfam dinner jacket, TimEEz is in the set of red flannel long johns, the bowler tilted at a jaunty angle.

"Not what I'd want to see when I'm whacked," says 8Handz. "Personally."

"The dignitaries don't like it either," says Felix. Indeed, Sal, Tony, and Sebert are backing up to the walls and staring in alarm.

"Ohh look," says TimEEz, pointing at them. "Monstrous! Monstrous! Ew, and what a fishy smell!"

"Fishy monsters," says Red Coyote. "I smell ... corruption!"

"We could put them on show," says TimEEz. "Gibbering lunatics. Street people. Addicts. Dregs of society. Always good for a laugh."

"People would pay good money to see this," says Red Coyote. "'Minister of Justice in Drug-Fuelled Meltdown.' Great headline!"

"Cue the Hag-Seed dancers," says Felix.

"Here we go," says 8Handz.

After a moment's pause, Caliban enters with his two backups, in matching Godzilla mashup headgear. They've written a new number especially for this occasion. 8Handz hits the button for the accompaniment, and the beat floods the room. Caliban begins to chant:

You been callin' me a monster.
But who's more monstrous than you?
You stole, you cheated, you bribed, you lied,
You didn't care who you kicked aside,
You called me dirty, you called me a scum,
You called me a criminal, a no-good bum,
But you're a white-collar crook, you been cookin' the
  books,
Rakin' taxpayer money, we know what you took,
So who's more monstrous
Who's more monstrous,
Who's more monstrous than you?

Monster, monster, gonna put you on show,
Monster, monster, from your head to your toe,
Monster, monster, so the world's gonna know
Just what a monster you are!

We know what you took! White-collar crook!
White-collar crook! We KNOW what you took!

"Demons!" shrieks Tony.

"I'm a monster!" Sal wails. He hides his face in his hands.

"What do they know?" says Sebert, looking wildly around. "Who told them? It was a legitimate expense!"

"Gentlemen, gentlemen!" pleads Lonnie from behind the table. "Get ahold of yourselves!"

"I know they're assholes and they're trying to snuff our Players, but this is too sick even for me," says 8Handz. "It's beyond a bad trip, they're scared shitless."

"It's part of the plan. Anyway, they had it coming," says Felix.

"Don't you feel sorry for them?" says 8Handz.

All this time Miranda has been hovering behind him – a shadow, a wavering of the light – though she's been silent: there haven't been any lines she's needed to prompt. But now she whispers, I would, sir, were I human. She's such a tender-hearted girl.

Has 8Handz heard her? No, but Felix has. "Hast thou," he says, "which art but air, a touch, a feeling of their afflictions, and shall not myself be kindlier moved than thou art?"

"Are we back in the play?" says 8Handz. "Am I supposed to say, 'I would, sir, were I human'?"

"No, it's fine," says Felix. "Just muttering. But you're right, that's enough vengeance. Not a frown further. Time to reel them in. Cue the Goblins."

I'll fetch them, sir, Miranda whispers. Do you love me, Master?

39. *Merrily, merrily*

In the midst of a phalanx of black-clad Goblins the captives are escorted down the hall to the main room, which is dimly lit with blue-toned floods. They've settled down somewhat: there is no more audible weeping, no yelps, shouts, or moaning. Whatever was in the grapes must be wearing off.

The rest of the cast is already assembled, except for Anne-Marie, still sequestered with Freddie in their cell, and 8Handz, who's at the computer behind the folding screen. Felix is there too, waiting for his entrance.

Once the four dignitaries have been courteously seated in the front row, surrounded by Goblins in case they lose control and try to run, 8Handz plays a drum roll and a trumpet call, kills the lights, activates a golden spotlight, and, ta-da!

Felix steps out from behind the folding screen with a flourish of his stuffed-animal magic garment. Raising his fox-head cane into the air, he cues more elemental music. For this 8Handz has chosen "Somewhere Over the Rainbow," played in slow chords, a minor key, and featuring two bass saxophones and a cello.

"A solemn air, and the best comforter to an unsettled fancy, cure thy brains, now useless, boiled within thy skull," he says portentously. The lights come fully up. "Thank you for your kind offices, Lonnie – you at least treated me with some decency in the past, unlike Sal, and especially unlike Tony here."

All four of them stare at him as if he's mad, or as if they are. "Felix Phillips?" says Sal. "Am I dreaming? Where did you come from?"

"The same," says Felix. "Though my name is Mr. Duke, in here."

"You vanished so completely I thought you must've died," says Lonnie.

"What's going on?," says Sal. "What have you done with Freddie? Are you real?"

"A good question," says Felix. "Maybe I'm an enchanted vision generated by this magic island. You'll sort it out in time. Welcome, my friends all!"

Tony is not pleased. "You did this," he says. His voice is still thick with fading chemicals. "Up to your tricks, grandstanding as usual. I always thought you were paranoid! You can kiss your precious Literacy Through Literature program goodbye." He pauses, making an effort to grasp his habitual manner. "You drugged those grapes, I suppose. That's illegal."

"If Freddie's been hurt," Sal says, "you'll pay big-time, I'll charge you with –"

"I think not," says Felix. "Sal, you're the Justice Minister, so I want some justice. First, I demand my old job back, at the Makeshiweg Festival. I was wrongfully dismissed so that Tony could take my place. It was an underhanded plot cooked up by the two of you, as you well know."

"You're crazy," says Tony.

"That's beside the point," says Felix. "Anyway, the experience you've just undergone is called 'artistic immersion.'

What you'll tell the world, Sal, is that the Fletcher Correctional Players presented a very creative piece of interactive theatre, and that, having tasted its benefits – not to mention its grapes – you fully grasp its educational potential and will in future back it to the hilt. Tony, as Heritage Minister, will announce a guarantee of five more years of funding – enhanced funding, I must emphasize. After that, Tony will resign. He can say he wants to spend more time with his family. As for Sebert, he will back out of the leadership race."

"This is insane! What makes you think –" says Tony.

"I've got it all on video," says Felix. "All of it. Sal mewing and boo-hooing in the corner, obviously stoned out of his mind; Sebert's dissolving-body speeches; you, Tony, yelling at invisible demons, buzzed to the gills. None of you would want any of this to go viral on the Internet, as it will should you fail to make full amends and act as required."

"That's not fair," says Tony.

"Let's call it balancing the scales," says Felix. He lowers his voice, addresses Tony directly. "And by the way, I've recorded that fascinating conversation you had with Sebert when Sal and Lonnie were asleep. It tells us a lot about loyalty."

"I'll have this place searched, they'll find the footage, they'll destroy –" Tony begins.

"Save your energy," says Felix. "The video's already stored in the cloud." This is a bluff – it's on a memory stick in his pocket until he gets the chance to upload it – but his tone is convincing, and Tony wilts. "So we don't have a choice," he says.

"That would be my read on it," says Felix. "Sebert?"

"It's enticement," says Sebert. "You set us up."

"I gave you time and space, and you made your own use of it," says Felix. He turns back to Sal. "In addition, I'll want an early parole for my special-effects technician. That said, under these conditions I pardon all of you, and we'll let bygones be bygones."

There's a pause. "Done," says Sal, the chief beneficiary of this arrangement. Tony and Sebert say nothing, but if looks could kill, thinks Felix, he himself would be dead ten times over.

"Good," he says, "I'm glad you all agree; and incidentally I've got that bargain we just made on video as well, as a further precaution."

"So the riot, the lockdown –" says Lonnie. "Were they – They weren't . . . Was it theatre?"

"And where's Freddie?" says Sal. "Is he really dead? I heard him scream. I heard the shot!"

"I sympathize," says Felix. "I lost my own daughter, in this late tempest. It's irreparable."

"But," says Lonnie, "that was at least twelve years . . ."

"Come with me," Felix says to Sal. Sal stands, and Felix links their arms. "I want to show you something."

"Here they come," Anne-Marie whispers. "It's Felix and your dad. Act surprised." She and Freddie are sitting on the floor of the cell, cross-legged, the chessboard between them. "In one second they'll be peering through the window. Got the lines?"

"All set," Freddie whispers back.

"Sweet lord, you play me false," says Anne-Marie at her most winsome.

"No, my dearest love, I would not for the world," says Freddie.

The door to the cell bursts open. "Freddie!" yells Sal. "You're alive!"

"Dad!" Freddie reciprocates. "You're alive too!"

"Thank God!" They fall into each other's arms.

The Bard provided more eloquence at this moment, thinks Felix, but they've covered the main points.

Once the exclamations of joy and the hugs and back-patting are done, Freddie says, "Dad, I'd like you to meet my new partner, Anne-Marie Greenland. She was with Kidd Pivot, and she just played Miranda."

Anne-Marie has scrambled to her feet; her dress has slipped quite far down her shoulder, the paper flowers are askew. She grins impishly, sticks out her hand to be shaken. Sal does not reciprocate. He narrows his eyes at her. "Business or romantic?" he asks.

"Both," says Freddie. "At least, I mean –"

"Hang on a minute," says Anne-Marie. "We haven't really talked! I need to think about this!"

"Dinner tonight?" says Freddie.

"I guess," says Anne-Marie. She hitches up her sleeve. She's even blushing.

Felix turns to Sal. "True romance," he says. "You can't fight it. Anyway, it's the best outcome."

Having taken their leave of the cast, the dignitaries are being escorted back through the hallway and out through the fail-safe doors to the reception area. Miraculously, their security pagers have reappeared on their belts.

They're due to share a drink with the Warden and some others at the high end of the hierarchy at a special reception, with photo ops scripted in. There will be wieners on toothpicks, less toxic than the grapes; there will be cream cheese on crackers; there will be an alcoholic drink or two. Estelle will be there, listening to everything. She'll tell Felix later how it went.

Will there be any talk of how thoroughly they were all

fooled? There will not, thinks Felix. Nothing about the so-called riot or the so-called lockdown. Nothing about the strange hallucinations. Nothing about the backstory of Mr. Duke. Nothing, in a word, discreditable to the visitors.

Instead the Warden will be complimented on the high standards of excellence achieved by the Fletcher Correctional Players. He will be assured that an announcement will be forthcoming, affirming the continuation of the program and an increase in funding. There will be handshakes and toasts. There will be congratulations all round.

Sal won't have any problem with lying: he's a practised politician. As for Tony and Sebert, they'll keep their lips zipped; that way, at least, they'll be allowed to maintain their reputations, unsullied by any viral videos, and will thus have some hope of seats on various corporate boards once they retire from politics. Maybe they'll even be hoisted into the Senate, one of these days. For services rendered.

Freddie and Anne-Marie have gone to the Warden's reception, but not before Anne-Marie has planted a kiss on Felix's bearded cheek. "You're the best," she says. "I wish you really were my dad. It would be an improvement."

"You did brilliantly," he tells her.

"Thanks," she says, "but Freddie helped. He understood it almost right away, he really got into it." She's glowing.

Young love, thinks Felix wistfully. So good for the complexion.

Felix stays behind to help 8Handz roll up the tech. The tiny mics have to be gathered, the speakers taken down; the special lights have to be dismounted. All of it has to be packed up, after which it will be returned to the rental agency.

Felix busies himself with the sorting, while 8Handz checks the quality of the last audio-visual he recorded – the scene in the main room, with Sal's acceptance of the conditions. That might prove crucial at some future time, because you never know.

"I think I'm picking up a radio station or something," says 8Handz. "Through my headphones. There's, like, singing."

"What kind of singing?" Felix asks.

"It's faint, but . . . wait. Okay. It's 'Merrily, merrily.'"

" 'Merrily, merrily, will I live now, Under the blossom that hangs on the bough'?" says Felix. It must be Miranda, prompting again. Clever girl, she's infiltrated Ariel's headphones! But she seems to be confused about the script. "We already did that part, it's in the video," he says for her benefit. They'd used the original Ariel song after all, with only a little change to get rid of the sucking. *Where the bees buzz, there buzz I.*

"No," says 8Handz. "'It's not that. It's 'Merrily, merrily, merrily, merrily, Life is but a dream.'"

A chill shoots through Felix. The hair on his neck bristles. "I used to sing that to her," he whispers to himself. "When she was three." Does she remember after all? Does she remember being three? Does she remember not ever being four? If so, then . . .

"What a coincidence," says Felix. "I was thinking of putting it in the backstory, but I didn't." He's making this up. "Maybe as a song Prospero sings to little Miranda when they're in the leaky boat. That's what you do when kids are frightened, you sing to them."

That's what you do while you hold their feverish hands and stroke their foreheads in the hospital room, but despite everything they slip gently away from you, into the dark backward and abysm of time.

"I know that song. It would've been nice," says 8Handz. "And seriously, thanks for getting me the early parole. That was genius."

"Happy to help," says Felix. "I couldn't have worked this whole thing without you. Is that music still coming in?"

8Handz listens. "Nope, it's gone."

"Can I try your headphones?"

8Handz transfers the phones. Felix listens, listens. Nothing there now, no singing. Only silence. Where is his Miranda? What is she trying to convey?

Outside, it's dusk. Felix trudges toward his car. The expected blizzard has already swept through, though it can't have been major: small drifts of white snow ripple the tarmac.

He drives down the hill in silence. If this were a real first night the cast and crew would all go out, eat somewhere, encourage one another while waiting for the reviews. As it is Felix will have an egg for supper; by himself, unless his Miranda decides to join him. She must be in the car somewhere, though there's no sign of her.

"Anyway I succeeded," he tells himself. "Or at least I didn't fail." Why does it feel like a letdown?

The rarer action is / In virtue than in vengeance, he hears inside his head.

It's Miranda. She's prompting him.

V. This Thing of Darkness

40. *Last assignment*

Friday, March 15, 2013.

On the evening before the final day of class, Felix purchases twenty bags of Miss Vickie's Sea Salt Potato Chips. Using a razor blade, he makes a small slit in the package of each bag, at the back, right underneath the crimped closing. Through each slit he inserts fifteen cigarettes, one at a time. Marlboros is the brand of choice: they seem to be popular. He can't perform this operation too far ahead of time or the cigarettes will taste like potato chips, and vice versa.

Then he reseals the slit, using a hand-held heat crimper. He's been doctoring bags of potato chips for the cast party of each of the plays he's produced at Fletcher.

He packs the chips into two Mark's Work Wearhouse carry bags and hopes for the best.

The next day, Anne-Marie meets him in the parking lot. She's attending the last session by special request. It's a cast party in a way, and as Leggs has pointed out, she's part of the cast, so why should she be left out?

"Thanks for doing this," Felix says to her.

"I wouldn't miss it," says Anne-Marie. "Freddie wanted to come too, but I said not this time. It's for the guys." From this Felix concludes that Freddie is still on the hook. Or that they are on each other's hooks. He smiles.

"Freddie's not jealous of WonderBoy?" he asks slyly. "Those scenes were pretty intense."

"You mean hot? Yeah, they were. But Freddie didn't see them, he was playing chess with me," says Anne-Marie. "Anyway, WonderBoy has backed off now. He's fine with it."

"Fine with what?" says Felix.

"Fine with it being just a play," says Anne-Marie.

The bags of chips sail through Security: who'd suspect them of containing contraband? Dylan and Madison, most likely, but if so they turn a blind eye. Maybe they think the Players deserve some reward for all the effort they've put in.

"That was a great video, Mr. Duke! That *Tempest* thing," Dylan says as he's handing Felix his security pager. "I wasn't expecting to like it, no battle scenes and all, but I really got into it."

"Yeah, everyone got into it," says Madison. "It was so weird!"

"You're right, Mr. Duke, there was no fairies in it," says Dylan. "That blue alien thing or whatever, and that Hag-Seeds rap number – they were wicked! You were awesome, Miss Greenland, ma'am. That Miranda was a stone cold fox!"

"Thanks," says Anne-Marie a little drily.

"What's in your bag?" says Dylan.

"Nothing sharp. Some chocolate cookies I baked for the guys, and just some dolls. You've seen them before."

"Nothing weird in the cookies?" says Dylan, grinning.

"Here, you can test them," says Anne-Marie. She doles out a cookie each.

"What're the dolls doing here?" asks Madison.

"It's a cast party," says Anne-Marie. "They were in the cast. In the video. You saw them."

"Oh yeah. Whatever," says Madison. He throws Dylan a look: ditzy artist. "Just make sure they come out with you. You wouldn't want them getting molested."

"They can take care of themselves," says Anne-Marie, straight-faced. What's she up to? Felix wonders. With the dolls?

"What play are you gonna do next year, Mr. Duke?" says Dylan to Felix.

"Haven't decided," says Felix.

"Well, merde, whatever it is," says Madison.

"A brilliant performance," says Felix to the assembled cast. "Flawless! It couldn't have gone better! A perfect example of the strengths of interactive theatre, an excellent demonstration of the practical uses of theatre arts, and" – he allows himself a heartfelt grin – "and, best of all, thanks to everyone here, the Literacy Through Literature program has been guaranteed for the next five years. The Fletcher Correctional Players are safe." Spontaneous applause, fist bumps.

"Whoreson fantastic!" says Leggs.

"Give yourselves five stars," says Felix. "Now a future generation of budding actors will be able to enjoy the privileges and acquire the skill sets of theatre in a hands-on way, as you have done. Let me add that this was the finest production of *The Tempest* I have ever mounted." Not for them to know that it's the only one. "It can't be bettered, so I will never attempt this particular play again. I have already congratulated the principal members of the cast separately, but I must say that, collectively, this was the most accomplished crew of Goblins anyone could wish for. Let's hear it for all of us!"

Modified cheers, more fist bumps.

"And a special round of applause for our plucky Miranda, Ms. Anne-Marie Greenland, who took on the role of Miranda despite conditions that would have compelled most actresses to refuse. She's a brave lass indeed!" This time, louder cheers, applause, and a chorus of "Yeahs!" and "Awesomes!".

Leggs raises his hand, receives a nod from Felix. "Want to say from all of the guys, thanks, Mr. Duke. You are the greatest. It was . . ." Under his freckles he's actually blushing.

"Fuckin' awesome!" says 8Handz. More applause.

Felix gives a little bow. "It was a pleasure," he says. "And now, your final assignment, for fifteen percent of the total marks. We'll hear your presentations on the post-play lives of your characters. Then we'll round things off with the cast party, including refreshments, such as potato chips. Everything's in order." He says this to reassure them that the cigarettes have indeed been safely smuggled in. "First up, Team Ariel." He gestures to 8Handz to take the front of the room, then sits down at the empty desk beside Anne-Marie.

41. *Team Ariel*

8Handz is ill at ease. He shifts from one foot to the other, clears his throat. He's looking younger than ever.

"This is the report of Team Ariel," he says, "which is me, WonderBoy, Shiv, PPod, and HotWire. We did it together. We all put in some ideas. You guys rock," he says to his teammates.

"We were supposed to figure out what happens to your team's main guy after the end of the play. So, our team's guy is Ariel. I know we all said at the beginning that he's an alien from outer space, but we changed our minds. Like Mr. Duke said, this play is about changing your mind, and it's Ariel who changes Prospero's mind, from revenge to forgiveness, because despite the crap they did, he feels sorry for the bad guys and what they're being put through, once they've suffered enough, so we take it that's okay – to change our own minds."

He looks around the room. Nods, a couple of thumbs-up.

"Great. So, we decided he's not an alien from space. If he was that kind of an alien he'd need to be picked up in a space vehicle, or else he could get beamed up, like in *Star Trek*. So we came up with a different idea.

"We figure he's, like, a holographic projection. That's

how come he can move so fast, go invisible, and divide himself up like that. It all fits, yeah?" He smiles. "You need to know what a holographic projection is? Should I, like, go into it?" he asks Felix.

"Briefly," says Felix.

"Okay, it's like 3-D, only you don't need the glasses. But if he's a projection, who's projecting him? Is it Prospero? Is Ariel coming from inside Prospero's head? It can't be that, we figured, because when Prospero says, 'To the elements be free,' and lets Ariel go, then he would just vanish. He would snuff out. That wouldn't be any way fair, after all the awesome stuff he did for Prospero.

"So we read up on elementals, thanks for the notes, Mr. Duke, and we figure he's a holographic projection of, like, weather systems. He's an air-spirit, plus he can do fire and water as well, so he's got a handle on those kinds of things. Like on the Weather Network, you can see those dust devils and waterspouts, and the way clouds generate electricity – that's where the energy comes from, the energy Ariel uses for all the jobs he does for Prospero. Because those would take a lot of energy, especially the lightning.

"So after the end of the play Ariel's not picked up by a spaceship, and he's not hanging out in flowers on a galaxy far, far away. Maybe he has a little vacation, with the cowslips and whatever – he's earned it, right? But after that he stays on earth, and he flies off to tackle climate change. Sort of like Storm in the X-Men, only without the white eyeballs, plus he's not a girl. He's really happy to be doing that kind of work because he wants to help, he's always been helpful, he just didn't like being told what to do all the time, he wanted a project of his own, and he's got more of a soul and feelings than Prospero used to think he had: it says that right in the play.

"We think our idea is a good one, and it all fits.

"Signed, 8Handz, WonderBoy, PPod, Shiv and HotWire."

8Handz waits, looking nervous. There's nodding and murmuring around the room.

"Unusual!" says Felix. "Very inventive! Wish I'd thought of that myself." This is not a lie: he does wish it, more or less. Never mind that climate change hadn't been heard of in Shakespeare's day: Felix told them to make their own interpretations, and they have. "Any objections?" There aren't: it's the last day and everyone is in a good mood. "Full points," says Felix.

Happy grins from Team Ariel. 8Handz returns to his desk, receives shoulder slaps from his teammates. "Next up is Team Evil Bro Antonio," says Felix. "Let's see how Antonio's fate plays out."

42. *Team Evil Bro Antonio*

SnakeEye swaggers to the front of the room, looking as if he's wearing an overcoat, collar up, and a fedora low over the forehead. There's an invisible gun in this picture some-where, under his arm. He pushes out his chin, lowers his eyebrows, lifts a corner of lip. Is he still in character? It's hard for Felix to tell. In every part SnakeEye has played over the years he's always been villainous, almost too villainous. He skirts the edge of comedy, but he's never fallen over into it. He's the dark double of everyone in the room, and as such he's scary. The air goes silent.

"So, Team Antonio is me, naturally," he begins, "plus King Alonso – I mean, Krampus – and Phil the Pill, who's Sebastian, plus VaMoose, who's my understudy and learned the part better than me. All of these guys got to know Anto-nio up close and personal, so they have a true take on what he's likely to do once the ship sails off for Naples with every-one onboard. We all wrote this, I only happen to be the one reading it. Thanks, Phil, for helping with the spelling, though I have to say you've got crap handwriting like doc-tors have, I could hardly read your notes." The tension breaks: laughter from the class.

"So here goes. The Report of Team Evil Bro Antonio.

"First, Antonio is the most hardcore evil guy in the play. You can't think of one non-evil thing he does. He's always out for Number One, namely himself. Even his plan to murder the King and Gonzalo so Sebastian can be King isn't done for Sebastian, it's done for Antonio, because their deal is that Milan, namely him, Antonio, won't have to pay no – won't have to pay any tribute, which is like taxes. So it's like a tax evasion, only with murder.

"But on Antonio's side, you need to add that it's partly Prospero's fault because he wasn't interested in anything but his magic. It was like leaving your car unlocked: he made crime easy for Antonio. So what can you expect, Prospero was stupid, he had it coming, though Antonio must've been evil to begin with or he wouldn't have taken advantage.

"But the more evil he did, the eviler he got; it was like Macbeth, for those of you who were in it. It was like the blood speech, right? 'I am in blood / Stepp'd in so far that should I wade no more, / Returning were as tedious as go o'er,' and some of us know about that first-hand, right, because once you get going on a thing you think it's chickenshit to back off, and you need to finish it. Get it done. Whatever it is." Sage nodding from the cast, or some of them.

"Anyhow, no risk to Antonio during his first evildoings, because Prospero don't – he doesn't notice, he's got his head jammed so far up his ass – sorry for the language, Anne-Marie – he's got his head buried in the magic sand like an ostrich or whatever, and he doesn't see a thing. He's so busy with bossing around the imps and what-not and making the dead bodies come out of the graves – why was he doing it, anyway? – that he's careless about his own body, close to home. He admits that himself, at the beginning. He would've been better to act like Antonio: Never trust nobody. Anybody.

"So that's the kind of guy Antonio is, love him or hate him, and I guess you mostly hate him. But he has his own take on things, like everybody. So, he gets onto the ship for Naples, and what does he do?

"Remember, Prospero forgives him in a way, and we wrote 'in a way' because Prospero says he won't tell anything about the plan to murder the King *at this time*. '*At this time* I will tell no tales,' he says, which means he'll most likely do it later, and then Antonio's cooked.

"Alonso the King tells Prospero he's sorry, but Antonio doesn't say sorry. He's not sorry. He's most likely mad as – really mad because he got caught, and so he won't be the Duke any more, and he could get life in prison or else his head cut off, the way they did with traitors like him.

"So he bides his time on the sailing trip, and when they're almost to Naples he starts up another plot with Sebastian, and they sneak into King Alonso's cabin and smother him. After that there's a sword fight with Ferdinand, who catches them in the act, but they win the fight and kill him because it's two against one, plus they cheat.

"Then they stab Prospero, because the stupid klutz has let Ariel go free by then, what an idiot, so Prospero's not magic any more. They go to deal with Gonzalo, who's halfway dead of fright anyway, but he has a stroke before they need to kill him, and he just falls over. Then they rape Miranda – sorry, Anne-Marie, but that's how it would go down – and they include Caliban in on the rape for extra punishment to her – raped by a monster – so Caliban finally gets what he wants.

"But then they start to throw the girl overboard so there won't be any heir to Milan, but Caliban hates that idea, he wants to keep Miranda around, rape her some more, and he tries to stop them, so they murder Caliban too. Stephano and Trinculo stay out of the way because they're cowards, plus they want to keep their jobs at the court or whatever. You can't blame them, they're like anyone.

"There. That's our report. Antonio acts like what you'd expect him to do, and Prospero doesn't see it coming because he never saw it coming the first time. We know this is not a nice ending for a lot of the people in this play, but we wanted to tell the truth in some kind of real way, and this is what it's like, this is what happens. Antonio is evil, what d'you expect? Thanks, guys," he says to the rest of Team Antonio, "for helping us stick to life the way it is, no sugar-coating." With the same defiant swagger, he returns to his seat. The class is silent.

"Excellent," says Felix. "You did a thorough job, and I can't say I dispute your conclusions, unpleasant though they are." Is there to be no mercy for Antonio? he wonders. It appears not. Shakespeare was not merciful either: after Prospero forgives him, Antonio is not awarded any more lines in the play.

"It's harsh," says Anne-Marie.

"Yeah. Life is harsh," says SnakeEye.

"I think Team Antonio deserves full marks," says Felix to the room. "Don't you?"

Nods and murmurs. The rest of them don't like this story: it's not a happy ending, and it contains no redemption. But all things considered they have to agree.

"What might save Prospero and Miranda?" says Felix. "And Caliban," he adds.

PPod puts up his hand. "The sailors," he says. "Maybe them. The Boatswain. He could do it."

"Maybe," says Felix. "It's not out of the question."

The class relaxes: a door of hope has opened. They like doors of hope. But then, who doesn't?

43. *Team Miranda*

Felix consults his list. "Next up is Team Gonzalo," he says. "Bent Pencil?"

But as Bent Pencil is gathering his papers together, Anne-Marie strides to the front. "If you don't mind," she says, "I have something to add. I know I don't get marks or cigarettes or anything, but I've been a part of this production, and by the way it was a pleasure working with all of you, but I need to say I can't let this rest. Felix? Mr. Duke?"

She's requesting permission, but that's a formality: it's clear she'll get whatever it is out of her system in any case. "Forge ahead," says Felix with an indulgent smile.

"You're talking as if Miranda is just a rag doll. As if she's just lying around with her legs open, draping herself over the furniture like wet spaghetti with a sign on her saying, *Rape Me.* But it wouldn't be like that.

"First off, she's a strong girl. She hasn't been tied up in corsets and stuffed into glass slippers and such at court. She's a tomboy; she's been clambering all over that island since she was three. Second, ever since Caliban tried to pull that rape number on her when she was maybe twelve, Prospero had to have been training her in self-defence, in case it happened again when he wasn't around. By the time she's on that ship to Naples she's got a lot of fast moves, all the better because those puffed-up gentlemen wouldn't be expecting that kind of fight-back from her. She's got some muscles too – look at the way she was heaving those logs around so Ferdinand didn't have to.

"But there's more. Prospero already said that he educated Miranda beyond what other girls like her would learn. But we aren't told what he was teaching her, apart from how to play chess, plus she knows what a womb is. My guess is, it was a bit of magic. She's certainly heard about spirits and maybe even seen some, because she thinks Ferdinand is one, and she's aware of other examples of what Prospero can do with his sorcerer powers, such as keeping Caliban in line. What do you think the girl was up to when Prospero was having his afternoon snoozes? She was hitting the books – Prospero's books! Like father, like daughter – she had the gift, she was learning the skills.

"But there's even more. She has a side deal with Ariel. Here's how she worked it. You know that song you all thought was so stupid? 'Where the bee sucks there suck I, In a cowslip's bell I lie . . .' Right. It does sound stupid. But the cowslips and bee stuff was what Ariel said he wanted to do once he had a choice. So Miranda heard that, and she took the precaution of digging up every single cowslip on the island and taking them all onboard with her. Her entire cabin was filled with cowslips! And since Ariel had a thing for bees, she used the enchanted bee on her arm" – Anne-Marie rolls up her sleeve, shows them her bee tattoo – "she uses some of the magic she's been studying from Prospero's books to create the illusion of a whole hive of bees. It's like a charm for Ariel, it's like an addiction, it's like a drug! He has to follow her, help her out. Then he gets his fix: cowslips and bees."

Ingenious girl, thinks Felix. She'll go far, but far in what? "They're only illusory bees," he says. "An illusion of bees."

"So what? Ariel doesn't care," says Anne-Marie. "It's the same thing for him: the illusory is real."

"This make any sense to you, Ariel?" Felix says to 8Handz. "Were you in on this, ah, this amendment?"

"I didn't think it up," says 8Handz. "But it sounds good. Why not? It's cool."

"This is how it really goes down with Antonio," says Anne-Marie. "When he makes his move." She peels off her shirt, kicks off her boots, slips off her jeans: she's in her dancer's skin-tight top, her green satin shorts. Up on her toes she stretches, down go her hands onto the floor. She straightens, stands on one foot, grasps the other foot behind her, extends her arm: archer pose. She's hooked every man in the room.

Now, both feet on the floor again, she leans forward, cups one ear, listening. "The two murderous villains approach Alonso's cabin. But Ariel sees them and warns Miranda, and she tells him to guard the cabin with lightning until she can get there. When she arrives on the scene, Ferdinand is trying to fight them off, but he's losing. So Miranda wades in, and with one high kick she breaks Sebastian's wrist." Anne-Marie demonstrates. She executes three pirouettes, does a swift arabesque, then lashes up and out with her right foot, heel first.

There's a subdued cheer from the class: they're leaning forward, and no wonder, thinks Felix. If he were their age he'd be leaning forward too. Actually, he is leaning forward.

"That's Sebastian's sword hand," says Anne-Marie, "but he's got a dagger in his other hand, and Antonio has a sword *and* a dagger. And now here's Caliban, claws out, so it's three to two, and Ferdinand's bleeding. So Miranda calls in the heavy artillery. Goddess Power!"

She pirouettes across the room to her large tapestry bag, whips it open. Out come Iris, Ceres, and Juno in their woolly knitwear, only now their eyeballs are painted an opaque white. She's got them rigged up with harnesses and attached to long thin strips of leather. "First, Iris! To the attack!" She whirls Iris around her head like a bolo. "Wham! Take that, Antonio! She's flying away with his sword! Now Ceres! Now Juno!" She twirls them around in a figure-eight. "Get 'em, Goddesses! The two of them go for it! Goddess Power, right in the nuts! Ssss-bam! Shrivelled up like raisins! So much for your little rape project for today, fellas!"

"Suck it, Toni-o!" calls PPod, and the rest of them cheer.

"But she still has to deal with Caliban. He lunges, leering and drooling. Watch out, creep!" Anne-Marie tosses the goddesses back into her knitting bag, springs up on top of Felix's desk, and stands poised on the edge. Then she bends her knees, raises her hands above her head, and does a 360-twist backflip onto the floor. Now she's horizontal, scissoring her legs, crossing them, rolling, sitting up, all smooth as iron caramel. It's a move from her Kidd Pivot routine.

"Dislocated both of his scaly Caliban arms," she announces. "Painful."

She jumps to her feet, raises both fists, and releases into the air two handfuls of glitter confetti. "Maestro," she says to Felix. Then she bows to the watchers. The applause is as thunderous as such a small group of men can make it.

"Thank you from Team Miranda and the Goddesses," says Anne-Marie. She does a stage curtsey. She's hardly even breathing heavily, though her forehead's a little damp. She sits down at her desk again and starts putting on her shirt.

"Well," says Felix. "That was a refreshing interpretation. I think we'll take a coffee break."

44. *Team Gonzalo*

They stand around with their paper cups of Felix's premium coffee, and Anne-Marie passes the chocolate cookies. Luckily there are enough to go around.

"These are poxy good," says Leggs.

"She is one whoreson of a cookie baker," says SnakeEye.

"Wish there was hash in them," says 8Handz. There are chuckles.

"A virtuoso performance," says Felix to Anne-Marie. "But would the goddesses really have that kind of power? They're just a show put on by Ariel. They aren't real goddesses."

"They are now," says Anne-Marie.

Felix checks his watch. "Okay, we need to move it along," he says. "Two more reports." The paper cups are collected and deposited in the trash, the cookies have vanished. "Next is Bent Pencil."

"I fear I will be something of an anti-climax," says Bent Pencil. "After Anne-Marie. I'm not much of a dancer." No one contradicts him. No one laughs. Gamely, he plods to the front.

"Thank you for this opportunity," he begins. "It has been instructive for me to play the role of the worthy

Gonzalo – thankless though worthy characters so often are – and also to have been able to take part in the, ah, innovative segment of interactive theatre to which you, Mr. Duke, have treated us this week to such great effect. I believe the VIPs who found themselves participating on the spur of the moment, as it were, found it eye-opening as well." He permits himself a retrospective chuckle.

"Dead right," says Leggs. "We learned them a lot!"

Bent Pencil flicks him a smile. "This report is by Team Gonzalo," he continues. "Gonzalo does not have any allies or confederates in the play, apart from Ariel, who prevents his murder, and Prospero, who is working behind the scenes. However, Colonel Deth, TimEEz, and Riceball have done me the honour of assisting me in compiling this report." He sends a thin avuncular beam their way.

"Report: The Life of Gonzalo After the End of the Play. By Team Gonzalo.

"We can divide the characters of *The Tempest* into optimistic characters and pessimistic characters. The optimistic characters are stakeholders in the more positive side of human nature, the pessimistic characters in the more negative side. So, Ariel and Miranda and Ferdinand are optimists; Alonso, Antonio, and Sebastian are pessimists. Stephano and Trinculo and Caliban waver back and forth, investing in the hope of fortune for themselves but willing, as well, to visit violence and death and/or slavery upon others.

"Gonzalo is at the extreme positive end of the spectrum, so much so that we wonder how he's survived as a councillor at the court of King Alonso, populated as it is by cynics, opportunists, and placeholders. That he *has* survived gives some credibility to the proposition that Alonso's repentance is genuine, that he means what he says, and that

Ferdinand and Miranda may therefore look forward to a safe and happy transition to their reign, supported by Alonso to the best of his ability. Unless Alonso had some good in him from the beginning – and despite his facilitating of the callous treatment of Prospero – he would not have employed Gonzalo as his councillor.

"But Gonzalo has little power. Except for Prospero, none of the positive characters – Miranda, Ferdinand, Ariel, Gonzalo – are in positions of power, and even Prospero's power is hardly of the usual kind. As Caliban says, without his books he's nothing.

"Is extreme goodness always weak? Can a person be good only in the absence of power? *The Tempest* asks us these questions. There is of course another kind of strength, which is the strength of goodness to resist evil; a strength that Shakespeare's audience would have understood well. But that kind of strength is not much on display in *The Tempest*. Gonzalo is simply not tempted. He doesn't have to say no to a sinfully rich dessert, because he's never offered one.

"What we in Team Gonzalo propose for the future life of Gonzalo is as follows.

"Let's suppose that our pessimistic friends are wrong – that Antonio does not win the day, that Prospero is not thrown overboard – in fact, that all goes as it seems to be planned at the end of the play. Let us overlook also the enjoyable fantasy about Miranda and her goddess friends that has just been created for us with such verve, in Anne-Marie's performance. I add this on my own, as Team Gonzalo was not aware in advance of this intervention." He smiles at Anne-Marie, not altogether warmly. "Back to our report. The play of *The Tempest* declares for second chances, and so should we.

"Thus, everyone sails back to Naples, enjoying the fair

winds provided by Ariel via Prospero, and the wedding of Ferdinand and Miranda is celebrated. Prospero bids them goodbye and goes back to Milan, where he takes up his dukedom again and no doubt incarcerates Antonio or otherwise neutralizes him. Prospero tells us that every third thought of his will be his death, but that leaves two thoughts out of three for governing Milan. Let's hope he's better at it this time around.

"At the court of Naples, Sebastian is held in check by Prospero's knowledge of his treasonous intentions toward his brother the King, which Prospero has written down and provided to Miranda to be used against Sebastian if needed. As for Gonzalo, so grateful are Ferdinand and Miranda, and indeed King Alonso, for the good deeds done by him over the course of time that they offer him whatever he wants.

"We, Team Gonzalo, decided to test Gonzalo's goodness. He chooses to go back to the island with a group of other people as good as himself, and there he sets up a kingdom-republic, with himself in charge, where there will be no differences of rank and no hard labour, and where there will be no immoral sexual behaviour, no wars, no crimes, and no prisons.

"That's our report.

"Signed, Bent Pencil, Riceball, TimEEz, and Colonel Deth." He beams around the room again.

"Thank you," says Felix. "And how does it go?"

"How does what go?" asks Bent Pencil innocently.

"Gonzalo's ideal republic."

"Team Gonzalo leaves that to your imagination," says Bent Pencil. "Let's say that Gonzalo is no magician. He can command no Goblins, nor can he bring the dead to life. Also he has no army. He depends on the better natures of other people. But maybe Bountiful Fortune, otherwise known as Auspicious Star, will smile on him. She's a character in the play too. Without her, Prospero would never have got his chance. She's very important."

"Quite right," says Felix. "She is. Well done! Full marks for Team Gonzalo. As my uncle used to say, it's better to be lucky than rich."

"I'm neither," says Bent Pencil mildly. He gets a laugh, which gratifies him.

"You're not lucky yet, maybe," says Felix, "but you never know with auspicious stars. Who's up next and last? Ah. Team Hag-Seed."

45. *Team Hag-Seed*

Leggs makes his way up to the front of the room, red in the face and more freckled than ever. He's giving it his best shot, taking a dominant stance, one leg forward, foot angled out, then a tilt of the pelvis and the other leg swinging as if welded at the knee. He surveys the assembled cast and crew, scowling his Caliban scowl. Then he slowly rolls up his sleeves.

Good theatre, thinks Felix. He's making them wait.

"Team Hag-Seed reporting here, sir," he says to Felix. The mode is quasi-military but at the same time subtly mocking.

"Here's the real clear truth," he begins. "Hag-Seed, I mean Caliban – nobody's on his team. Even his so-called friends and allies, those two drunk assholes – they're not loyal to him, they make fun of him and call him names, they're out to make a buck off him. So inside the play, he don't have a team. His only team he ever had is dead, which was his mother, who other people called a witch. But she must've loved him enough to at least not drown him like a kitten. She did the bare essentials, she kept him alive. You gotta hand it to her, considering. She was all alone on the island, birthing the baby and so forth.

She maybe had her failings, but she did what she could for him. She was tough."

Nods from the audience: tough though fallible mothers are being remembered.

"Then she died and Caliban grew up on his own. He was welcoming to Prospero at first, but now Prospero's on his back 24/7, and Ariel's not gonna help him out either, though they're both slaves in a manner of speaking. They're both kept in line by threats of torture; only difference is, Ariel sucks up and Caliban holds out, so it's only Caliban who gets the pinches and cramps.

"But I'm glad to say I have a team helping me with this report, and that is the Hag-Seed backup group and costume designers for the numbers we did, namely PPod, TimEEz, VaMoose, and Red Coyote. You guys were great, I couldn't of done it without you, we really scored, and this will always be a great memory in my life." He pauses. Is it a studied pause or is he choking up? I've taught him too well, thinks Felix, if even I can't tell the difference.

"So this is our report," says Leggs. "Report of Team Hag-Seed. What happens to Caliban after it's over? At the end of the play he's left dangling, so we don't really know. He's going to be a good servant to Prospero, or what?

"Okay, we thought of various ways it could of gone. First, Caliban's left on the island and the rest of them sail away. He gets the island and he's the king of it, like he wanted, but there's nobody else on it any more, so what's the point? You can't be a king unless you're the king of somebody else, right?"

Nods from the cast. They're listening intently: they really care what happens to Caliban.

"Okay, so we tossed out that one. Next – that's number two – he sails on the ship for Naples with the rest of them.

Prospero gets killed and Miranda gets raped, like in what Team Antonio said – sorry, Anne-Marie, but in real life there wouldn't be any goddesses, so that's what would happen – only she's not raped by Hag-Seed. It's only by Antonio, because he's so evil, like he said. After that he kills her because he wants to be the Duke and he can't have any rivals, so she has to go, it makes sense. Caliban's pissed off by that, but he can't do nothing because by this time Stephano and Trinculo have him chained him up in the bottom of the ship.

"When they get to Naples, they put him on show for money, just like they said they would. They tell folks he's a savage from the jungle, a part-fish monster, and also he eats people. Everyone throws things at him like a gorilla in a cage, and they call him shit names, like Prospero and Miranda and Stephano and Trinculo did, and they poke him with sticks to make him snarl and curse, and they laugh at him. Plus they feed him crap food. So after a while of this he gets a bunch of diseases – he's never been vaccinated, right? – and one day he comes out in spots and a fever, and then he flops over and dies."

Silence in the room. It's all too plausible.

"But that was too dark for us," says Leggs. "Why should the other ones in this play get a second chance at life, but not him? Why's he have to suffer so much for being what he is? It's like he's, you know, black or Native or something. Five strikes against him from Day One. He never asked to get born."

More nods. Leggs has the audience. Where's he taking them? Felix wonders. Somewhere strange, you can see it in his eyes. He's about to spring a surprise. "So here's what we're thinking," says Leggs. "We're thinking about that line, said by Prospero: 'This thing of darkness I acknowledge mine.' What's he mean by it? Just that Caliban works for him or is, like, his slave? It's gotta be more than that." He leans forward, making eye contact, then more eye contact. "This is what we think. It's gotta be true. Here it is: *Prospero is Caliban's dad.*"

Murmurings, small head-shakings. They aren't convinced. "Stick with me," says Leggs. "Let's walk it through. His mom is a sorceress, right? Sycorax. She's wicked! Prospero is a sorcerer. They do a lot of the exact same kind of things – charms, spells, changing the weather – including putting the twist on Ariel, except that Prospero does those things better, and we're supposed to think it's okay for him but evil for her. Suppose they met earlier at, like, a sorcerer type of convention, and they had a thing together. One-night stand. He knocks her up, skedaddles back to Milan; she's up the spout, she gets caught, they dump her on the island.

"Prospero washes up onshore. Sycorax is dead by then, but he takes one look at Caliban and he knows right away whose kid this has to be. He slangs the dead mother, that's natural; he doesn't own up to the kid, but thinks he might make something of him anyway – the kid must have some good qualities, right, because it's half his. Proud of him at first, because Caliban's self-reliant, knows his way around the island, comes up with food, pig-nuts and fish, whatever – eager to please. So Prospero humours the kid, teaches him stuff. Language, and that.

"But then the kid takes a crack at Miranda. That's natural too, maybe not nice, was there consent, who knows, he said she said, but whose fault was it anyway, letting Miranda prance around in full view? Prospero should'a seen it coming. Should'a locked her up, if it was that important. Prospero ought to eat some of the blame for that number.

"But that's not what he does. Instead he gets in a twist,

piles on the insults, starts with the tortures, overlooks the good points Caliban's got, such as musical talent. But by the end, Prospero's learning that maybe not everything is somebody else's fault. Plus, he sees that the bad in Caliban is pretty much the same as the bad in him, Prospero. They're both angry, both name-callers, both full of revenge: they're joined at the hip. Caliban is like his bad other self. Like father, like son. So he owns up: 'This thing of darkness I acknowledge mine.' That's what he says, and that's what he means.

"So after the play, Prospero tries to make up for what he did wrong. He takes Caliban onto the ship, runs him under the shower, scrubs off that fishy smell, orders him some fancy new clothes, makes him, like, a pageboy or something, so he can learn to eat from a plate. Says he's sorry and they need to start fresh. Appeals to the artistic side of Caliban, what with the beautiful dreams and all. Once Caliban is cleaned up and well dressed and has manners, people don't think he's ugly any more. They think he's, like, rugged.

"So Prospero sets him up as a musician, back in Milan. Once he gets a break, the kid does really well. He can bring out, like, the darkness emotions in people, but in a musical way. He has to keep away from the booze though, it's poison to him, turns him crazy. So he makes the effort, and he stays clean.

"Next thing you know he's a star. Prospero's really proud of him. The kid is top billing at all the duke-type concerts. He's got a stage name, he's got a band: HAG–SEED AND THE THINGS OF DARKNESS. He's, like, world-famous.

"That's our report. We hope you like it."

This time the class is in full agreement. There's a chorus of "Yeahs" and "Way-to-gos," and a round of applause that swells to a rhythmic clapping, then a stamping of feet. "Hag-Seed! Hag-Seed! We want Hag-Seed!"

Felix stands up. This shouldn't get too far out of control. "That was excellent, Team Hag-Seed. Full marks! A very creative interpretation! And a fitting end to the formal part of this class. Next up, cast party! Are we ready?"

46. *Our revels*

The bags of potato chips and the cans of ginger ale are handed
out. There's talk, the clinking of ginger ale cans, an air of
muted celebration. In a few minutes they'll sidle up to Felix
one by one and cough up some form of bashful thanks. It's
what happens at these parties, every time. That, plus the opening of the chip bags and the swift pocketing of the cigarettes.

The number of cigarettes in each bag is the same, and
why not? They've all done so well. Once Felix is out of sight,
the bargaining and trading will begin: cigarettes are an
unofficial currency, desirable for bribes and the obtaining
of goods and favours.

"Not my usual brand," says Bent Pencil. Chuckles: everyone knows he doesn't smoke.

"If there's a hole in one end and fire at the other, I smoke
it," says Red Coyote.

Shiv: "You're talking about my woman." Laughter.

"Yeah, but which end is which?" More laughter. "Sorry,
Anne-Marie."

"Watch it," says Anne-Marie. "Don't forget, I've got that
goddess power."

"By the way, well done, Anne-Marie," says Felix. "I didn't
see that coming."

"You always say magic should be unpredictable," says Anne-Marie. "I wanted to surprise you."

"And you did," says Felix.

"We're really grateful to you. Me and Freddie. It's –"

"No need for gratitude," says Felix. "I was pleased to help out."

"We got a surprise for you too," says Leggs, who has ambled over to join them.

"Oh?" says Felix. "What kind of surprise?"

"It's an extra number we wrote," says Leggs. "Me and the Hag-Seeds. We all wrote it together. We're working on, like, a musical."

"A musical?" says Anne-Marie. "About Caliban?"

"Yeah, about what happens after the play's over. Doing that report got us thinking: why shouldn't Caliban have a play to himself?"

"Go on," says Felix.

"Okay, so, it begins at the part where Stephano and Trinculo put him in a cage and show him off for money. But in the musical, he gets out of the cage. That's this number we did – where he gets out, and he says he's not doing any more slave work or living in a cage."

Boom boom boom, the Hag-Seeds start the beat. Leggs chants:

Freedom, high-day! High-day, freedom! Freedom,
    high-day, freedom!
Got outta my cage, now I'm in a rage –
No more dams I'll make for fish,
Nor fetch in firing
At requiring,
Nor scrape trenchering, nor wash dish;
Ain't gonna any more lick your feet

Or walk behind you on the street,
Ain't gonna get on the back of the bus,
And you can give our land right back to us!

Ban-ban, Ca-Caliban,
Don't need no master, I am not your man!
So stuff it up your hole, gimme back what you stole,
Tellin' you it's late, I'm fillin' up with rage,
I'm gettin' all set to go on a ram-page!
Ain't gonna work for less than minimum wage –
Live in a shack and piss in a pail,
You earn yourself money by puttin' me in jail!

You kick me in the head, you dump me in the snow,
Leave me there for dead,
'Cause I'm nothin' to you.
Ban, ban, Ca-Caliban,
You think I'm an animal, not even a man!

Now Hag-Seed's black and Hag-Seed's brown,
Hag-Seed's red, don't care if you frown,
Hag-Seed's yellow and Hag-Seed's trash white,
He goes by a lotta names, he's roamin' in the night,
You treated him bad, now he's a sackful of fright,
Hag-Seed!

Ban, ban, Ca-Caliban,
Don't need no master, I am *not* your man!
Move it, man! Let it go, let it flow –
Don't need no, need no, need no! No no no!

"That's powerful," says Felix. "Very powerful."
"More than powerful!" says Anne-Marie. "It's got – it

could be really – But what happens after he escapes from the cage?"

"We figure he might go after everyone who used to treat him in such a bad way," says Leggs. "Do a whole revenge thing, sort of like Rambo. Pick them off one by one, beginning with Stephano and Trinculo."

"What about Prospero?" says Felix.

"And Miranda?" says Anne-Marie.

"Maybe they're not in the musical," says Leggs. "Or maybe they are. Maybe Caliban forgives them. Maybe he doesn't. Maybe stalks them, jumps them, goes to work with his claws. We're still working on it."

Felix is intrigued: Caliban has escaped the play. He's escaped from Prospero, like a shadow detaching itself from its body and skulking off on its own. Now there's no one to restrain him. Will Prospero be spared, or will retribution climb in through his window one dark night and cut his weasand? Felix wonders. Gingerly, he feels his neck.

"Think you'd maybe direct it, Mr. Duke?" says Leggs. "When we get it done? You'd be, like, our first choice." He smiles shyly.

"If I'm still alive," says Felix. He's absurdly pleased by the offer, though of course this will never happen. Or will it? "It's possible. You never know."

47. Now are ended

As Felix is finishing his ginger ale, 8Handz, Leggs, and SnakeEye come over to him.

"There's one more thing," says SnakeEye. "About the coursework and all."

"What's that?" says Felix. What has he forgotten?

"The ninth prison," says 8Handz. "We only counted eight. Remember?"

"You said you'd tell us if we didn't guess," says Leggs.

"Oh. Yes," says Felix, gathering his scattered wits. "It doesn't come out all that well for Prospero at the end, does it? He gets his dukedom back, but he's not very interested in it any more. So he wins, but he also loses. Most importantly, he loses the two beings he loves: Miranda, who is now paired with Ferdinand and will live far away in Naples; and Ariel, who leaves Prospero's service without even a backward glance. Prospero will miss him, but Ariel himself shows no sign of missing Prospero: he's happy to be free. The only one who might stick with Prospero is Caliban, hardly a big treat. Still, why would Prospero need him, now that he's leaving the island? He will have other servants back in Milan. Maybe he'll take the thing of darkness with him out of some feeling of responsibility: it's his, not anybody else's.

But at this moment Prospero's feeling guilty about a different thing."

"Where do you get all that?" says Leggs. "About him feeling guilty?"

"It's here," says Felix, rooting through his playbook. "He says, 'Let me not dwell / In this bare island by your spell.' Prospero has undone his charms and is about to break his magic staff and drown his book, so he can't perform any more magic. The spell is now controlled by the audience, he says: unless they vote the play a success by clapping and cheering, Prospero will stay imprisoned on the island.

"Then he says he also wants them to pray for him. He says: 'And my ending is despair, / Unless I be relieved by prayer, / Which pierces so that it assaults / Mercy itself, and frees all faults.' In other words, he wants a divine pardon. The last lines of the play are 'As you from crimes would pardoned be, / Let your indulgence set me free.' It has a double meaning."

"Yes, it's in the notes," says Bent Pencil.

"I forget that part," says SnakeEye.

"An indulgence was a get-out-of-hell-free card," says Felix. "You could buy those once."

"Still can," says SnakeEye. "It's called a fine."

"It's called bail," says Leggs. "Only that's not free, right?"

"It's called early parole," says 8Handz. "Only you don't pay for that. You're supposed to kind of earn it."

"What was the guilty thing?" says Anne-Marie. "What's Prospero done that's so terrible?"

"Indeed, what?" Felix asks rhetorically. More of the cast have gathered around. "He doesn't tell us. It's one more puzzle in the play. But *The Tempest* is a play about a man producing a play – one that's come out of his own head, his 'fancies' – so maybe the fault for which he needs to be pardoned is the play itself."

"Elegant," says Anne-Marie.

"I don't get this," says SnakeEye. "A play's not a crime."

"A sin," says Felix. "Not a legal lapse. A moral one."

"I still don't," says SnakeEye.

"All those vengeful emotions? All the anger?" says Felix. "Making other people suffer?"

"Well, yeah, maybe," says SnakeEye.

"Okay, but what about the ninth prison?" says 8Handz.

"It's in the Epilogue," says Felix. "Prospero says to the audience, in effect, *Unless you help me sail away, I'll have to stay on the island* – that is, he'll be under an enchantment. He'll be forced to re-enact his feelings of revenge, over and over. It would be like hell."

"I saw a horror movie like that," says 8Handz. "On Rotten Tomatoes."

"The last three words in the play are 'set me free,'" says Felix. "You don't say 'set me free' unless you're not free. Prospero is a prisoner inside the play he himself has composed. There you have it: the ninth prison is the play itself."

"Okay, cool," says 8Handz. "That's neat."

"Crafty," says Anne-Marie.

"I'm not sure I'm entirely convinced," says Bent Pencil.

"What play're we doing next year?" says Shiv. "You're coming back, right? We saved the program?"

"I promise you there will be a play next year," says Felix. "That's what we all worked for."

"I feel kind of weepy," says Anne-Marie as they walk down the corridor together. "Because it's over. The revels now are ended. And that was a fucking good revel!" She takes Felix's arm. The security door locks behind them with a dull thunk.

"Revels end," says Felix. "But only these revels. You'll have others. How's it going with Freddie?"

"Not bad so far," says Anne-Marie, understated as ever. He surveys her profile: there's a definite grin.

They pass through Security, where Felix says goodbye to Dylan and Madison. "It's been awesome," Dylan tells him. "Fantastic cookies," he says to Anne-Marie.

"See you soon, Mr. Duke," says Madison. "Same time next year?"

"Triple merde, eh?" says Dylan.

"Looking forward," says Felix.

In the parking lot he thanks Anne-Marie once again, then drives out through the gates in his wheezy car and winds down the hill. Dirty heaps of snow line the road, meltwater trickling from them. All of a sudden it's the beginning of spring. How long has he been inside Fletcher Correctional? It seems like years.

Did his Miranda leave the cast party too, did she come out through Security, is she in the car with him? Yes, there she is in the back seat, over in the corner: a shadow within the shadow. She's sad to have seen the last of all those wondrous people inside their brave new world.

"'Tis new to thee," he tells her.

Epilogue:
Set Me Free

Felix is in his shanty, packing; not that there's much to pack. Some odds and ends. A few elderly clothes; he folds them neatly, lays them in his black wheeled suitcase. It's officially spring; outside, the ice is melting, the birds are already tuning up. Sunlight streams through the opened door, which is just as well because Felix's electricity has been cut off.

When he'd trudged over to the farmhouse through the damp snow to ask about that, he'd found it deserted: the Maude family had decamped, leaving – presumably – a stack of unpaid bills. They'd made a clean sweep. It was as if they'd never been there at all; as if they'd manifested themselves only as long as Felix had needed them, then turned to mist and blended into the fields and woodlots. Ye elves of hills, brooks, standing lakes, and groves, he murmurs to himself. But most likely they're in Bert's truck, heading west to better pickings.

He got his revenge, such as it was. His enemies had suffered, which had been a pleasure. Then Felix had strewn forgiveness around while listening to the clenching of Tony's teeth, which had been a greater pleasure. And as long as he keeps that video footage in the cloud where he's stowed it, Tony won't be able to cross him any time soon, much though the conniving asshole would like to. But he's resigned from his position, so he's lost his credibility. He has no leverage, no power platform; he's no longer among those who matter. Tony is out and Felix is back in, which is as it should be.

Specifically, Felix has his old job back: Artistic Director of the Makeshiweg Theatre Festival. He can stage his long-lost *Tempest* of twelve years ago, if that is his pleasure.

Strangely enough, he no longer wants to. The Fletcher Correctional Players version is his real *Tempest*: he could never better that one. Having pulled it off so spectacularly, why would he bother with a lesser attempt?

As for Artistic Director, he's accepted the position but in name only. He'll be an *éminence grise*, he'll work behind the scenes. He'll break his staff, he'll drown his book, because it's time for the younger people to take over.

He's hired Freddie as Assistant Director: let him learn by doing. Felix will help him out for a while, though in essence he'll be handing over the keys, a process he's already begun. The boy's a fast learner. Freddie can't thank him enough, and that too is a pleasurable feeling: never to be thanked enough.

Anne-Marie has been taken on as the chief choreographer for the musicals Freddie wants to add to the Makeshiweg repertoire. *Crazy for You* is the first one they're doing: it's got enough dance numbers to stretch Anne-Marie's talent. She can go to town on it, raise the roof, and he has no doubts that she will.

They're working beautifully together, those two. It's as if they were made for each other, like a pair of ice-dance champions. Watching them as they pore over the costume sketches and solemnly discuss their aesthetics and mess around onscreen with their digital set designs, Felix finds himself choking up, as if at a wedding: that strange mixture of nostalgia for the past mixed with joy for the future; the joy of others. He himself is only a bystander now, a well-wisher, a flinger of virtual rice. Their path won't be easy because theatre has never been easy, but at least he's given them a start. His life has had this one good result, however ephemeral that result may prove to be.

But everything is ephemeral, he reminds himself. All gorgeous palaces, all cloud-capped towers. Who should know that better than he?

He'd thought Sal O'Nally would kick up about Freddie: his adored first-born son snatched out from under his nose by Felix, whisked away from the world of lawyerdom and politics in which Sal had wanted to encase him and matched up with a hoyden like Anne-Marie. But if anything, Sal seemed relieved: the boy's future had a direction, he was happy, and, best of all, he wasn't dead! All plusses for such a doting father. But even doting fathers have to let go sooner or later. From now on the boy will be working out his own destiny, as much as anyone can.

Felix pauses in his packing to take stock. *Shabby* is hardly the word for his wardrobe, and for himself, come to think of it. He'll get a haircut and eventually some better teeth; very soon he'll go shopping. He needs fresh garments, because he's embarking on a cruise.

Estelle has fixed it up for him. Among the many people she knows are some who run cruise companies. Seize the moment! she'd said. Grasp Fortune by the forelock, because after the strenuous time he'd been having, wouldn't it be a fine idea for him to take a relaxing break? Lie back in a deck chair in the sun? Be restored by the salt air?

No cost to him: all he'd have to do is give a couple of lectures about his wonderful theatre experiments at Fletcher Correctional. He could even show the videos, if he thought it appropriate; people would be fascinated, his approach was so novel! Or if he couldn't show them due to privacy issues concerning the actors, then at least he could discuss his methods. And the Caribbean would be lovely at this time of year, she said. She herself would be going on the cruise too. They could do some line-dancing and other things together. It would be fun!

At first Felix balked. A cruise ship filled with old people, people even older than himself, snoozing in deck chairs and doing line-dancing – that was his idea, if not of hell exactly, then at least of limbo. A state of suspension somewhere on the road to death. But on second thought, what did he have to lose? The road to death is after all the road he's on, so why not eat well during the journey?

So he'd said yes, but with one condition. 8Handz had been granted early parole, and Felix could not find it in his conscience – he tells Estelle – to leave the young fellow at loose ends. From what he's heard, the day after getting sprung from prison is even more terrifying than the day after getting locked up in the first place. So 8Handz must come on the cruise as well. He could recite some of his Ariel speeches during Felix's presentations; he's got them down pat, he's a born performer. And on such a cruise, the boy might well meet some influential businessman – someone in digital tech – who would recognize his extensive talents and give him the creative scope he needed. The lad deserved a break, considering all the hard work he'd done for Felix.

Estelle's bangles jingled as she gave his arm squeeze: they were now on definite arm-squeezing terms. No problem at all, she said, beaming full upon him. She would pull the necessary strings. It sounded to her as if young 8Handz deserved some good fortune, and the sea air would be so liberating for him.

Felix folds up his stuffed-animal garment: take it or throw it out? On a whim he packs it into the suitcase. He'll bring it on the cruise with him, where it will add a colourful and authentic note to his presentations. The aura it once held for him is dimming, like holiday lights at noon. Soon it will be nothing but a souvenir. And there's his fox-head cane as well. It's no longer a magic staff, it's only a wooden stick. Broken. Should he bury it certain fathoms in the earth? That would be histrionic. Anyway, who'd be the audience?

"Farewell," he says to it. "My so potent art."

It comes over him in a wave: he's been wrong about his *Tempest*, wrong for twelve years. The endgame of his obsession wasn't to bring his Miranda back to life. The endgame was something quite different.

He picks up the silver-framed photo of Miranda, laughing happily on her swing. There she is, three years old, lost in the past. But not so, for she's also here, watching him as he prepares to leave the full poor cell where she's been trapped with him. Already she's fading, losing substance: he can barely sense her. She's asking him a question. Is he compelling her to accompany him on the rest of his journey?

What has he been thinking – keeping her tethered to him all this time? Forcing her to do his bidding? How selfish he has been! Yes, he loves her: his dear one, his only child. But he knows what she truly wants, and what he owes her.

"To the elements be free," he says to her.

And, finally, she is.

The Tempest: *The Original*

In a storm at sea, a ship is floundering. Alonso, King of
Naples; his brother, Sebastian; his councillor, Gonzalo; and
his son, Ferdinand, are onboard, as are Antonio, the Duke of
Milan; Stephano, the butler; and Trinculo, the jester. As
lightning strikes and the ship begins to sink despite the
efforts of the Boatswain and sailors, all fear for their lives.
This scene is usually played with the elemental spirit, Ariel,
visible in the rigging.

On the shore of a nearby island, fifteen-year-old Miranda
pities the drowning ones, but her father, the magician Prospero, says no one has been harmed, and all has been done
for her welfare. He then explains why he has raised the
tempest. He, not Antonio, is the rightful Duke of Milan.
Because Prospero was wrapped up in the study of magic, he
delegated the practical affairs of his dukedom to his brother,
who took advantage of the situation to league with Prospero's political enemy, Alonso. The latter invaded Milan, and
Prospero and the three-year-old Miranda were put into a
leaky boat with nothing but some clothing and Prospero's
books, supplied to him by the good councillor, Gonzalo.
They drifted ashore to the island, where they have been
living in a cave-like "cell" for twelve years.

Now an auspicious star and the deity Lady Fortune have brought Prospero's enemies within his reach. He has ordered the illusion of the tempest to land them onshore. His purposes are twofold: revenge and the betterment of the fortunes of Miranda.

Prospero puts Miranda to sleep, dons his magic robes, and calls upon his chief attendant spirit, Ariel. Ariel serves Prospero in return from having been released from a cloven pine where he had been imprisoned by the witch Sycorax because he wouldn't fulfill her loathsome commands, but now he wants his freedom. Prospero scolds him for ungratefulness, but promises that if his present plan against his enemies works out with Ariel's help, Ariel shall be free. Ariel then describes the "tempest" he has created. Three groups of travellers have been landed in different places onshore: Ferdinand by himself, Stephano and Trinculo as a pair, though separated, and the court party together.

Next command for Ariel: to dress as a sea nymph, to render himself invisible to all but Prospero, and to find Ferdinand – who believes his father has drowned. Ariel is to lead him with music to the place where he will see Miranda.

Prospero wakens Miranda and they go in search of Prospero's other enforced servant, Caliban, the ugly and brutish son of Sycorax. Caliban, Prospero, and even Miranda trade curse words and reproaches: Caliban accuses Prospero of stealing the island from him, and Prospero points out that Caliban has tried to rape Miranda. Caliban wishes he had done so, and peopled the island with Calibans; then, enforced by the pinching of Prospero's spirits, he goes off to collect wood.

Ariel leads in Ferdinand, who is awestuck by Miranda, as she is by him. So that things won't be too easy and thus lightly valued, Prospero sets an ordeal: he magically disarms Ferdinand, accuses him of being a pretender and a traitor, and says he will imprison him. Ferdinand claims he can bear that if only he can glimpse Miranda once a day.

Ariel is sent off to keep tabs on the court party: Alonso, Sebastian, Gonzalo, Antonio, and other lords. Alonso is certain that his son has drowned and is very dejected. Gonzalo tries to cheer him up by praising the island and describing the utopian society he would set up if he had the ruling of it. Antonio and Sebastian scoff at him. Ariel appears and puts Alonso and Gonzalo to sleep, whereupon Antonio proposes to Sebastian that they murder them, thus making Sebastian the King of Naples. Ariel, however, wakes the sleepers just in time and speeds off to report developments to Prospero.

Meanwhile, Caliban is gathering wood when he sees the jester Trinculo approaching. Fearing he is a tormenting spirit, he hides under his cloak. A storm approaches and Trinculo hides under the cloak too, despite its fishy smell and the monster underneath. Stephano the butler approaches, reeling drunk. He gets Caliban drunk too, and Caliban decides to worship Stephano like a god, and serve him as master instead of Prospero. He sings a song to this effect.

Meanwhile, Ferdinand has been put to work hauling wood. Miranda appears and pleads with him to rest – she will do the work for him. They pledge their love and promise to marry each other. Prospero, unseen, is happy.

Caliban, Stephano, and Trinculo are now even drunker, and after a fight engineered by Ariel, Caliban proposes that they murder Prospero and set up Stephano as the island king, with Miranda as the queen. Ariel leads them astray with music, and Caliban tells them not to be afraid, as the island is often filled with ravishing sounds.

Alonso, Gonzalo, Sebastian, and Antonio are resting in their search for Ferdinand when a banquet is presented to them by some oddly shaped spirits. Prospero watches, invisible, as they approach to eat; but the banquet vanishes and Ariel appears in the shape of a harpy, upbraiding Alonso, Antonio, and Sebastian for their criminal mistreatment of Prospero, and implying that the loss of Ferdinand is Alonso's punishment. The three culprits are then driven raving mad, and suicidal as well in the case of Alonso.

Prospero now visits Ferdinand, releases him from bondage, and greets him as his future son-in-law, but warns him against premature intimacy. He commands Ariel to present another illusion – a masque of three goddesses, who shower the young couple with blessings.

The show is interrupted when Prospero recalls Caliban's plot to murder him. He explains to Ferdinand that the beings he has seen were spirits, and have vanished, as everything must eventually – being at heart equally insubstantial and dream-like.

Ariel describes to Prospero how he has led Caliban and his two co-conspirators astray. He and Prospero hang out some gorgeous garments to further entrap and delay them. Stephano and Trinculo want to steal these, though Caliban urges the murder first. The theft is interrupted by a pack of spirit dogs who chase the culprits away, egged on by Ariel and Prospero.

At Prospero's command, Ariel is now to fetch the court party. When he describes to Prospero how much they are suffering and says he feels sorry for them, Prospero is impressed that a mere air-spirit can feel pity and decides to follow Ariel's example. He orders Ariel to release them from their madness. Then he says it's time for him to abjure his "rough magic," break his staff, and drown his book of spells.

The court party is led in by Ariel. Prospero confronts Alonso and Antonio and their confederate, Sebastian, with their treachery toward him, but says he forgives them. He warns Antonio and Sebastian, in an aside, that he knows about their plan to murder Alonso, but won't say anything about it just yet.

Alonso is still grieving the loss of Ferdinand. Prospero says he too has lost a child – a daughter – but then brings him to his "cell" and reveals Ferdinand and Miranda playing chess together. Alonso, amazed and grateful, embraces the marriage of Ferdinand and Miranda. Miranda, for her part, is astonished that there is suddenly a new world filled with such amazing people. Prospero remarks that they are new to her. (He himself knows them for what they are.)

The Boatswain enters, fetched by Ariel, and explains how he and the mariners have awakened to find their ship safely in harbour. Enter Caliban, Stephano, and Trinculo, bedraggled and sore; they are suitably chastised and repentant. Prospero acknowledges that Caliban, "this thing of darkness," is in some sense his.

Plans are made for the return to Italy and the impending wedding. Prospero will have his dukedom again. Miranda and Ferdinand will eventually be the Queen and King of Naples. Ariel will ensure calm seas for the voyage.

Prospero finishes the play with an epilogue, in which he tells the audience that since his magic spells have now been overthrown, he must remain imprisoned on the island unless the audience pardons him, and sets him free by using its own magic to applaud the play.

Acknowledgments

It has been a great pleasure to work on this book, partly because it gave me the opportunity to read so much about Shakespeare and *The Tempest*, and also about the value of literature and drama within prisons.

The following books and films were particularly helpful:

Julie Taymor's film of *The Tempest*, with Helen Mirren as Prospera.

The Globe on Screen's version of *The Tempest*, with Roger Allam as Prospero.

And the Stratford Festival's version of *The Tempest* – which I also attended in person – with Christopher Plummer as Prospero.

The *Shakespeare Insult Generator*.

David Thomson's suggestive book, *Why Acting Matters*.

Northrop Frye's essay on *The Tempest* in his book *On Shakespeare*.

The excellent and highly useful edition of *The Tempest* in the Oxford World's Classics series; the editor is Stephen Orgel.

Isak Dinesen's story "Tempests" in her collection *Anecdotes of Destiny*.

Andrew Dickson's book *Worlds Elsewhere*, which explores

the many varieties of Shakespeare performances world-wide and across time.

There is a very long tradition of prison literature. I have read in it here and there, both while writing my novel *Alias Grace* and more recently while working on *Hag-Seed*. Apart from such well-known contemporary books as *Orange Is the New Black*, I was particularly interested this time around in books that dealt with literature and drama being taught or being experienced within prisons. Stephen Reid's collection of essays, *A Crowbar in the Buddhist Garden*, was generally suggestive, as was Rene Denfeld's astonishing novel *The Enchanted*. Avi Steinberg's account of working as a prison librarian, *Running the Books*, was helpful, as was Andreas Schroeder's *Shaking It Rough*. More particularly, Laura Bates's memoir, *Shakespeare Saved My Life*, was encouraging. It was helpful too to learn of the prison college programs run by Bard College and, through that knowledge, to learn of many others.

That being said, it must also be said that Fletcher Correctional is of course a fictional institution. It's doubtful that any place exactly like it exists, though many share some of its features.

Felix Phillips borrowed his last name from the late Robin Phillips, long-time theatre director at the Stratford Festival in Ontario, Canada. To see his magic at work, view the excellent documentary *Robin and Mark and Richard III*, in which he transforms an unlikely actor into the sinister Richard before your very eyes.

Anne-Marie Greenland plays the part of Miranda thanks to an auction run by the Medical Foundation for the Care of Victims of Torture.

And much about conversing with dead loved ones and

other strange experiences can be learned in *The Third Man Factor,* by John Geiger.

My gratitude to my longsuffering editors, Becky Hardie of Hogarth and Louise Dennys of Knopf Canada, who nudged me to tell more; and to my copyeditor, Heather Sangster of Strongfinish.ca. Also to my editor of over twenty-six years at McClelland & Stewart, Ellen Seligman, who passed away in March 2016 without having been able to read this book.

Thanks also to my first readers: Jess Atwood Gibson; Eleanor Cook; Xandra Bingley; Vivienne Schuster and Karolina Sutton of Curtis Brown, my U.K. agents; and to Phoebe Larmore, my longtime agent in North America; and to Ruth Atwood and Ralph Siferd.

And to Louise Court, Ashley Dunn, and Rachel Rokicki, of Penguin Random House, who sped me on my way during publication time.

Thanks also to Devon Jackson, who helped with some primary research on prisons. Also to my assistant, Suzanna Porter; and to Penny Kavanaugh; and to V. J. Bauer, who designed my website at margaretatwood.ca. Also to Sheldon Shoib and Mike Stoyan, who keep track. And to Michael Bradley, Sarah Cooper, and Jim Wooder, to Coleen Quinn and Xiaolan Zhao, and to Evelyn Heskin; and to Terry Carman and the Shock Doctors, for keeping the lights on. Finally, my special thanks to Graeme Gibson – an old enchanter, though happily not the one in this book.

HOGARTH
SHAKESPEARE

The world's favourite playwright
Today's best-loved novelists
Timeless stories retold

For more than four hundred years, Shakespeare's works have been performed, read, and loved throughout the world. They have been reinterpreted for each new generation, whether as teen films, musicals, science-fiction flicks, Japanese warrior tales, or literary transformations.

The Hogarth Press was founded by Virginia and Leonard Woolf in 1917 with a mission to publish the best new writing of the age. In 2012 Hogarth was launched in London and New York to continue the tradition. The Hogarth Shakespeare project sees Shakespeare's works retold by acclaimed and bestselling novelists of today.

Margaret Atwood, *The Tempest*
Tracy Chevalier, *Othello*
Gillian Flynn, *Hamlet*
Howard Jacobson, *The Merchant of Venice*
Jo Nesbo, *Macbeth*
Edward St Aubyn, *King Lear*
Anne Tyler, *The Taming of the Shrew*
Jeanette Winterson, *The Winter's Tale*

penguin.co.uk/vintage